MIRACULOUS FAUNA

TIMMY REED

Underground Voices
Los Angeles, California
2016

Published by Underground Voices
www.undergroundvoices.com
Editor contact: Cetywa Powell

ISBN: 978-0-9904331-5-6

Printed in the United States of America.

MIRACULOUS FAUNA

Still born

On the day she was born, Rachel came out in several pieces with skin like a bruised cantaloupe. There was no pulse, but she was crying softly. The delivery room smelled like sulphur and beef stock.

The doctor had been ready to induce a typical stillbirth. His schooling and experience had not prepared him for such an extraordinary delivery, but he was a good physician with a deep regard for the value of life. He ordered his staff to sew the girl back together and take her pulse again.

There was still no heartbeat.

But there was no denying Rachel was an active baby. She pursed torn, grey baby lips and nibbled the doctor's latex-gloved finger with tiny, yellow teeth.

She's hungry, the doctor said. That's always a good sign.

Rachel's broken, undersized body was placed in the arms of her teenage mother, Bobbi. Bobbi also looked small and broken but alive with the tired, glowing eyes of a new mom. The nursing staff nervously watched Bobbi look into her child's face, deep blue and white like the ocean. A ball of gas rattled the infant's body, trying to escape, and her lips parted as if she were exhaling an actual breath. Bobbi was woozy from the drugs and the pain but felt full with life, protein. She saw a tiny star of light flash above her child's forehead.

My baby, Bobbi sobbed.

She's like an angel or something.

Rachel's body was still warm from being inside her when they placed it on Bobbi's chest. Her heart throbbed against the infant's weight. She looked into her child's flattened eyeballs and saw herself in the reflection. When Bobbi's eyelids grew too heavy to keep open, nurses took Rachel away. She was delivered to a laboratory in a small clinic outside the city, where she was examined overnight by a group of expert pathologists who spoke mechanically into recording devices and used the word mystery a lot.

Throughout the autopsy, Rachel wailed for her mother. She was placed on an evidence sheet and radiographic images were taken of her body. A sample was plucked from a patch of black and white hairs poking out around a deep wound that reached across her scalp from ear-to-ear. The doctors combed over her little body with their instruments, reporting imperfections and birthmarks, each pustule, wound, and abscess, into their voice recorders. Radiated gunk was pumped into Rachel's intestine while the doctors crowded in front of the X-Ray screen and watched it pass through her system. Food — a milk formula and bits of mashed peas — came out only partially digested. Finally her back was arched over a body block and the stitches were temporarily removed from her chest so the doctors could poke around in her heart and lungs with metal sticks. It sounded like a plumber cleaning a drain. After an exhausting three nights of tests, they sewed her whole again.

In the end, a conclusion could not be reached in the argument about whether Rachel should receive a birth certificate, a death certificate, or both. She received no formal documentation at all.

Bobbi's own mother died without leaving her daughter any memories other than a vague feeling of having once been loved and a small yellow diary. The diary had always been empty except for a holy card and a wrinkled photograph on printer paper of her mother's hands cupping her own, as if teaching her how to pray.

It was the only photograph her mother left her. Bobbi treasured it. The holy card was lost during a move when she was a girl.

She always wanted the hands to be her mother's, but she was also wary. The picture wasn't printed on photo-paper. It was printed on plain white printer paper, wrinkled and torn at the edges. The hands in the picture had make-up on them and were manicured. The lighting looked professional. A part of herself she didn't like had always suspected the image was from an advertisement and not her mother at all. But why would she be left a photo copied from a magazine?

Her father hadn't left her anything. He'd just left.

When Bobbi was handed her child in the morning, the baby was stitched together like an old doll. Bobbi wanted more than anything to nurse her child but the doctors, concerned about Rachel's teeth, warned against it. They prescribed a high-vitamin formula, which Rachel refused. Bobbi fed her liverwurst instead. She massaged ointment into the infant's wounds, which never healed completely. She doted on the child. She spent her free time trying to craft baby clothes from yarn, which seemed to fall apart on Rachel's rotten flesh overnight. When Bobbi could not find a priest to baptize the baby, she performed the ceremony herself.

Conception in the Tombs

Eight and a half months before Rachel was born was the last time Bobbi visited the garden.

Every spring when the flowers came out, she started making up lies to visit the prayer garden after school. Her foster mom at the moment was a woman named Miss Grundlich, who disliked the place and didn't understand why Bobbi would want to spend so much time there alone.

Both prayers and gardens only distract fools from realizing how foolish they are, she said.

Bobbi lived with Miss Grundlich in a small single home in northeast Baltimore with a front porch and brown vinyl siding that reminded her of an earthworm's skin. The house was a few blocks away from a large Catholic cemetery next to a small church with a prayer garden that stunk of roses each spring. On breezy days, the odor overtook the graveyard and filled the rows of white crosses like syrup in a waffle. It made Bobbi's guts go soft, thinking: Nobody is alive to smell this.

She wondered if ghosts could smell flowers. Bobbi had never seen a dead body, although the only love she could ever imagine came from a woman who had been a corpse her whole life.

She had come to the prayer garden each spring since she moved from her last group home to Miss Grundlich's three years earlier. Bobbi had not been raised on religion, but she wanted it. She was drawn to the little plot of red roses and white lilies in the shadow of the cemetery.

The small hexagonal nook was empty day after day. The emptiness made her feel safe, like all the monsters in the world had been chained up and fed with slabs of bacon. It was just Bobbi and the flowers, waiting for God to join them.

Bobbi's pale blonde hair was cut into a bulb. It was lopsided and resembled an oversized military helmet sitting atop the fine skeletal features of her face. Miss Grundlich cut it herself and fancied it made Bobbi look like a flapper. Bobbie never had a haircut she was proud of. She never felt like she owned anything. Even her body and hair was on loan.

The garden became her place to rest, a place where she could own herself. The first spring after she discovered the place, she found a book called *The Canon of Saints* at the library. The book contained biographies, as well as beautiful images from holy cards. She began to learn the lives of the saints, study their faces in the cards. Their lives were marked by ordeals and miracles. She related to and admired the ordeals. She saw beauty and hope in the miracles. Saints were men and women set aside from the world, people who had heard God's calling. The stories spoke to her, even though God had not. She wished to be called by someone.

She prayed for her life to be part of a plan. She began to write prayers in the yellow diary, which she kept wrapped in plastic bags beneath a paving stone in the garden, next to a miniature statue of the Virgin, her tiny foot on the neck of a snake with an apple in its mouth.

Bobbi lived in single-sex group homes most of her life, so she had known very few boys. The ones in her class terrified her and she avoided them, even though several were secret admirers. They sometimes approached her in the corner of the asphalt playground during free periods. She would sit with her back against the chain-link fence and read about the saints from her book. The boys would approach her in packs and make noises, blow her kisses or reach out to touch her hair. It made her feel like she was trapped in the gorilla enclosure at the zoo.

She chewed her fingernails until they bled. They often swelled with green pus that smelled like her fingers were dying. She bit her cuticles with her front teeth and yanked them from their sockets. Skin peeled off around the edge of the nail and scabbed. When she touched anything at all, her fingers burned.

She almost only wore a purple sweatsuit in those days, which everyone made fun of.

Bobbi was afraid of boys, but she was more afraid of her foster mom. She was afraid because her foster mom was proof of the dissatisfaction she suspected in all living things.

Miss Grundlich was a sad woman who lived to spend her afternoons reenacting the villainous roles in musicals with the donkey-faced nephew she occasionally babysat. Otherwise she lived a plain, frugal existence that seemed like a penance to Bobbi. Bobbi admired her for it. Sometimes she encouraged Bobbi to apply for college scholarships, but for the most part she had given up on everything.

One night Miss Grundlich got half-drunk on rum punch near a moon-bounce that was set up for her nephew's birthday party and said, Life is over for you, Bobbi. It will always be like that. Life barely even exists for me.

Miss Grundlich's home was near Bobbi's high school, a mile or so past the far end of her campus. Bobbi hated both places, but that mile in between felt good. The prayer garden existed within that mile.

The lies she told Miss Grundlich usually involved boys.

Miss Grundlich went out of her way to meet boys for Bobbi when she was running errands. Some of them sounded too old for her. Maybe even illegal, although Bobbi wasn't exactly sure how the law worked. Bobbi believed she was being pawned off because she would be a legal adult soon. Miss Grundlich would no longer receive a monthly stipend for taking care of her. She needs somebody to take me off her hands, Bobbi thought, and she thinks only a man would be interested. So Bobbi made up lies about after school dates, in order to be alone in the garden.

The day it happened Bobbi woke up sleepy, almost still in a dream. The night before, a bat had entered the house through her bedroom somehow while she was sleeping – or had she dreamt that too? — and Miss Grundlich had thrown a fit. She screeched at the terrified animal, which banged itself into the ceiling fan and sent dust falling like snow onto Bobbi's head. Miss Grundlich hid under a white macramé tablecloth, which made her look like a panicked ghost. She shouted directions at Bobbi from the floor of the dining room. Eventually the bat was trapped in the kitchen, where Bobbi let it out the back door. She could hear the bat cursing as it flew away. It took her an hour to get back to sleep and by that time, the sun was nearly up.

Bobbi slipped through the school day in tired silence. She never spoke a word and no one ever asked her to. Her knees buckled twice on the way to the prayer garden. When she got there, she had to lie down, even before she checked on her diary. She curled up in a spot near the roses and fell asleep, listening to the breeze squeak the gates of the cemetery.

She heard her name as if it were being called out through the walls of a tomb.

Bobbi rolled over on her belly and put her face in the grass. The blades felt sharp on her cheeks.

The voice gurgled through the muck of her dream.

Wake up for me. I want to show you something.

His voice — it was a male voice — was low and phlegm-soaked, urgent like someone struggling to breathe. It pulled on her.

I want to teach you about life and death.

When she woke up, the garden was empty and the sun was tipping over the edge of the steeple, threatening to set.

Bobbi, the voice said. Hi.

A large boy or a small man was standing at the edge of the garden in a dark, hooded sweatshirt. She could barely make out his face, even though it wouldn't be dark for more than an hour. All she could see were yellow teeth in the shadow of his hood. A little moustache like a silver caterpillar.

Bobbi's heart wriggled when she heard her name. It was as if it had stepped from the Stranger's mouth, declaring itself to her. She thought of the diary and panicked. She went to reach for it but stopped. She had never written her name inside the book. The only mark her mother had made for her had been the outline of a small red heart with a dot inside. Even if he had found it, there was no way of knowing it belonged to her.

Are you looking for your prayer book?

It's not a prayer book, Bobbi was quick to answer, then caught herself. She had never been quick to answer anything in her life.

I don't have a book, she said. And it isn't prayers anyway. Or it wouldn't be.

She was embarrassed of her prayers.

The smell of roses in the garden was deeper than usual. It made her dizzy, nauseous. A wind blew over the fine blonde hairs on her cheek. Bobbi edged herself closer to the paver stone where she hid her diary. She could see a yellow corner peeking out, blurred by the plastic bag.

You don't need that, the Stranger said. I don't want to read it anyway. I don't need to read your thoughts on paper.

He sounded bored all of the sudden. She wasn't sure why, but for some reason that bothered her. He cracked his knuckles one-by-one and yawned. He is making a big show of it, she thought.

Books are dead trees, he said. I like things that are alive.

He sat down next to her and removed his hood, but even then she had trouble telling how old he was. He had silver hair and a face that was flat as a tombstone. His eyes twinkled like aluminum foil in a microwave. His skin was smooth and white. When he smiled at her, it cracked like old plaster. Bobbi thought of a clown trapped inside make-up.

Do you want to hear a joke? he said.

No. Do we know each other? She was trying to be defensive without being impolite. She realized her hands were shaking. She held them together, as if in prayer. Do you know me? she asked.

He appeared to be considering the idea.

I think so, he said.

Bobbi thought that was a weird answer. She squinted at him. For a second she thought she saw a face much like her own, a sort of male version of her face, but then it passed. He was blank and unfamiliar again. He lit a cigarette and offered her one.

I don't smoke, she said and it felt good. It was a line she had used before. Being offered a cigarette was something she knew she could handle.

There's a first and a last time for everything, he said. Last time I checked, teenagers did things like smoke.

Yeah. Well I'm not that good at being a teenager, I guess.

No. I don't guess you are.

His cigarette smelled funny. It was a thick chemical odor like the one released in Biology when her lab partner opened the small pink stomach of their fetal pig. It smelled like it had been dipped in the fluid the dead pigs were packaged in.

No worries, the Stranger told her.

That was how she thought of him: the Stranger.

You're a special girl and that's better than being a typical teenager any day or night. It's what I liked about you.

The Stranger's use of the past tense — Liked — gave her the creeps. Bobbi couldn't look at his face. She watched his hands instead. He began to pick lilies and take them apart with fingers that looked as if they were carved from bone. He was meticulous in his dismantling of the flowers. First he plucked the petals from the stem. Then he yanked each stamen with his thumb and forefinger and flicked the tiny, pollen-dusted anthers from their tops with his thumbnail. All that was left was the stem and the stigma, the female part of the flower, which he then ground into the dirt near his knee.

Bobbi watched the procedure with rapt attention, horrified but unable to look away. The Stranger noticed and gave her a flower that he had been about to dissect. She accepted, still too captivated to think, but was pulled from her trance by the way the flower looked in her hands. He had just picked it. It was still fresh. It wasn't dried out or wrinkled the way she thought of a dead flower. But still, there it was: Lifeless.

Bobbi let the flower fall. She stared at it in the patch of grass between them. She hoped that when she looked back up, the Stranger would be gone. When he wasn't, a tiny part of her was glad. He was sort of interesting, she thought, and he is interested in me. He had been nothing but friendly so far. Still, she hated herself for that tiny part.

You don't like your family, do you? the Stranger asked.

I don't have a family.

She stared down at her chest and waited for him to respond. The silence was making her even more uncomfortable.

Of course you have a family. He said it just when she needed it.

She felt comforted by his remark, but also irritated. Who was he to tell her about the family she did or didn't have?

I do not. I've never had one.

Right away she felt guilty again. In some ways, Miss Grundlich, as sad as she was, had tried to be her family. And her mother — even though she was dead, had always been dead — she was Bobbi's family too. Bobbi felt like she had betrayed them both. She was alone.

Would you like a family?

He moved closer. She wanted to slide away, but couldn't. It was like the grass was tugging on her skirt. It gripped the bottom of her thighs as though her tights were rubber. His eyes were flickers in a well. She looked down at her chest.

Do you want a family? he asked her again.

She started to say maybe she did want a family but she corrected herself.

What I really want is sainthood, she said.

The Stranger laughed.

What do you want something like that for?

Bobbi had trouble answering. Her thoughts raced. Why did she want to be a saint? There were a million reasons — she was sure of it — but she couldn't think of any on the spot like that, which also made her feel guilty. Maybe she wasn't cut out to be a saint after all.

It's better than whatever I am now, she said. She was surprised to hear so much confidence in her own voice.

Good answer, he coughed. But what's that? What are you now?

This line of questioning exhausted Bobbi. She couldn't remember why she had ever started coming to the prayer garden in the first place. None of her prayers had been answered. She was as lonely as she had ever been. It's only a hiding place, she thought. For a loser girl with no God or family. She felt ridiculous. It killed her to feel that way in front of the Stranger.

He repeated himself. What are you? he asked.

I would do anything to blink my eyes and find myself somewhere else right now, Bobbi thought. I want to turn into clay and be stomped into the dirt.

Relax, the Stranger said. He stood up and held out his hands. They looked almost translucent. She felt like she had been staring at those hands her whole life. Her own palms were pink and slimed over with sweat and dirt from the garden. She tried to pray, but forgot how.

Let's go for a walk, the Stranger said. He was already leading her into the cemetery. She never went back for her diary.

Rachel's First Home

Miss Grundlich allowed Bobbi to bring Rachel home to live in a space above the garage.

Despite her condition, Miss Grundlich said.

Bobbi was grateful but nervous about the situation. She didn't want to be the burden she was certain she was. Moment to moment it was as if she were stepping across a glass coffee table, waiting for it to shatter beneath her.

She was also grateful, in a confused way, to the Experts who had examined Rachel after she was delivered. Upon their request, Bobbi went back for a visit. A deal was struck between them, in which Bobbi would be paid in return for participating in a long-term research study. The study would last an indefinite amount of time. The only requirement was that Rachel be available for semi-regular examinations. Bobbi tried not to imagine what went on during the examinations.

She had trouble telling the Experts apart. Only a week after leaving the hospital, she found herself outside a medical clinic in an otherwise vacant strip mall, ringing a buzzer. There was a camera over the entrance. An old woman in a black cardigan answered the door. She smiled and for a second Bobbi thought her jaw had become unhinged, like a snake. The woman explained that she had just put false teeth in to answer the door and they were still off-center. Bobbi apologized for being startled.

They were led through swinging doors in back of a tiny waiting room with a white foam-paneled ceiling, where the old woman had been watching television. They walked down a white hallway. A clump of people waited for her at the end of the hall.

The Experts had sweat on their foreheads. Some of them were in lab coats. Others wore dark grey suits. They smelled of latex and disinfectant. Bobbi thought they looked educated. Like men guarding ancient secrets.

One of the Experts in the front seemed to have been nominated spokesman for the group.

We would like to continue our studies as long as … He was having trouble coming up with Rachel's name. Apparently, they had been calling her something else.

Rachel, Bobbi said.

As long as Rachel, he continued. Remains … How should I phrase this?

He glanced at his colleagues, searched for the perfect delicate word to explain the situation.

Animated, someone chimed in from the back, proud to help.

Fair enough, he said. As long as she remains animated.

Bobbi regretted the contract as she was signing it. She was desperate and terrified and for the first time in her life, it was not for herself. She had never taken care of anything, much less a daughter. She remembered the time she was given the responsibility of looking after the gerbil, Doug, who lived in her group home. She had been eleven-years-old. The hairs on her forearm tingled when she got to hold him. She could feel his tiny heartbeat and it almost made her cry. She was proud to hold him, to be given a chance. She could tell he liked her. She was sure of it. She could feel his tiny heart beating in her hands.

Doug was a nervous wad of fur that shook and burrowed his face in her skin. She tried to calm him down by petting him. It was working except he was so soft and nervous that she couldn't stop. After about an hour of furious petting, Bobbi accidentally pushed Doug's little body from her hand. She watched the animal fall like a lump of Play-Doh onto the tile floor and break his neck. The other girls in the home said she did it on purpose. They called her a witch. Not long afterward, the social workers moved her again.

The blood pumping through her chest curdled when she imagined the prospect of being responsible for another human being. Bobbi had never held a real job before. It never occurred to her that she might one day have a kid. None of the saints she could think of had given birth. The only one she came up with was Mary, Mother of God. And Mary was a virgin.

The initial income from the study allowed her to rent the space above the garage, though Miss Grundlich specified that the undocumented lease would require renewal on a bi-weekly basis. Inside there was an industrial sink, a toilet, and a small mirror, but no shower. There was a hot plate but no stove. Bobbi still had an old single bed from the house, but Miss Grundlich insisted she take her double. Bobbi refused, but the old woman demanded it. She suspected Miss Grundlich still held onto fantasies of the child's father reappearing in her life. She cloaked Rachel's crib in mosquito netting to protect her from flies. She kept all their clothes in the same trunk she had been carrying around since she was a little girl. The trunk was covered in stickers, most of them peeled off fruit.

There was no other furniture in the garage apartment. Bobbi was afraid to buy any. Movement felt impending. She purchased items for the baby but everything else was baggage. I will never own anything again, she told herself. She began to keep a new diary, on paper napkins that she carefully folded into the leaves of a Bible, which she stored at the bottom of the purple book bag she used to carry to school. She could only fit a few lines on each napkin. On one napkin, she wrote: *Only live for her, because she can't live for herself.*

Although Rachel was an infant and would not remember, Bobbi could tell she already felt something wrong with herself. Her little body grew and decayed simultaneously, like a plant that struggles on despite dead limbs. Her body digested itself. The muck that leaked from her cells loosened the skin until her tiny hands looked as if she wore over-sized gloves. Her fingers were black.

Bobbi had to adjust her daughter's position frequently. She held her upside down, stretched her out, anything to combat gravity. She lined the crib with trash bags to catch the yellow fluids of her daughter's decay. She massaged gas and partially digested lunchmeat from Rachel's distended tummy. Rachel groaned in appreciation. Rachel's tongue and genitals collected bacteria that caused bloat. Bobbi scrubbed them with a wet cloth. She injected saline to prevent the infant from drying.

She must see the world around her and be terrified, Bobbi thought, just like any other baby. She cried like any baby too. She cried because she was hungry. She cried for love. She cried because she wanted her mother's attention. She cried because something inside was already telling her that she belonged hidden beneath the earth.

Rachel lay in her crib beneath a mosquito net pulled tight and held in place with clothespins. Three flies crawled on its surface, trying to work a way inside. She reached up toward the flies as if to eat them. Bobbi brushed the creatures away and inhaled the thick, sickly-sweet odor that came from inside the crib.

Shoo, she whispered.

Parental Guidance

Bobbi went to the library for research. She bundled Rachel in a onesy with mouse ears and surrounded her with a number of blankets, then tucked her deep into the darkness of her stroller. She would rather have spared Rachel — and the reading public — the whole experience altogether, but Miss Grundlich felt uncomfortable watching the baby.

I'm not sure that would be appropriate, Miss Grundlich said.

Bobbi noticed her lip trembling.

Rachel would have to go outside someday, Bobbi thought. She felt sorry for Miss Grundlich but filled with a gust of vitality at the same time.

Outside. That's where the world was. They were going to have to deal with their lot in life. Life would find ways to deal with them, too.

Rachel liked the world outside the hospital and the garage. She breathed the air even though she didn't have to. Bobbi listened to her make a noise like laughter, as if the breath inside were tickling her. Rachel coughed; a wormy hunk of meat popped out of her mouth. It didn't look like anything Bobbi had fed her yet that day. She reached under the mosquito netting and wiped Rachel's face, then wrapped the meat in Kleenex and began to look for a trash can. She did her best to ignore the birds that circled above her daughter's stroller or the dogs that strained their leashes when she rolled past.

Bobbi's research was like the research that all new moms do in some ways, but not in every way. She learned a number of facts about death she had never planned on knowing. Dead flesh offers more resistance to x-rays, for instance. A corpse's eyeball flattens and glazes shortly after death. Embalming hardens tissues, makes the muscles stiffer and less pliable. Putrefaction is a generative process. It allows bacteria, mold, and larvae to live. The course of decay depends on the environment and situational factors.

She learned how to stitch and apply Superglue to Rachel's wounds, to hold Rachel's mouth open with retractors so she could brush her teeth and gums. She learned how to administer formaldehyde intravenously at the neck and as a light bath. She recognized the odor of the embalming fluid. Fetal pig. It made her cough.

She covered her mouth with a rag when she bathed Rachel. Occasionally she puked into the bathwater and had to start over. She spent hours scrubbing herself after Rachel's first bath. She scrubbed her forearms until she had wounds on her wrists that burned when they touched the long sleeves of the shirt she wore to cover them. It was painful, but she felt a rush of satisfaction when Rachel looked even a little rejuvenated.

Each time she was embalmed, Rachel's cheeks filled out and stretched taut the stitches in her face. Some pinkness entered her skin after the treatment, but never quite the hue of someone who once lived. Bobbi had to be careful not to use too high a concentration or Rachel would turn into a pickle.

Although there was no shower in the garage, Miss Grundlich requested that Bobbi bathe Rachel there. Bobbi thanked her for permitting so much.

Bobbi was certain her nostrils would be filled with the smell of embalming fluid — and the flowery, rotten smell that Rachel's body gave off — for the rest of their lives together. She read something about how formaldehyde was found in nail polish, hair-straightener and wood paneling. One website said it was the reason new houses smelled the way they do. Bobbi had never been in a new house before. She told herself formaldehyde was a minor penance. She tried to think only of the body it preserved.

On her first trip to the library, Bobbi encountered stares. She'd figured out she had more than enough from her stipend to purchase a home computer, but the library was an excuse to visit the world. Being near books and people, just surrounded by them, in their vicinity, Bobbi knew that was important somehow, too. Nobody could see Rachel tucked into the baby carriage as deep as she was tucked. Bobbi was sure of it. I'm being paranoid, she thought. She felt naked. Like an earthworm. Like a piece of sushi.

At the adjacent computer station sat an orange-haired woman with very tight lips like a beak. Her hair was badly dyed the color of blood on asphalt and had been placed with great care on top of her forehead like a rooster's fan. When I am that age, Bobbi thought, I will wear my hair like that. She meant it, too. She imagined it would keep people from getting close to her.

Bobbi could feel the woman's eyeballs probing the stroller at her side. She tried to ignore her, which was difficult because the woman was sniffing her and the stroller like she had discovered a long-lost pile of dogshit.

Maybe she has, Bobbi thought.

She focused on her own research. There was so much she didn't know and desired to learn. About life. About everything. But first about death.

She learned that young physicians learn to think of corpses as objects. She learned that for this reason anatomy lab personnel go to the trouble of swathing cadavers in gauze so dissection students can unwrap them as they work. She considered herself in the act of dressing Rachel in her onesy. The same way she was probably dressed as a girl, only without the extra care that was taken to avoid tearing Rachel's sutures. And Bobbi was dressed by a stranger, without the love a mother would give.

The rooster-headed woman was still sniffing her. Bobbi smelled the air with the curiosity of someone who has been alerted to the passing of gas. The stares began to make sense. Without knowing it, she had already gotten used to her daughter's odor. Or at least momentarily forgotten it in public. She listened, her muscles tense. More sniffing.

Pardon me, the rooster woman said.

Bobbi stared at the screen. Don't talk to me don't talk to me don't talk to me, she thought. The woman poked at her shoulder but stopped just short of touching her, as if Bobbi were carrying something contagious.

Excuse me, but I am having trouble with your … aroma. She fanned the air in front of her. An awkwardly polite laugh slipped from her beak.

I'm sorry, Bobbi whispered without looking up from her computer.

She was keenly aware of library rules all of a sudden. She turned back to her research.

I don't know what it is, she said.

She could feel the rooster woman's concerned expression fluttering against the back of her head. It's probably my perfume, she added.

The rooster considered this idea. But the smell is coming from the carriage, too? she asked.

It's her scent also, Bobbi said. Only she wears it better than I do.

She counted silently to herself. Without realizing it, she counted more than six-hundred banana before she pushed Rachel out of the library, rushing down the handicap ramp outside with tears on her cheeks.

We're not ready for life.

She was praying and talking to herself at the same time.

We're not ready, she said.

We don't want it yet.

Thanks

Early in life, Bobbi had nightmares. She was always scared. She learned to say the words "Sorry" and "Thank you" on every possible occasion. She used these two phrases even when they were not entirely appropriate. The words proved useful — like spells — for survival, but never helped her make any friends.

When Bobbi was 6 years old, she saw visions of ancient, wrinkled women giving birth to snakes and wondered if they were poisonous. She saw tiny featherless birds chomp on bloody egg yolks like they were gummy candy or dehydrated fruit. She saw spiders living in the shells. Worlds gave birth to rotten worlds. As soon as she learned the word "Fuck" she woke up screaming it. She never woke up screaming "Sorry" or "Thank you" but they remained the easiest things to say when she was awake. And she always meant them, without ever knowing why.

Mimicking a Heartbeat

For some reason, even though they were living in a one-room garage apartment, Miss Grundlich purchased Bobbi and Rachel a baby monitor. Maybe wishful thinking, Bobbi thought. She hopes it will prove useful somewhere else, after we have moved away. Bobbi used it anyway. Even as she fell asleep holding Rachel's chilly body, she kept the monitors nearby — one clipped to the neckline of Rachel's sweatshirt, right in front of her mouth, the other on the pillow by her ear. She listened to the sound of her own breath, which Rachel softly mimicked into the microphone. As she fell to sleep she thought she could hear the slow pulse of her heartbeat play back through the speaker, but it was only static. Rachel couldn't mimic a heartbeat. And Rachel did not sleep.

At night, neighborhood dogs barked at the garage. Some howled. Bobbi lost sleep over the embarrassment it caused Miss Grundlich. Bobbi lost sleep for all kinds of reasons.

The neighborhood dogs are acting up again, Miss Grundlich said over breakfast one Sunday. She and Bobbi were having oatmeal. Rachel was eating red ground beef from a plastic bag.

They've been acting crazy every night since… Miss Grundlich paused. She chose her words carefully. Since recent history, she finished.

I hear them too, Bobbi said. I'm sorry.

Why? It wasn't you that was barking.

I'm sorry anyway.

Bobbi mixed some of her oatmeal in with Rachel's mush. Rachel didn't even pause to notice. She just pushed it into her mouth and stared ahead with flat, blank eyes. Miss Grundlich gagged a little and excused herself.

Happy Birthday

Bobbi watched Rachel grow. It confused her. *How does my daughter work?*

The Experts seemed to know very little.

It's a good sign, I think, one told her. Growth. At least it often is … Excepting things like cancer. When cancer grows, it's always bad.

Rachel's brain scan looked like a tie-dyed tee-shirt. Her heart was a balled-up sock. She was one years old.

Bobbi planned an intimate birthday celebration, centered on a piece of pound cake that Miss Grundlich agreed to let her bake in the oven. She copied the recipe off the Internet at the library. Visits to the library were getting easier. She just pushed the stroller in a direct line to the same computer in the back each time. Whenever they showed up, her computer and the ones stationed around it were empty. At first, Bobbi dangled air-fresheners from the mosquito netting in the stroller but after one or two visits she gave that up. The air-fresheners made her feel silly and ashamed. On Rachel's birthday, Bobbi got her ready in the garage. She wiped No Tears baby shampoo on clear blue patches of skin that danced underneath with grubs like grains of long rice. Bobbi made a mental note: Rachel needs more fluid.

When they got home from the library, they prepared and ate the pound cake alone. Miss Grundlich had left for the weekend, saying she needed to visit her sister and nephew. Even though Miss Grundlich wasn't home, Bobbi decided to eat in the garage.

Rachel didn't like the pound cake. Bobbi wrapped a very small piece in bologna for her and put a candle in it. She placed the candle in front of her daughter and lit it.

Rachel looked down at the tiny flame, enchanted. She leaned forward and gnashed her teeth at the flap of slimy meat. Bobbi made a thousand wishes for her daughter, then blew out the candle.

Bobbi didn't like the pound cake either. It came out of the oven hard and white like a slab of marble. After blowing out Rachel's candle for her, she picked the cake up off the table with both hands and dropped it into the wastebasket with a thud. She sat back down on the bed next to Rachel.

I always wanted a mother who could bake me treats on my birthday.

She was starting to cry.

You deserve one, she said. More than me. Even if you don't eat cakes, you deserve a mother who makes them.

Rachel pawed at Bobbi's arm like a cat investigating a dumpster, then opened her mouth wide. Her little teeth had flecks of pink meat in them. Bobbi picked her up off the bed. If she wants to bite me, Bobbi thought, I will let her. But the baby's head only fell into her chest, mouth open, and laid there. Bobbi could feel teeth on her skin. She took hold of Rachel's tiny hand and squeezed gently. Rachel squeezed back.

Early next morning before sunrise, Miss Grundlich came home and went directly to bed before Bobbi could see her. Bobbi heard her pull into the driveway. It sounded like a broken train. She waited in bed holding Rachel's tiny limp body until she was sure Miss Grundlich wasn't coming back out. Then she got up to look.

In the driveway was a worn, brown Honda Odyssey mini-van with a tear-drop trailer attached to a hitch on the back end. In black electrical tape, across the side of the trailer, it read: HAPPY BIRTHDAY! There was a shiny combination lock attached to a chain on the trailer's door handle. The combination was hanging next to it on a tag.

Bobbi knew Miss Grundlich couldn't afford to buy her something like this but she took the hint, or at least thought she did: Miss Grundlich felt like she couldn't afford not to buy it.

In the moments just after sunrise Bobbi stood in the driveway and said to her daughter, You are one of the special things in the world. And our job, *your job*, is to go out there and find all the other special things.

She put Rachel in the gently used car-seat Miss Grundlich had attached in the back and walked around to the driver's side door. The keys were in the ignition.

Just a year and a half ago, Miss Grundlich and the man from school were teaching her how to drive. She had been so bad at it. She was a death machine on wheels. She was sure of it. Miss Grundlich told her so, in those very words. She wanted to quit, but Miss Grundlich told her driving would be important when she was grown up and had to support herself. The van and the trailer signified that day had come.

There are going to be plenty of other special things out there, Bobbi told Rachel as they made the turn at the end of the block. The world is full of them.

Over Bobbi's shoulder, Rachel was gnawing on the straps of her car seat. I am talking to myself, Bobbi thought, and kept talking. The world is made of special things. At least, I think it is. And the special things can be found anywhere. Everywhere maybe. If we only bother to recognize them. You know?

At the first rest station Bobbi passed on I-95, she purchased a map. She locked the trailer and left Rachel alone for three minutes. Schnauzers were barking at the trailer when she returned. This is only temporary, she told Rachel.

She felt like she was lying.

New Beginnings Are Everywhere You Look

The teardrop trailer was silver. It looked to Bobbi like an armored beetle following in their rear-view mirror. She thought about the flesh-eating beetles she first read about on the Internet. They are commonly known as Skin Beetles and they feed on decaying animals. They are so good at it that they are used in taxidermy and in natural history museums to clean the skin of animal skeletons. The same beetles are also known to dine on natural fibers like silk, or fur. Because of this, they are sometimes called Carpet Beetles and considered pests. Bobbi had learned all this stuff on that first nervous trip to the library, after she had been picking them off Rachel for several days.

The trailer was five-foot-wide and ten-foot-long with a hatch in the back that opened to reveal a small outdoor kitchen. The door to the hatch acted as a cover when you were cooking in the rain. The roof was five-foot-seven inches tall, so Bobbi's head almost hit the roof when she was standing. In the center of the low, rounded ceiling was a small square skylight that opened up so you could see the stars while you were lying in bed, framed as if they were in a painting. The only other windows were portholes the size of pie tins on either side door. Each porthole was leaky and the bottom halves collected water. Bobbi sometimes felt like she was looking through the windows of a sinking ship.

Inside there was a bed, four drawers, and a little compartment just tall enough to store a man's overcoat. Bobbi filled the drawers with Rachel's stuff. She kept her own trunk in the mini-van's cargo space, underneath more of Rachel's stuff — diapers, bandages, tarps, embalming fluid, buckets, sewing kits, insecticide, mosquito nets, a meat cooler, syringes, an IV pump, large and small capacity hazardous waste disposal bags, disposable wipes, fold-up bassinet, bibs, and a stuffed lamb named Mary.

On their first night in the trailer at a truck stop outside Ashland, Virginia, Bobbi discovered a note Miss Grundlich had taped to the small refrigeration unit in the outside kitchen: *I'm sorry, Bobbi. I was wrong. Your life has only just begun.*

Disneyland

The worst thing Bobbi ever did was kiss the boy who raped her. When she looked into her daughter's black milk eyes, she was certain of it. She tore herself to pieces at night, bundled against the wall of the trailer with Rachel's body cold like a watermelon in her lap. She took hold of Rachel's hand and said a prayer to Saint Joseph, the patron saint of Happy Death. Outside was a loud buzzing sound. It was February. The air was too cold for most bug swarms, Bobbi figured. It sometimes felt like she was making all of this up, every fact she knew, even life in general. The light was fading in the porthole of the trailer. Rachel was yawning, or biting the air. Bobbi thought about the buzzing until nothing else mattered. She couldn't tell if the noise belonged to a swarm of insects or an overhead lamp in the parking lot. One or the other, she thought. She was afraid to look.

I've never been to Disneyworld, she whispered, talking to herself in order to drown out the sound.

Or is it Land? Which one is in California? Which one is better?

Would you like to go to Disneyland, Rachel? When are you big enough for the rides?

Bobbi made a note on a napkin and slipped it in between the leaves of her Bible. The note said:

Bobbi, you've just beaten death but life is still in front of you. What are you going to do now?

We're going to Disneyland!

Learning to Walk

The girls were in the back corner of a Wal-Mart parking lot the size of a galaxy, where Rachel was learning to walk. Bobbi had taken Rachel inside the megastore earlier that morning, when she thought fewer customers would be around. The place was full of people anyway. She hurried through the store with Rachel's stroller. In no time, she picked up beach chairs, a Dell laptop computer, a travel router for WiFi, and a bag full of Disney movies on DVD. None of the customers even bothered to look at Rachel. They shambled, still sleepy, through the aisles with their mouths open, transfixed like drugged livestock by the giant boxes and vibrant displays. They looked a lot like Rachel does now, Bobbi thought as she watched her daughter scuffle and totter around the parking space behind their trailer.

She couldn't help but laugh. The laughter bubbled up from her chest and surprised her. It was like fruit in her mouth. She had forgotten what laughter tastes like.

She laughed because she was proud.

Rachel stumbled and the asphalt tore a flap of skin from her wrist. Her bone shined through like a hunk of yellowed quartz. Bobbi plunked down in a chair behind the trailer and tended to the loose skin with a sewing kit and glue. Rachel sat very still on her lap while she worked. Bobbi's hand slipped anyway; she pricked her left thumb with the needle. A red bead appeared. Rachel's face stirred in the direction of the blood. She stopped short and moaned a little, like a scolded dog. Bobbi shoved the bloody thumb in her daughter's mouth.

Careful, she said. Mommy needs you to be careful. Rachel nibbled a moment, then only sucked. Bobbi could feel her baby daughter's confusion through the vesicles in her thumb. She worried about what such confusion would mean for the future.

The walking lesson continued. Bobbi sent Rachel out like a boomerang into the cracked lot, but the little girl just kept going and not coming back. Bobbi chased after her. She turned Rachel around then ran back to the silver trailer ahead of her, like a child training a puppy. Rachel hobbled back toward her mother, stumbling slightly but relentless, dragging her left foot like she had forgotten it was attached. Bobbi offered her part of a cookie as a reward. Rachel only ate a little. She let most of it fall out of her mouth onto the ground.

I'm sorry, Bobbi said. She kicked the wet crumbs under the trailer.

It's no good? she asked.

She meant Rachel's life, but didn't know it.

I ruined it, she said. It's my fault.

She bought a bloody slab of skirt steak from the Wal-Mart and the lesson kept on going.

Rachel bobbed about the parking spaces in back of the trailer. She wobbled through the area between the yellow lines in a nervous way that made Bobbi think of a duck on a tightrope. She admired Rachel's cheeks and the tight stitches that she had recently woven into them, which barely hid yellow blobs like egg yolks. Bobbi thought she was smiling.

Bobbi never knew the story of how she had learned to walk. There was no one consistent enough in her life to tell it to her. She could only imagine it was an awkward experience from watching videos of other baby humans, goats, and kittens on the computer. Bobbi liked watching animals learn to walk. Giraffes were the most awkward. Rachel walked even worse than that, Bobbi had to admit. Rachel walked like an amphibian, not sure on which part of the earth she belonged. Rachel walked adorably.

Wet Death

Bobbi and Rachel had been at the campsite two and a half months on the evening she caught Death in the shower. In that time, Rachel's walking improved considerably. She still hobbled and dragged her feet, but she moved with a greater sense of direction. Her interest in the world around her told her where to go. It told her to go everywhere.

Rachel's diet also expanded during their time at the campground. It was springtime. There were all kinds of creatures in the woods around her, on the outskirts of the Shenandoah National Park. She spent most of her time lumbering and crawling after them. She ate earthworms and wolf spiders in the little enclave where they parked their trailer, tucked away down a service road at the back of the campsite.

Mister Courtney Tomball, who ran the place, put them up free of charge. He first came across the pair stranded at an overlook on Skyline Drive. Bobbi was nervous about accepting help from the old man. It was raining hard and the sky was growing purple. Nobody had stopped at the overlook in the hours they'd been stuck there. Bobbi felt alone on the mountain, like the cars driving past on the wet road were a mirage. Mister Courtney Tomball was a thin man and rusty-looking like a railroad spike. There was something in his face that reminded Bobbi of a crow, which caught her off-guard. She tried not to imagine viscera hanging from his lips like a gummy worm. Bobbi was also frightened of his driving. Mister Courtney Tomball was a little blind. He careened into the overlook then climbed down from his Jeep with a cane, wearing Aviator sunglasses even though the sky was dark grey and purple. He approached the wrong side of the minivan, moving with the slow caution of someone unearthing a mummy. Bobbi reached across the passenger seat to roll down the window. He offered to help.

Bobbi wanted to help him, but she couldn't. She accepted his charity instead.

I'm sorry, she told Rachel. We have to trust somebody.

She wrapped Rachel in a tarp before getting in for the ride to the station to fill up a gas can. The tarp was to guard against Rachel bloating in the rain.

Sometimes the only thing left to do is trust someone.

Bobbi insisted on paying for their use of the campsite, but the old man wouldn't allow it. As a compromise, he agreed to let Bobbi help out around the campsite, sorting compost and cleaning out the restrooms. Bobbi enjoyed the work. She told herself that work was a kind of prayer. She told Rachel the same thing.

Several days after she arrived, Mister Courtney Tomball appeared at the door of their trailer with a backpack designed to hold babies. The backpack had been sitting in the shed for years, he told her. It was old and brown but spotted with red flannel patches that looked fresh and clean.

Rotting a little bit, he said. Waiting for you, I guess. All patched up now.

I can't possibly take that, Bobbi said. You've already done so much.

Doing me a favor, he said. Need the space. Not carrying little people around too much at my age.

Rachel fit the backpack neatly. Bobbi had to line it against seepage with newspaper and trash bags. The two went for a hike in the woods that afternoon. Bobbi found a bird's nest with tiny blue eggs in it. She was careful not to touch the nest. She remembered learning somewhere that mothers abandoned eggs that had been touched. She left after only a glance. Rachel was perched on her shoulders, moaning like a hungry dog.

In the time since, Bobbi had taken tea with the old gentleman each day and grown to enjoy his company. He would arrive around three each afternoon carrying a hot brown mixture he called WitheRod Tea. They sat on a pair of stools made from cut logs while Rachel scrambled around in front of them. One day Rachel looked up from the dirt with the bloody front end of a baby mole sticking from her mouth. She was delighted to show off in front of someone new. Mister Courtney Tomball petted her softly around the ear. Bobbi pulled her back just before she began to gnaw on his wrist.

Bobbi and the old man talked a lot during their afternoon tea times, but never about Rachel's condition. Mister Courtney Tomball acted as if he didn't notice, even though it was impossible to miss, even half blind. Bobbi appreciated his sensitivity about the issue. It made her feel safe.

Instead they talked about their favorite colors. Brown, him. Blue, her. They talked about wild herbs. He told her about geosmin, the compound that provides the odor of root vegetables and the earth's must when it rains. They talked about birds. Bobbi liked hearing about birds and Mister Courtney Tomball seemed to know a lot about them. Their bones are hollow, he told her. Bobbi felt like she could relate. They talked about what trees at the campsite were old and it just so happened that the Eastern Hemlock behind their trailer was the oldest.

A thousand years, Bobbi repeated him in a whisper. She gazed at her daughter who was trying to poke a stick in the dirt. Struggling with a keyhole in the side of the earth.

Mister Courtney Tomball told her that the mountains themselves were the oldest in the world.

And the tallest once, too, he said. 460-million years ago they were born. Size of the Himalayas. Now they're just lumps.

Bobbi tried not to imagine all the ghosts that lived there, but she did anyway. They were ancient things. Things deeper and older than the religion she wanted. She imagined monsters, but she couldn't picture their faces. She was afraid to. She glanced at Rachel, who was at her feet chewing a piece of something squirmy with black blood that was caked all over her face.

Mister Courtney Tomball liked to talk quietly, in clipped sentences that made him sound like a prehistoric man. He liked to listen. His ears were red and full of hair like steel wool.

Bobbi never saw his eyes.

He asked Bobbi about her future, but never about her past.

When you grow up, what do you want to be? Not that you're not grown up already, he said.

He was trying to be polite. Bobbi knew she was not grown up.

Need something to look forward to though, he said. None of us is grown up really.

He stopped himself, as if he had said something wrong.

I know what you meant, Bobbi said. She wasn't sure that she did. Everyone looked adult to her. She was only interrupting to spare him the embarrassment.

I always wanted to be a saint, she said. Or at least a really good person.

Bobbi took a sip of hot tea. It burned in her throat. She pushed out her lower lip and blew her bangs up off her forehead. I sometimes think it's gotten too late for that, she said.

No moping, he said, adamant. It's never too late for sainthood. No matter the religion. Saints don't need religion in my book.

What he said about lateness was already true in her mind. It had to be. Bobbi could think of several saints off the top of her head that had been late bloomers. There was Saint John of God, patron saint of alcoholics and publishers, who spent forty years as a runaway, soldier of fortune, and a vicious overseer of slaves in Morocco before opening a Christian bookshop and flagellating himself in public until he had to be institutionalized. And Saint Francis of Assisi who lived the high life as the metrosexual bachelor son of a wealthy cloth merchant before he began to have the strange visions of Christ that led to his ecclesiastical awakening. Saint Margaret flitted about the streets and castles of Cortona as a sex pervert until she came to realize the value of her soul and turned to God. She battled the condition the rest of her life as a holy woman. Or Saint Moses the Black who led a gang of thieves and murderers in the Nile River valley before his conversion. And even Saint Paul tortured and executed Christians, other saints even, before he met Christ on the road to Damascus.

But Mister Courtney Tomball didn't talk about religion. He talked about natural things like plants and animals. They were new subjects to Bobbi but they made her feel comfortable nonetheless. There was a part of her that thought of Rachel — and sometimes herself — as little more than a plant.

She trusted the old man to know about life. After all, Mister Courtney Tomball spent thirty years as a Ranger for the National Park Service before he retired to open the campsite. Thirty years seemed like forever to Bobbi.

Bobbi spent the day in the same way that she had spent almost all of her days since she and Rachel came to the campsite. She woke up at 5:30 am and looked into Rachel's eyes, wide open and opaque like filthy marble.

Rachel had lain still next to her mother most of the night. After Bobbi woke up, she massaged the ooze from Rachel's belly and fed her a quarter-packet of scrapple from the trailer's mini-fridge. She set about repairing Rachel's wounds and applying calendula and balsamicum ointment to new places of rot. Mister Courtney Tomball had given them to her. Rachel let out a soft moan as Bobbi ran her hand down her spine.

After she got Rachel ready, Bobbi brought her into the woods to pray. She was scared of being in the woods alone, but every day she was at the campsite the tiny family — Just us two, Rachel! — went to pray. They prayed to no one in particular, no specific god or saint, but they prayed. Bobbi held Rachel's hands in her own. They prayed a prayer of thanks for being able to pray.

The woods spoke to Bobbi in a strong voice when she prayed. Her scabby fingertips caused a slight pain when they touched.

You're no good, something told her. There is evil in the world and it is your fault. It is everybody's fault.

And you're one of them. You're the worst one of them.

The woods also whispered, too quiet for Bobbi to understand. The whispers suggested beautiful and terrifying things, like the soundtrack to a dark fairytale movie. She prayed through it, uncertain but hopeful that she was aiming for the right God with her prayers. Rachel prayed along with her, she thought, probably thinking of food.

Then Bobbi did her chores as the sun rose to a peak in the sky.

In the afternoon, she began another walking lesson with Rachel in the space outside their trailer. They both grew distracted. She bit her nails and looked at the trees. Rachel couldn't help digging for worms. Bobbi gave them a break for lunch. Afterward she sang to Rachel who stared, drooling worm flesh, at a cloud in the sky that was shaped like a human kidney. It was a moment of rest.

Saw two birds collide, Mister Courtney Tomball said when he arrived for tea. This morning. Near my office trailer. Dropped like stones.

You *saw*?

Bobbi was thinking of his bad eyes. Then she remembered the birds' lives — she felt bad that she had not thought of them first.

I mean, that's horrible, she said. Are they okay?

Heard them right off. Like hitting a golf ball. Then saw them. Dead on the earth. Heads bashed together. Brains co-mingling in the dirt. Ran square into one another.

Bobbi liked the way Mister Courtney Tomball talked. It was hard not to laugh, even when he was talking about death. He sounded like a gentle giant, aged and shrunken from a time out of books. Or a chief from an old Indian movie. Bobbi liked both ideas. So long as they distracted her from death.

Still, these birds were dead. Bobbi thought of the nest she had seen in the woods and their deaths became more important than other deaths at the moment. She felt for a second like she was going to cry.

Mister Courtney Tomball sensed this.

All apologies, he said. Did not mean to upset a young lady. Makes me sad when birds die too.

They sat in silence for a moment. Bobbi could hear all the birds that were still alive singing in the trees.

Finally Mister Courtney Tomball said, Like to have a funeral?

Bobbi had never been to a funeral before, at least not that she could remember. She assumed she had been present at her mother's service as a toddler but she had no memories of the day. She always had the idea that her mother had been cremated and her ashes thrown in the sea, but she didn't actually remember anyone telling her that. It was just something that she always remembered knowing. Bobbi looked down at Rachel in her lap. She was still, wrapped in gauze rags like a silkworm in a cocoon. She didn't blink. Her mouth hung open. Bobbi took Rachel's hands in hers.

I think I would like that very much.

Mister Courtney Tomball led a slow pace down the trail to the spot where the birds had collided. Rachel strained Bobbi's hand, pulling ahead as if she knew the way by scent. Bobbi had to pick her up in order to keep them both from falling.

Little girl's excited for the bird funeral, Mister Courtney Tomball said. Already smells like dead bird around here. Not a good smell.

They weren't even close to the dead bird yet.

He smells my daughter, Bobbi thought.

When they got to the spot where the trailhead meets the parking lot, the birds were lying on a bed of brown pine needles. Their skulls were broken like Christmas tree bulbs. Rachel kneeled down and began to lick at their brains immediately. Bobbi swooped her up, bundled in her arms, still biting.

We're going to have a funeral, she said. Yes we are. Yes we are.

Mister Courtney Tomball disappeared into the office trailer. When he reappeared, he was holding a shovel and a worn, green toolbox.

Gonna dig a hole, he said to Bobbi.

He wrapped the birds in an oilcloth and led the way to a shady area in back of a volleyball court, net half-buried in the sand. The shade was provided by twenty-foot apple trees with big, clumsy yellow fruits shaped like hearts.

Sour, he said, nodding to the apples. Birds love them though.

In the clearing, there were already several small graves marked with blank pieces of slate. Bobbi wondered if this was the first time two birds had run into each other at the campsite.

As if he could read her mind, Mister Courtney Tomball said, Two birds hitting each other in midair. Bad sign. Death is near. Been hanging around here a little while now. At least it seems that way.

The old man's head was turned up toward the sky. Bobbi wished he would take off his sunglasses. She wanted to see his eyes.

Has this happened before? she asked, nervously. Two birds hitting each other?

Rachel strained against Bobbi's arms. She reached out toward the dead birds. She grunted.

Ever? he said. You bet. Lots of birds gone down in history; some must've done it this way. Around here though? Only once that I ever knew of. Just before my wife died. Two little blue fellows like these ones here. Warblers. Right smack into each other.

Bobbi didn't know Mister Courtney Tomball ever had a wife. He had never mentioned her in any of their conversations. She wasn't sure what to say.

I'm sorry. For your wife … And the birds … And everything.

Rachel made noises. The deepest part of her voice made a gurgle sound like fresh clay being squeezed.

Its okay, he said. I don't let myself feel too bad about it. Or I try not to. That's how death gets you twice, he said. If you get caught up with a worry about it.

Mister Courtney Tomball set about digging the grave with the confidence of a well-sighted man half his age. Bobbi offered to help.

Hold onto the tiny one, he said.

Bird, Bobbi whispered to her daughter. She directed Rachel's gaze away from the dead birds below to a hawk in the sky that had been following them all day. Rachel, she said and touched Rachel's chest. Mommy, she said and patted herself on the head. Love; and they held hands.

Mister Courtney Tomball led the service. Bobbi watched to see if he would remove his sunglasses when he spoke. He didn't. Bobbi held Rachel in her arms and bowed her head so their cheeks were touching.

Two birds stopped flying today, Mister Courtney Tomball said. He used a deeper, more formal tone than usual. It made him sound like a politician.

Suddenly and not on purpose. At least we cannot assume that it was on purpose and we are certain that it was sudden. Unless they'd been planning it for months; birds are often more intelligent than we give them credit for. No matter.

He cleared his throat.

Bobbi tried not to laugh. Mister Courtney Tomball sounded so different when public speaking.

Today, two birds are here only in memory. We are here at the moment existing only to bury them. We mark the occasion in order to make sure they stay in memory.

He went on like that for a while.

When it was time to bury the birds, Mister Courtney Tomball handed a carcass to Bobbi. Several feathers came out its skin and drifted to the ground. It was as if the bird was melting in her hand.

She quickly placed it in one of the little holes Mister Courtney Tomball had dug and noticed for the first time that the bird was missing an eyeball. Rachel hissed at the bird as Bobbi placed it in the earth.

Afterward, her palm ached where the bird had been sitting. She could feel its weight and feathers like a phantom wound. Like she was being tickled with electric fronds. Somehow touching Rachel in far more intimate ways felt normal. More than normal. Clean. Wholesome.

Now she wanted to take a shower.

Should we be worried about the bird flu? she asked Mister Courtney Tomball, who was on his hands and knees, patting down the earth over the graves.

Bigger things to worry about than that. If you're going to worry anyhow, that is. These birds weren't sick. Died of *navigational* difficulties, he emphasized. No bird flu here. Isn't it all the way in China?

I don't know, Bobbi admitted. I don't know anything about it.

Don't either, he said. Hope it stays that way.

When they got back near the trailer, Bobbi excused herself to put Rachel inside while she went to the outdoor shower.

Mister Courtney Tomball would have nothing of it.

Nonsense, he said. Little one's easy enough for me to watch after. No good reason to lock her up in that trailer. Had kids myself. Watched them just fine. Eyes are a little worse, but I figure children mostly look the same as they did back then anyway.

Bobbi had never considered that Mister Courtney Tomball might have children of his own. He had never mentioned them before. They had to be very old now, she thought. He seemed like he had been an old man forever. He was so good at it.

It was the first time Bobbi had asked anyone to watch Rachel alone since Miss Grundlich. She was nervous for both of them, but Mister Courtney Tomball's voice was smooth and reassuring, hard to refuse. Somehow he sounded like milk. To be careful, Bobbi tied Rachel's toddler safety leash, reinforced with so much duct tape, to a log bench in the clearing outside the trailer. She also put a binky wrapped in bacon in Rachel's mouth to keep her jaws busy. She was only going to take a fast shower and then she'd be right back.

Let yourself feel clean, Mister Courtney Tomball said. Go on. Little one is safe. No use to worry about an old mummy like me.

There were three outdoor shower stations on Mister Courtney Tomball's property. There were two near the front of the campground where several cabins and most of the campsites on the property were located. Bobbi and Rachel had been using the third shower, deep out in the woods, a moderate hike past their already remote location. Mister Courtney Tomball had once explained why he put the shower out there.

For lovers, he said. Built it supposing lovebirds might want to come up here for a getaway. Most times it just stays empty though. Turns out people don't like to walk so far for a shower.

Bobbi's hands felt raw as she got closer to the shower. She had been rubbing them together and as she walked little rolls of dead skin came off her palms like black Play-Doh. She blew them into the forest. She wrung her hands like dirty washcloths. She was rushing to get back to Rachel and Mister Courtney Tomball, but the walk dragged on. The shower stall felt much farther away than it had these past two-and-half months. She looked out for landmarks, trees she recognized. For a short while, they felt familiar but soon her worry started to rise — she felt as if she were being watched, like she had always been watched and was now just starting to notice — and all the foliage went strange.

Bobbi moved through the forest at a clip. She clutched the towel against her shoulder to keep it from falling in the dirt. The sunlight was going dim, as if controlled by a lever. Dark mushrooms bubbled up alongside the trail as she rushed past. Old trees hid faces in their rotting bark. At one point she stumbled and fell, then sprang back up again. The dead-bird feeling that had been crawling over her skin since the funeral grew stronger, as if she were still holding their carcasses. She wiped her hands on the towel. She stopped to spit at her hands but her mouth was like sawdust.

She heard the water in the distance. Someone was already in the shower. She stopped, considered going back. Germs danced on her fingertips. Her pores tickled. Bobbi was growing feathers. Turning into a dead bird. She needed that shower. She took a deep breath and kept moving. Whoever it is are only normal campers like me, she told herself. She searched for courage, buoyancy. She didn't want to appear afraid.

It's probably lovebirds, she said as cheerfully as she could, in case something was listening.

The light grew dimmer. She could hear the sucking of the drain and the pipe leading bathwater away down the mountain. It was still cold out for spring, but she smelled roses.

The four adjoining showers were made of white cedar. The stalls were only partially covered by a grooved vinyl roof in order to let light in, but the sun had sunken below the treetops and filled the stall with a fuzzy orange glow. Bobbi had to paw like a raccoon to find the bar of soap she had left inside the door. The water was running in the shower on the other side, but she couldn't see anyone's feet beneath the stall when she bent down to look. The smell of roses was overpowering. Bobbi hung her clothes on the nail. She bit her fingernail and turned on the warm water. She tried to cut the silence between them.

Somebody has fancy shampoo, she said. It smells good.

Somebody has fancy shampoo, her voice echoed back only with a smarmy edge, like it was mocking her.

Through the hot water, she felt a chill. Bobbi squeezed the soap, dug her swollen fingertips in. The bar slipped from her hand. It skidded beneath the partition.

She waited a moment to see if the other bather would kick the soap back over. Nothing happened, except the smell of roses began to turn rancid in her nose.

Excuse me, she said and shook off a fearful thought. My soap got away from me, would you mind sliding it over?

No answer.

Excuse me?

Bobbi knelt down on the wet floor and reached under the stall, padding around for the bar of soap. She felt nothing but water and wet cedar.

Do you think you could help me? I'm filthy. I've got a kid at the campsite. I've got to wash up and get back to her. It's almost dark.

Child?

It was a taunt. Her own voice again, but deeper.

She inched forward and peered through one of the narrow cracks between the boards. She saw the edge of a black cloth and a tight sliver of smooth white that looked like the skin of a statue. A flash of yellow teeth. A shiny little moustache. An orange glow burning inside the hood. The stall stunk of formaldehyde now. She saw smoke trailing out into the forest.

Child? the voice said in a way that sounded pleasant on the outside, but nasty as thorns beneath. With a full life ahead of her?

Excuse me? Bobbi said. Her own voice was choked with tears. She knew she was crying, but she didn't know when it had started.

Do I know you? Do you know me? Do I know you? she kept asking. She repeated it over and over again.

You're still a child, said the Stranger, who she already knew and he already knew her and she knew in her heart was Death itself.

Life hasn't shown itself to you yet, he said. You and life don't meet until the end. Nobody does.

Bobbi howled in tears and burst from the stall still repeating herself as she ran through the woods. Do I know you? Do you know me? She was wet and dirty. She heard something like the sound of dead leaves crackling in a large fire. Nighttime noises croaked in the forest. It was almost dark all around her. She fell twice. She bruised her thigh and her wrist, tore the skin on her tiny left breast. Mud glued her hair to her face. She fell again. She kept running. The campsite was much closer than it had felt on the way to the shower. She was almost there.

Outside the trailer she found Mister Courtney Tomball with his face in the dirt next to Mary, Rachel's stuffed lamb. Mary the lamb was covered in dark brown gunk. Mister Courtney Tomball wasn't moving. Bobbi ran to his side. She was still crying from her encounter with Death.

Do I know you? Do you know me?

The old man's neck was open up to his cheek, which was also missing. One of his earlobes was on the ground. The dirt was muddy with blood. Bobbi tried to remember what she'd seen on TV. All she could think of was CPR. She knew it was a stupid idea — his jugular was torn and his cheek was missing and he was dead. She tried it anyway. She was uncertain what death meant at this point. She had no clue.

The lamb had witnessed everything, she thought.

Bobbi spun around toward the trailer. Rachel was underneath in the back, wedged against the inside of the tire like a dog. She was bent over something. Bobbi could see her little body moving. She ran to her daughter.

Rachel was not on her belly. She was on her wobbly, decomposing toddler knees. She had one hand in the dirt. With the other, she was holding a piece of Mister Courtney Tomball that she was chewing on. Bobbi scooped her up and wiped the meat from her lips.

She slapped the girl. The smack was almost gentle by living standards, but a small piece of Rachel's chin came off in the process. She growled and bit the air, then froze to look at her mother. Her eyes widened for less than a second before her face scrunched into a knot. Bobbi was on a rollercoaster that had just stopped upside down. She froze and placed the softest kiss on her daughter's scalp, then dropped to her knees. She turned her face to the dusk that seeped down into the woods around her. The clouds looked hollow, like plastic bags drifting in the sky. She prayed but felt nothing.

Bobbi left Mister Courtney Tomball by the bloody stuffed lamb. She didn't know what else to do. She only knew to take Rachel and move on.

A God Who Could Forgive

Bobbi worried the world did not conspire against her. She was bothered by the thought that things might happen for no reason at all. She wanted there to be a God somewhere who made the world a good place even if it did not always turn out that way. She held Rachel's hand at night in the trailer. She hoped to pass the thought along somehow through touch.

Months passed, up and down the highways of the eastern seaboard, sometimes in circles, sometimes repeating themselves, never stopping anywhere for more than a week at a time, until the whole world looked the same. They stayed north in the warm months because rot loves heat, but far enough south — Maryland, Virginia, North Carolina — in the winter that it would be comfortable to cook meals outside the trailer. Bobbi pictured herself trapped in a video game, pacing similar territory all the time without ever quite finding the edge of her world. She lived a routine, most of it inside the trailer. She washed Rachel outside, under the moon, and tried not to be afraid of love. If there was a God who made the world a good place that wasn't always good, then there was a God who could forgive.

We Don't Pick at Ourselves

The way all toddlers learn to copy the world around them, Rachel learned to mimic the ways of living things as best she could. Bobbi sat in the dark trailer with Rachel on her lap and they watched videos on the computer. She iced Rachel's flesh, stroked the leather around the exposed tendons in her wrist, whispered to her as they watched cartoons Bobbi had mostly only heard about from other kids or seen in fragments as a child in group homes. The outside of the teardrop often crawled with flies that made a loud buzzing sound. The buzz was like an electrical tower, an orb of energy that hugged their tiny world. Rachel stared at the flickering screen, through it. She croaked. She reached toward it and missed like it was a mobile spinning above her crib. Bobbi worried about her, what she was reaching for, but tried her best to ignore those thoughts. She couldn't ignore anything. Instead, she prayed. Often she worried she was praying to nothing. The skin that separated her prayers and worries was thin.

Bobbi spoke to Rachel near constantly now, after reading a blog post about speech development in toddlers. According to the article, the average two-year old can speak fifty or more words and is on the verge of an explosive increase in verbal capability. Rachel only gurgled and spit, strung together little noises and ground her teeth to make a sound like her mouth was full of glass. Bobbi worried that Rachel wasn't exposed to enough conversation to learn the basics of being human. Even if her rotten vocal cords would never talk, Bobbi knew her daughter should be; she *was* understanding things, shaping a world around her, collecting words and objects in her mind. It was hard to tell what Rachel thought most of the time. Bobbi was still struggling with the basics of being human herself.

Rachel's body was changing too, Bobbi thought almost as a parody of other toddlers. She was still decomposing and growing all the time, but she seemed to be doing all of it more *quickly* than before, if that was possible. Like her body was repeating itself in fast forward. Her skin grew constantly tough in some places and soft in others. It cracked, then rotted, then peeled and healed again. In that way, Rachel was more alive than anything else Bobbi had ever seen. She was a log made of the earth, eaten and reproduced, turned to energy by mushrooms and bugs and algae and moss. Rachel's eyes did not widen, but eroded. Her cheeks did not plump like fruit, but blisters ready to pop. There were no curls around her hollow temples. Bobbi bought Rachel thrift store wigs she cut to match the full heads of young hair on other kids her age, kids she had never met and probably never would. The wigs were made of dark hair, much darker than Bobbi's, to disguise staining. The wigs fit on Rachel's head like a helmet. The hair came from a horse.

Bobbi's body had also changed as a result of her time with Rachel. There were certain moments, flashes of deep age in her face. She was bent in places — knots that throbbed in the center of her back or lines that creased at drooped corners of her lips. She sensed age coming like a storm off-course.

Love, love, love, she said into the spot above Rachel's ear. The word vibrated like a beehive between her lips and her daughter's skull.

Did you know that I love you? she asked, repeatedly. Do you now? Will you always?

Rachel reached toward the computer screen. A large, winged rat was flying toward a fancy party in a cartoon. The other rats below were singing. Bobbi hesitated, turned on a nature video. It was about snakes that left their skin on granite stones like shriveled ghosts.

One of the key methods for encouraging speech in toddlers was called modeling. Modeling basically meant narrating your life as you live it in front of your child. It was supposed to familiarize the child with the common objects, actions, thoughts, and feelings they would encounter as they grow. Bobbi had not thought of herself as much of a talker, but she quickly took to modeling and soon found herself speaking almost all the time, often without realizing it.

Mommy is washing your skin with a special towel, she said of the disposable ripped t-shirt material she had purchased in bags from a hardware store in Rhode Island.

She sang The Alphabet Song in a soft, deliberate voice. She sometimes imagined she was voicing the password outside a large black gate, although she didn't know why. She often peppered a lesson or a bit of information into her descriptions of the daily routine, usually about the saints.

Objects that come in contact with sacred remains become sacred themselves, she said. That's why this towel and our trailer and your drip bottle and your nightie and your bonnet and everything, maybe even Mommy, is special.

That means everything you meet will become special just from having known you, she said.

Rachel dug at a hole in her neck, working her finger inside. Bobbi brushed her hand away.

We don't pick at ourselves, she said. Mommy is going to give up biting her nails too.

Bobbi looked down at her chewed up fingernails. They were pathetic. She had wanted to quit biting her nails her whole life but it felt impossible to her, like a drug that kept her from falling off the edge of something. Rachel liked to suck on her mother's fingers and nibble the scabs and Bobbi told herself it was a reason not to quit biting them. Now it seemed less virtuous to suffer painful, tender fingertips and let Rachel suckle than it was to resist the temptation to bite them. Bobbi thought about it, but decided too much contemplation of her own habits was self-obsessive. It was better to avoid the issue altogether. Let God decide whether she bites her nails or not.

Mommy is having an argument with herself and it is making her uncomfortable, she said, yanking off a cuticle in her teeth.

Somehow Living a Life

When Rachel was three-and-a-half, Bobbi was robbed in a grocery store parking lot in southeastern Pennsylvania. The robber was only a boy, not yet old enough for high school. He was carrying a small folding knife with a wooden handle. It looked like something passed down by a relative. Bobbi prayed for him as he slipped the book bag from her shoulders.

You didn't need that knife, she said before he ran away.

I would have given you anything.

The boy kept running.

Rachel was safely locked in the trailer when it happened, but all of their money and identification was taken. Bobbi made a desperate trip to the Experts for help. She begged for gas money along the way.

I'm sorry, she said when she got there.

Don't waste anyone's time feeling sorry for too long, they told her, but reminded her gently that she had not been to visit them in too long.

Bobbi's eyes were watering as she handed Rachel to a man in a white coat. He was wearing a facemask and a shower cap, a thick rubber guard buckled around his arms. Another man slipped a mask and shower cap over Rachel's head.

Adorable, he said.

Bobbi thought she saw Rachel smile.

The Experts put Bobbi up for two weeks in a room with a hospital bed, a television, and a plant.

People kept visiting her, especially the old woman in the black cardigan, offering her Jell-O and Kool-Aid and sandwiches. They brought her magazines. Otherwise, she was alone.

She asked about Rachel.

She's a little trooper, they said.

We'll be finished with her soon, they said. For now.

One time they offered to examine Bobbi.

Bobbi said no, but they kept offering. The old woman in the black cardigan stood in the room nodding as if she were trying to send Bobbi a message, telling her it was the right thing to do.

We would love to look at you, an Expert said. We really would.

Bobbi just shook her head.

The day Bobbi left, she wrote a note on a paper towel and slipped it in between the leaves in her Bible. The note said: *This life will be lived somehow. This life will be lived somehow. This life will be lived somehow….*

She wrote it one hundred times in red pen.

It hurt to live off Rachel. Bobbi needed work. She would not come back here, she told herself.

Life will go on fixing itself if we let it, she said aloud, balancing Rachel on her shoulder as she climbed into the van.

If it doesn't, Mommy will help it.

Pulling Ribs

Bobbi went online to search for internet-based jobs. She found one writing video descriptions and adding tags for a company that created pornographic websites. It was not her dream job — saint — or even a step in the right direction, but the hours were flexible and it was the only one to get back to her. The footage made her uncomfortable at first but she didn't have to watch for very long in order to write accurate copy. Mostly she just lifted language from existing video descriptions. None of it mattered so long as the videos got clicks. They always did.

Bobbi worked at night, in the dark. The images on the computer screen painted the inside of the trailer in pink light. It was hot in the trailer. She wore headphones so Rachel wouldn't be exposed to the sounds the actors were making. The videos were noisy with headphones on, like a wad of the jungle being crammed in her ears. Sweat formed in droplets at her hairline as she watched. Her clothes moistened at the armpits and crotch. When she was working Bobbi hid the computer screen from her daughter, who lay on her back in silence like a doll put away in a box, dead eyes fixed on a constellation in the skylight above.

Bobbi watched the bodies on the screen thrust into each other like gears in a machine and it made her feel alone. She was an oddity among the human race, a person who had forgotten or never quite understood some simple truth everyone else took for granted. She knew the bodies on the screen were only playing at the sexual act for the camera but it still felt like a kind of worship. She was reminded of God reaching into Adam's side to pull out his rib. The image confused her. Humans were obsessed with making new life, she thought, pretending to make life, even watching each other pretend. She understood as well as anyone the instinct to protect; but the instinct to create remained somewhat of a mystery. She had never set out to make a child. Life was too hard a gift to put on a stranger, much less someone you would love forever.

Bobbi never worried about her own lifespan until she became a mother. Now she thought about Rachel and staying around for her seemed like the only reason for her own life to exist. She thought of an online video she'd seen about a baby who was born with a brainstem but no brain. The child lived two years without a single thought passing through his head before he died in his mother's arms. The constant smile on the boy's face made sense to Bobbi. When stuff like this became too much for her, she turned the pornography off and reached for Rachel's hand. She considered the stars that glowed like bits of glass through the sunroof. The constellations she had never learned. Those stars are all dead, she thought, and on fire.

Monstrum

Bobbi did an online search for the word *monster*, which led her to its Latin root: *monstrum.* Monstrum not only meant a monster but also an evil omen. A warning from God.

Washing Clothes

Bobbi washed Rachel's clothes in Laundromats with yellow lighting, hunched in the corner behind a magazine as the garments spun. She held Rachel close, dug her head into her armpit while they waited. She watched people look away from them. Rachel's clothes eroded quickly. Bobbi bought new clothes at thrift shops and megastores.

She wanted to buy a washboard. I want to wash our clothes in creeks and rivers, she whispered in Rachel's ear, as they watched the colors topple over one another in the wall of machines. I want the dirt from our skin to sail away into the sea.

Delicate Fingers

Bobbi held Rachel's forearms in each hand with two delicate fingers and operated them like the stick arms of a puppet. They were trying to play paddy-cake. Rachel did not understand the game. She trusted her mother to be in control. She knew very little, Bobbi thought, except to have faith in her mother.

Bobbi could not make herself trust Rachel in the way she wanted, needed in order to feel worthy of any kind of life, motherhood, death. It was as if she were nursing a tiger cub, loving it while trying to ignore what it would become. She prayed for forgiveness for her thoughts but no one responded, even to tell her whether or not her thoughts were something she needed to be forgiven for.

Advice From the Angel Babies

There were many websites in existence to provide support and information to parents who suffered stillbirth. Bobbi visited them from time to time, but never left a comment or asked a question. She felt like her situation was different, like she had done something — was doing something — that made her less than the other bereaved mother's on the message boards. Like she was carrying a toxin that might reveal itself if she typed so much as the phrase: Still Grieving in a subject line.

My loneliness is a sin, she thought.

The websites provided bits of information, facts that were not useful except as trivia to the mothers of the dead. One in every one-hundred and sixteen babies is stillborn. There are 26,000 stillborn Americans each year. These statistics felt unrelated to Bobbi's situation. She realized they existed to make her feel normal, as if she were part of a group, but she was skeptical that reading them made anyone feel less alone.

The websites had names like Angel Baby and Still Grace, Born Too Soon and Be Not Afraid. They featured whorls of lavender forget-me-nots and wisps of grey seedlings that sailed across the screen. There were blue and pink ribbons, typography ripped from the hospital gift shop. The websites always told her not to be afraid. They taught new mothers about their options before burial. They said things like: Don't be afraid to name your baby. Don't be afraid to take photographs, make a video. Don't be afraid to dress your baby if there were special outfits you wished to see your baby wear. Don't be afraid of life because you are still alive and must live it. Don't be afraid to cry.

Bobbi thought the websites should be altogether different. They should feature crushed flowerbeds and animal carcasses. Molestation. They should drip from the screen in cold puddles on your lap. They should be written in a code, black letters on a black screen, that only the mothers of the dead could read. They should fill the room with cold and the stink of bad fruit. They should turn your muscles to pus. Instead of telling you not to ask yourself: Why did this happen, the websites should confront you with the answer.

Life is full of dead things, they should say. It is your fault for participating.

You are not a mother, they should tell you. You are all alone.

The Imaginary Mother

When Bobbi was six-and-half-years-old, she had a brief friendship with a girl named Tayana who lived in her group home. Tayana's mother was very much alive. She lived a few neighborhoods away from the home. For the time being, she had been deemed unfit to care for her daughter but she was allowed to visit with gifts from the family, like candy and little plush animals that Bobbi coveted.

Before Tayana moved to the home, Bobbi had not once considered targeting another girl for friendship. She stared at her hands or her feet like they were foreign objects when the social workers tried to gather the children together or partner her up for an activity on the Magic Carpet, a colorful Astroturf rug laid out with shapes and numbers, where the children spent nearly all of their time.

She chewed on her fingers, which trembled. She acted as if she couldn't hear the social workers' directions until she thought she actually couldn't. Voices began to sound like waves breaking an object to bits in a faraway place. The air in her lungs felt too substantial when she was being spoken to, like hot syrup or goo. It was hard to talk.

Mostly, she had been ignored by the others so far and that came as a relief. Bobbi was scared, but she didn't know of what, or where she might hide from whatever it was. She looked out for love as if it was something tiny that would bump into her and rescue her. Otherwise, she kept to herself.

The truth is that as an adult, Bobbi didn't remember much about her relationship with Tayana except that it was short and made her feel like a person while it lasted, that Tayana had a mother and it ended when she went to go be with her again. What Bobbi remembered most was what happened after Tayana left. She remembered the Imaginary Mother.

The Imaginary Mother was the new friend she invented to replace Tayana.

The Imaginary Mother was not only Bobbi's mother but the mother of many girls just like her, spread around the world, girls who she would meet one day. They were her Imaginary Sisters, but she did not know them. She only knew the Imaginary Mother, who was her best friend and had come to be with her while she was in the group home, or while she was a child maybe, or until life got better somehow.

The Imaginary Mother did exist. She was a deep part of Bobbi, like a wound or infection. Imaginary things could both heal or become rancid, but Bobbi was too young to recognize either. The Imaginary Mother was a friend who would hold her close if she pretended.

There was no moment, no single instance when the Imaginary Mother entered her life, no haloed embrace on the Magic Carpet.

This was not a rescue, Bobbi knew that much. It was more like the Imaginary Mother was the same as her real mom and had been with her always and never left her alone in the world. That was part of the pretending.

Bobbi woke up in her bunk with the Imaginary Mother as a blanket. They talked mostly in her head (though she hummed slightly) throughout her morning ritual: brushing her teeth, sliding into her corduroys and poking her head through a turtleneck, picking at a generic toaster pastry while the other girls at the lone cafeteria table chattered like birds in a tree, each in front of a tiny cup of juice. The Imaginary Mother spoke in whispers, as if her voice was fading away. Her breath was a feather inside Bobbi's chest. She told Bobbi to never feel special and that would mean she always was.

But *you* are special, Mom.

No, I'm not. I don't even exist.

The Imaginary Mother's hair was dark like an oil slick, the opposite of Bobbi's. Bobbi thought she was beautiful. Bobbi thought they looked nothing alike.

We all look alike in some ways, whether we like it or not.

But I want to look like *you.*

Someday, *you* will.

Bobbi thought about sand on the beach. She had never been to the beach, but she had seen it on TV and in pictures. Her teacher said white sand was made from coral and fish skeletons, all ground up. Animals that had not only died, but almost disappeared.

Adjacent to the former glass factory that housed the girls' home was an annex reached by a hallway that went over a little bridge. The annex was where girls who had what the paperwork called Emotional and/or Behavioral Issues — which was almost everybody — went for therapy sessions. The Imaginary Mother stayed in the hallway during therapy. Most times therapy was spent quietly drawing or playing checkers. Bobbi had made a promise not to talk about her.

Of course, Bobbi wasn't the only girl at the home with an imaginary friend. The place was teeming with them. Invisible siblings, BFF's, and family pets paraded the hallways like ghosts, marching alongside the younger children wherever they went. Some of the ghosts, and the children they belonged to, demanded an enormous amount of attention. Bobbi preferred to keep the Imaginary Mother a secret. The Imaginary Mother made it clear this was the right thing to do. Secrets are best kept close.

I will always be with you, she said. A tiny spot in your heart.

That isn't enough, Bobbi said.

But that's all there is.

Bobbi hated to hear what she already knew.

The future seemed unreal to Bobbi as a child. The Imaginary Mother would take her there, or at least accompany her.

At snack time, Bobbi shared her sugar cookies and apple juice with the other girls. She would save half a cookie, not for herself, but for the Imaginary Mother to eat. Even though she had never had a family, Bobbi had an instinct that told her it was important for them to share. She also had an instinct for depriving herself, though she didn't know it yet.

During recess Bobbi sat alone with the Imaginary Mother on the splintered wooden bench where the other children laid their coats, humming. They talked about things Bobbi would not talk about in therapy. They talked until she felt sorry for herself and wanted to peel up the asphalt and hide beneath the playground. The Imaginary Mother changed the subject to nicer things, like what was Bobbi's favorite animal?

Bobbi felt guilty choosing.

When she prayed in her bunk at night, the Imaginary Mother prayed alongside her. They prayed to the same God, but Bobbi could not be sure if He heard her. She tried to feel a change when she prayed, anything at all. Sometimes she thought she did feel something but mostly she just felt strange, like there was a pocket inside her brain where God should be but wasn't. She watched the Imaginary Mother to see if she was doing something wrong.

The Imaginary Mother had her eyes closed gently, like a person who was sleeping. Slow breaths crawled in her nose and out her mouth. Every so often the skin near her temples would twitch as if she had been touched but otherwise her face was still. When she was finished, she would smile at Bobbi in a way that felt like a hug then she would actually hug her, drift off to sleep and leave Bobbi awake in her bunk. Sleep was elusive. Bobbi imagined everyone was talking to God but her.

The Imaginary Mother stayed with her for several years after the other girls Bobbi's age had already disposed of their own imaginary partners. Bobbi believed they would be together forever, or at least until the future came. She figured she would know it when the future was here.

One night after they had finished their prayers, Bobbi fell asleep before the Imaginary Mother. She was tired because she had been crying very hard earlier in the evening. When one of the social workers asked her why she was crying, Bobbi stopped gasping long enough to admit she didn't even know anymore. I understand, the woman said. You are tired. We all get tired.

In Bobbi's dream that night, she lived in a house with a bedroom that had her name painted on the door. Painted with love by the Imaginary Mother. The bedroom was dark but her eyes were adjusting to the light. The walls of the bedroom were decorated with posters of people with faces she did not recognize, but they felt appropriate like they should belong to a normal girl, like a girl on television with a family and friends in the neighborhood who dropped by to sit on the bed and look at magazines. There were stuffed animals (a duck, a bear, a pig) by her pillow. She was not joyous or excited or sad in the dream, but content. She dreamt she had just woken up in the middle of the night after a nightmare and was relieved to find herself at home. The walls of the house were constructed of feelings that made her warm inside. She listened for her family. They are all asleep, she thought. Having their own dreams. That idea also made her feel warm.

She heard a loud noise downstairs, not just the front door but the sound of the whole house opening up and then her bedroom door swung wide and a bright light flooded the room. The Imaginary Father was there, with an Imaginary Sister. They were as familiar as they were unfamiliar, which made sense to Bobbi in the dream, and there was something wrong with their faces. They had been crying.

She's dead, they told her.

Bobbi's chest ached like a ghost was trying to escape. Not dead. Only sick. Or injured. Not dead. A tragedy had occurred but someone, an expert, could help. There was still time to snap into action and do something because there was no way her mother was actually dead. There was always something that could be done.

All Bobbi could do was disagree with them.

She's dead, the Imaginary Father repeated.

Bobbi felt like she could disagree forever.

They found her bones, he said.

The Imaginary Sister stood at his knee in a yellow dress that made her look like a baby duck. They both kept nodding. Silent tears ran down their cheeks.

When Bobbi woke up in the morning the Imaginary Mother was gone, not even an imprint left in the sheets beside her. She went about her day like nothing had happened, and the next day, and so on until it felt like nothing had.

But as an adult with a young child, Bobbi sometimes wished the Imaginary Mother was there with her and Rachel, even as a disjointed skeleton. The Imaginary Grandmother's Bones.

The Cam Girl

Sometimes while Bobbi was tagging videos (Amateur, Asian, Teen, Cocksucker…) she would click on something and would get hit with a pop-up advertisement. Some of these pop-ups contained women who were willing to masturbate and have sex with objects for you as part of a private chat if you paid them for their time. Once a woman came onscreen and she looked tired. Bobbi saw her yawn.

Bobbi considered paying for the woman's time so she could take a nap, telling her to go ahead and sleep, but she thought better of it. She was afraid the woman might be offended, like someone was criticizing her performance. Bobbi thought she looked tired, but proud. It was pay-by-the minute anyway and it wasn't cheap. She wondered if God was watching us all the time like we were His own personal webcam subscriptions. She wondered how much He would pay to watch us. How much per minute, she thought, how much would He give per second of our lives?

Flotsam and Jetsam

Bobbi and Rachel parked in truck stops, garages, visitor centers, parks, and used car lots, on mountaintops, access roads, lookouts, and fields, outside twenty-four hour grocery stores, gas stations, nightclubs, apartment complexes, casinos, train stations, schools, churches, and Wal-Mart. They avoided police. They avoided anyone in uniform. They avoided anyone who looked interested in knowing them at all. Bobbi could see no benefit in being known. Loneliness was a comfort. Loneliness kept everyone safe.

I won't grow up, I will never grow up, Bobbi wrote on a fast food receipt and slipped it in between the leaves of her Bible, which she hadn't read in months. *We will all grow up.* She had been thinking about Little Orphan Annie. It was only later she realized the lyrics were from Peter Pan.

After Bobbi shut off her computer for the night, she would put Rachel in her lap and pick bugs from her spine like a chimpanzee. They listened to children's songs about fruits Rachel would never enjoy and numbers she would never understand. Through the skylight, they watched the ice blue fingers of thunderstorms stretch their tendons to reach inside the trailer. In winter they saw blizzards paint them into a coffin white flake by white flake. They looked at the moon and they looked at the stars until none of it made sense anymore, if it ever had.

When Bobbi was a girl, she was taken on a camping trip to a team-building retreat with a number of other girls from the home. It rained two of the nights, but the last night of the trip was clear. The counselors at the retreat took the girls to a nearby hilltop to view the constellations. Bobbi had never seen or heard of a constellation. She imagined a giant moving image in the sky. Something in color, like flesh. Something that might turn its head in her direction and whisper or growl. All she saw were tiny dots.

The children were handed photocopies of astronomical maps to look at under their headlamps, along with transparencies that had lines to connect the dots. The lines helped her see. The shapes made sense until Bobbi removed the plastic; then it was as if they had never been there to begin with. Bobbi pointed and gasped with the other girls anyway, utterly confused by their excitement but wanting more than anything to be a part of it. She wanted to see animals in the sky.

She tilted Rachel's head toward the skylight. She needed her to understand the constellations. To experience something she had been unable to herself. She pointed out stars above the trailer and made up her own constellations. Even those lacked sense to her eyes. Rachel didn't seem to mind.

They were parked in the lot outside a drab brick apartment building on the night of the mid-summer storm. The building was a monolith under the gathering afternoon clouds, a block of brick and concrete balconies with sliding glass doors that throbbed in the humidity. She had been driving north to escape the heat, but stopped for rest. When the power went out that evening, the building disappeared. Rain came at the trailer from the top and the sides. The walls were whipped by leaves, garbage, flowers, gravel, dirt, and small animals. Several times the trailer jumped. Or maybe the van in front of them jumped; it was hard to be sure because the whole world around them was moving, whisked into a hazardous stew. Wind and lightening split trees and took down traffic lights. Rachel hissed at the constant flashes above them. She reached for the violent blue light as if she wanted to strangle it or pull it to pieces. She shrieked through ruined vocal chords until it almost drowned out the storm. The sound was like needles on the brain. Bobbi covered her own ears with pillows then held her hands over Rachel's. She didn't want either of them to hear.

Bobbi prayed until she could only dream she was praying and then she continued to pray. Rachel strained but never rose or left her mother's arms until the morning came. At one point the trailer shook like it was in God's hand but then afterwards, nothing.

The storm battered the surrounding infrastructure throughout the night. Several were dead. Homes all over the Mid-Atlantic were broken or left without power. Gas stations and markets were closed. Trees standing for generations were splintered and thrown in the road. The heat wave that brought on the storm continued. Bobbi's forehead was burning. The parking lot smelled earthy, like beets.

The thick, needly top of a pine tree landed across the trailer's roof in the night, but did not break the skylight. Except for some scratches and a broken side mirror, they had been spared. The same could not be said for many of the other vehicles in the parking lot, including the four cars next to her that bore the brunt of the fallen pine. They were smashed, as was the rest of the world from the way things looked. The building stood tall but several of its sliding glass windows were in shards and there was an uprooted dogwood sticking out of the lobby entrance. Birds were singing. Bobbi couldn't imagine how they had survived. Some clearly hadn't. The first thing Rachel did upon being let down from the trailer was stumble along a trail of feathers in an attempt to find its source.

It was steamy but Bobbi wrapped Rachel in a small purple hood anyway. She had cut slits in the back to let her torso air out, but left the hood intact to cover Rachel's face. There were workmen gathered around vans and cherry-pickers that blinked in the street and there were a number of residents, some of them half-dressed or in pajamas, milling about the other end of the lot near the entrance. The people stared up at the building. They were peeking into cars and kicking at sticks with their slippers. Some had dogs.

One man carried a pet lizard. Bobbi used a short Nylon leash to keep Rachel close.

Nicole Armrest first appeared from behind them wide-eyed like a lemur, her face pointed through the foliage pressed against the side of the trailer. She was struggling to break through, caught by her black ponytail and the many rosaries around her neck and bangles on her wrists, tangled in branches, pinecones, and the sap of the broken tree. Bobbi held tight to Rachel's leash and moved near to help. Rachel was confused. She showed her teeth, but in the wrong direction. She was ready to attack the sky.

Nicole's mouth moved like she was chewing ten things at once. She looked very annoyed, not with Bobbi but with the storm or life in general. She cursed things so quickly that Bobbi could not understand her, but felt a need to help her stop. Bobbi tried to assist with one hand. She scooped Rachel and held her tight with the other.

Nicole brushed herself off. She looked them up and down.

You're parked in my spot, Chick, Nicole said once free.

Bobbi rushed to apologize.

I'm just fucking with you, Nicole said. We don't have reserved spots in this dump. Cute kid.

She hadn't even bothered to look at Rachel. She was too busy talking to herself now, scoping out the roof damage on the smashed Beetle one spot over.

You have no idea who you are fucking with, Bobbi thought. Really, you don't, or you would never even speak to us. We will never be cool like you.

There was something alive about Nicole that attracted Bobbi, an effervescence that bubbled from her giant eyes and constantly moving lips. She was at least ten years older than Bobbi, but somehow gave off the energy of a healthy child. Later Bobbi would learn it was prescription amphetamines and marijuana, but now the quality seemed almost supernatural. She imagined Nicole's insides filled with shining crystals. She pictured Nicole handing her one of the crystals in a walk-in closet while they prepared themselves in black dresses for a night on the town. Bobbi didn't know it, but she was more badly in need of a friend than ever.

Nicole introduced herself as they watched several men, disheveled tenants, wrestle with the dogwood tree blocking the front door of the building. It felt as if steam was rising from the pavement and tickling her calves. Bobbi held Rachel close and pet her forehead, unsure whether she was trying to comfort her or hide her face. Nicole said her real last name was Jennifer, but she didn't like having two first names.

Armrest is like my stage name, she said. My alter-ego, my nom de plume. I'm a writer, she said. Well, aspiring.

Bobbi didn't understand exactly. Why Armrest?

Nicole anticipated the question before Bobbi had gotten comfortable enough to ask it.

It's because I figure one day some super-cool Prince Charming-type with major assets, maybe a yacht and some famous friends, will read one of my stories and decide he wants to rest his arms on me, she said. Might as well put the thought in his head from the start. Or her head. I guess it doesn't matter as long as they're rich.

Nicole shrugged. I think about changing it sometimes but I've been blogging for a while now and I'm afraid of what it might do to my, you know, *brand.*

Bobbi watched the parking lot. She ran a gentle hand up and down over Rachel's face. She realized she was supposed to laugh at what Nicole was saying and allowed herself a chuckle. She thought of Miss Grundlich and sainthood and her mother, the ghost. She watched the people in the wet parking lot help each other pick up pieces of the earth, of their scattered lives, as if everyone agreed an old world or life had expired in the night and it was time for a new one to start fresh. She half-expected to lift her hand and find Rachel alive, pink and smiling, like their whole life up until now had been a dream. Instead she kept petting, afraid to look down.

It's so weird, Nicole said quietly as she scanned the parking lot. She was chewing on one rosary and fidgeting with the others. None of these people ever talk to each other on most days. We all just walk past and kind of nod. Now, because the wind blew a bunch of trees around and the power is out, it's like everybody all of a sudden cares.

Bobbi nodded. She had been alone too long to relate with what Nicole was saying but she was excited someone else had noticed some kind of change with the storm.

Weird, Bobbi said. She had goose bumps when she said it. She wondered if Rachel was capable of goose bumps and it made her sad again.

It's like all those stories, Nicole said. You know the ones you see where some person is being interviewed about how he saved some other person's life, like pulled them from an inferno or jumped in front of a bus or became a human shield after gunshots were fired into a crowd, and the interviewer is always like: *What made you do it?* Well, I don't know what makes animals care about other animals, like ants saving other ants or farm animals acting as surrogate mothers or whatever, but it's probably just nature. Biology. Whatever. I'm pretty sure they should be interviewing all the people who did nothing, right? Isn't there more to be learned from them? From the people whose instincts were *not* to help?

Bobbi wasn't sure if she was supposed to answer. It was hard to tell whose benefit these questions were for. It seemed like Nicole was talking to herself, like she had forgotten Bobbi and Rachel were there. Bobbi had no answers anyway. It occurred to her that they were just standing around themselves, watching other people do all the work. A woman and her daughter, not more than five years older than Rachel, had brought down pitchers of lemonade and tiny paper cups. Some people had branched off and were removing a bush from the road leading up to the lot. A spot near the front of the building had been taped off and several old men in work gloves and cooking aprons were trying to help a workman sweep up the glass.

Maybe we should help? Bobbi said. She hated herself for asking it as a question. I mean if you want to, she fumbled. She hated herself for that last part too.

Nicole was lost in a daydream brought on as if by the slow movements of her neighbors.

Maybe we should help? Bobbi repeated.

It looks like you've got your hands full with a pretty, uh, sick kid right there, Nicole said in a foggy voice. I should probably help though.

Bobbi couldn't help notice that Nicole was still just standing there next to her, watching, not joining her neighbors, not getting inspired to join.

She touched her cheek to Rachel's forehead. Sick, she thought. My sick kid.

Bobbi felt as if she had been pushing against a sheet of clear, suffocating latex that had finally broken as she marched Rachel toward the building. Broken glass twinkled like galaxies on the wet asphalt lot. Even if I cannot do anything to help these people, she felt, I will do the right thing. The storm the night before and this morning's soft display of healing had her in a powerful state of excitement, a trance. Her senses were altered. It was as if someone had turned the sound off. She could not even hear her new acquaintance calling out behind her. She could barely hear Rachel gurgling in her ear.

Was this how the saints felt? Was this how it felt to be called? To live your life for others? Even as she thought these things, she realized that in thinking them, in wondering, in allowing her thoughts to stop and turn inward, she had been less than selfless. Her doubt was immediate. What help could she provide these people that was not already being taken care of by neighbors and workmen and insurance companies? Of what use was she to anyone, even if she wanted so badly to be? Who, in the long run, was she doing anything for but herself?

By now she was on the broad sidewalk that led up to the lobby entrance. People were scattered about her. She stood in the center of the activity. She felt alone like a stranger that wandered uninvited into a party and was waiting for someone to notice. A strange girl carrying a dead child.

Her chest deflated. She was dizzy. The world tilted beneath her. Rachel screamed. There were eyes all around her, burnt holes in the spinning landscape. She saw spots. They sizzled, retreated. Bobbi couldn't tell if the whooshing that filled her head was made by the gasps of those around her or the wind or something inside her brain. It was too hot for a breeze, she thought. She saw the woman who was dispensing lemonade put down the pitcher to pull her daughter close, protect her.

Rachel reeked in her mother's arms. Stink filled the air in lines and bubbles, like something drawn in a little girl's composition book. There were dark wet spots on Rachel's sweatshirt. The spots caught Bobbi's vision. They also looked like eyes. They blinked at her. She would've gotten sick if she hadn't lost consciousness first.

It hurt her to know Rachel's clothes would never be more than a bandage.

Bobbi came to in a circle of people. Her head pulsed. It was a wide circle and the people in it weren't getting any closer.

Rachel held onto her mother's shirtsleeve with an outstretched arm. She lurched at the people who stood around them. Their mouths were open, unsure whether to help or run away. Rachel looked equally unsure. She reached out toward them with one hand while the other clung to Bobbi's shirt like a talon. A rough, gravelly noise escaped from her little mouth. A noise like a village being crushed into sand.

Bobbi could feel hands on her back, under her armpits, helping her up. Plastic beads on her neck like drops of cold water from the ocean. There was a burning sensation behind her face, her eyeballs. They had only just met but she knew it was Nicole who was helping her up. She wanted that badly to trust someone.

Bobbi slurred an apology at the crowd of neighbors around them.

I was trying to help you, she told them.

The back of her head was wet with hot blood from where she hit the pavement. She could feel Nicole's hand on it. She wasn't sure if Nicole was trying to stop the blood or hiding the head wound from her neighbors.

Rachel's attention was now drawn between the crowd, her injured mother, and the woman who was touching her mother. Her head twisted back and forth in near complete circles. She looked frightened, confused, like a nocturnal animal caught in sunlight. Bobbi pulled her close and held her. Nicole pulled them both off the curb and toward the wrecked revolving door of the building.

She's fine. They're fine. Nicole repeated herself in a loud, casual tone that did nothing to reassure her neighbors. Vicious hangover, she called out as she guided Bobbi through the door. We had a super late night. Plus, all this heat, am I right? And the storm. They're fine. I've got this. It happens all the time.

Bobbi's head was foggy enough to almost believe the things her new friend — or rescuer or something — was telling the people out front of the building. Rachel clung to her mother's neck. Sucked on her wet hair. The next thing Bobbi knew, she was inside a room swirling in posters and ripped concert flyers, on some kind of spongy lump, a soft boulder or maybe the back of a fattened, humped animal, unable to keep her eyelids open.

When she woke up, the dim room was fluttering with bats whose large flapping wings had images of faces and rainbows plastered all over them. Her brain throbbed against the inside of her face. There was the sound of her daughter wailing in her ears. She couldn't tell if the noise were in the present, a memory, or a dream. A white light shone from beneath a door on the other side of the room. The sound was coming from inside. Nicole — how did she even remember that name? Where from? — stood above her like a concerned totem pole, holding a pair of boxing gloves that looked as if they had been torn apart by eagles.

There was the vague memory of a tornado or hurricane — she didn't know the difference — but the prospect seemed unlikely. Nothing in life seemed likely. She knew she had a daughter nearby somewhere and that called for an attempt to get off the pair of bean bag chairs where she had been resting and find some answers.

Rising didn't work so well. She had to lie immediately back down. Rachel's crying was the sound of a loved one close to death. She got up again but the swollen pulse in her temples pushed her back down into the mound of vinyl and Styrofoam pills.

Nicole nudged her with one of the shredded boxing gloves. Rachel howled. Questions bounced around in Bobbi's head. Was the room painted, covered in mirrors and photographs, or alive with bat wings? Other things too, harder to define. Unpreparedness mostly. Irresponsibility like a sin.

She fought sleep, but impossibly, like a very old woman trying not to die.

When she woke again the lights were brighter and there was loud music playing as if to drown out the sound of crying. It worked, more or less. She could still hear Rachel behind the door, but softly. She was now making a kind of mucus-filled gurgle sound accompanied by a whistle, like it was coming from a hole in her chest. The noise was not as loud as her cries, but more disturbing.

She felt woozy as she stood up and touched the back of her head, which was wrapped tight in a pair of worn Lycra leggings with toilet paper sticking out the sides like feathers. She was taking an uneasy step toward the sound when Nicole came out the bedroom door and turned down the music. They looked at each other, listened to the sounds coming from behind the door.

I put her in there because she was kind of freaking out in a big way, Nicole said. She nodded at the boxing gloves on the floor near Bobbi's feet. Don't worry. I didn't punch her in the face or anything. I just used those to pick her up. She got a little, you know … Bitey? Great kid though. *Great kid.* So sorry she's feeling so … Gross?

Nicole chewed on the plastic rosaries around her neck, scanned the posters, magazine photo collages, and show flyers that filled the walls of her apartment like a teenage girl's bedroom. Bobbi thought that if she could read her mind it would say, Sorry your baby girl is dead. It must be very awkward for you.

And how are *you* feeling, I should ask, Nicole said. You hit your head pretty hard when you fainted. Don't worry, I played nurse. I cleaned it out with some vodka and then made a super-stylish bandage for you. The Internet said you weren't supposed to sleep but, you did, and you're up now. So that's good.

Bobbi had stopped listening. She had her hand on the bathroom door. Nicole turned off the music with a remote control. The room was still, except for the blowing of the window unit. Rachel had gone silent. What did that mean? Something inside Bobbi's veins was frozen, terrified at the prospect of losing her daughter — to what, and how? She was only in a bathroom and already dead — but something else, a tiny something that she hated, felt a tinge of relief. It burned like her heart had been tapped with a cigarette that was quickly pulled away. Her brain throbbed inside the Lycra wrap. She still thought she might be dreaming. She opened the bathroom door.

Rachel was on her belly with her face crammed in a crack in the tile border that lined the wall next to the shower stall. As they entered the room, Rachel lifted her head. Bobbi thought she saw her eyeing Nicole's calf muscles. Her mouth was covered in dead ants and a foamy black and yellow fluid. She saw Bobbi's feet and followed them up to her face with wide grey eyes that looked full of love and hope to Bobbi. Rachel pushed her face back into the cracked tile and sucked loudly. There were dead and dying ants all over. The wriggling ants mixed with her spittle to form a black jelly. Bobbi noticed Nicole gag a little.

I'm sorry. Both women said it at the same time like a chorus.

Jinx, said Nicole.

The apartment remained quiet. Even Rachel obeyed the jinx.

I think she's hungry, *Bobbi*, Nicole said, and with that name released her from the jinx.

Bobbi didn't remember telling anyone her name.

I need to get back to our trailer, Bobbi said. She was talking to herself.

I will come with you and help, Nicole told her. I'd like to help.

The Fasting of Spiders

Blood. Spiders. Bobbie thought about these things whenever she was bit or sometimes when she couldn't sleep at night. Spiders sunk their fangs into her skin to suck blood. She assumed that was what they were doing even though she had never watched one do it. She had seen the bites they left.

Bobbi wondered if spiders fasted. They were weird. They crawled on Rachel, in and out of her like they were drawn to there, but she had no blood to suck. Only a residue of blood, gunk like grease in a nearly dry sponge, and was that enough to press your mouth against and feed on? Bobbi worried. Was that enough to live?

Presents

Nicole Armrest reminded Bobbi of girls at her high school that she had avoided on instinct. Not that it ever mattered, she thought. She couldn't have been friends with them if she tried. These were girls who seemed like they were trying to be too grown up at the time. It was funny because Nicole was older but came off so youthful to Bobbi and she still seemed like one of those girls. It was like Nicole had stopped aging, at least mentally, during her adolescence.

Bobbi had always felt she didn't fit in with any age group.

Everything was an animated and distracted event for Nicole, from putting on clothes to picking out music to listen to while putting on clothes, to planning out her meals for the day, to leaving status updates on her social network. She was frenetic. She paced the apartment typing things into her computer, scribbling on notepads, changing channels on the television, trying on accessories, checking herself in the mirror, rolling joints, opening windows, fidgeting or adjusting her hair. Each action was usually punctuated by a little dance with her hips, as if everything was part of the preparation for a complicated spell. She often talked about being famous, and what that was like, and how it happened, and who it happened to, and why. Bobbi nodded a lot, and smiled.

She wasn't sure what to make of any of it. For the first few days while her head was still ringing, she held

Rachel tight in their beanbag nest and fed her from a cooler at the foot of the couch, which held meat products from the trailer. Nicole did not allow meat in her refrigerator. They kept the lights off during the day and waited for Nicole to get home from work at the salon with carry-out inari or packs of vegan beef jerky. She would already be talking as she came through the door, as if they had been with her in the hallway or even at work before that. Bobbi thought she sounded like a tree full of baby birds. She also sometimes thought of bats.

When Nicole didn't talk about being famous, she asked Bobbi a lot of questions. Sometimes she wrote things down as they talked, which she told Bobbi was normal for a writer. Rachel growled at Nicole, but quietly, and stayed close to Bobbi when all three of them were home.

She'll, um, warm up to me eventually, Nicole said. Everybody does.

Bobbi was glad for everybody's sake that Nicole moved around so much when she talked and never tried to sit right next to her and Rachel. Bobbi felt like she was carrying someone on a tightrope, but she wasn't sure who. By the third day she was at the apartment, she felt she was a burden but Nicole insisted she stay at least one more night. The same thing happened the day after that. Against her instincts, Bobbi started to get a little bit comfortable. She knew this meant it was time to leave, but she didn't.

You guys are good for conversation, Nicole told them one night as she stood in front of the TV. She flipped through channels so fast Bobbi thought she might be playing a game with herself. I need someone to talk to when I'm not writing, she said.

Bobbi had not seen her write anything except when they were talking. Then she scribbled away. Her pen sounded like claws on the page.

Bobbi closed the windows during the day because one of them didn't have a screen and the other's screen was broken. She was protecting Rachel against bugs. Nicole reopened them first thing when she came home in the evening. She turned on the fans, slid open the balcony door. She never mentioned the smell but Bobbi could see her swallowing, sometimes covering her mouth as she spoke, like someone trying to politely avoid a poisonous gas. Then she would roll a joint and pour a glass of pink wine from the box in her refrigerator and find ways to interview Bobbi as if it were a casual conversation.

You're so young. I'm jealous. And a mother too? Nicole asked. What's that like?

Oh my god did it hurt? Giving birth? Were you a virgin? Was he? I'm sorry. Don't answer those questions, but seriously what was it like? Did you consider the, you know, alternative? Sorry. But did you? I guess adoption was out of the question. I didn't mean it like that, but was it? I mean, was there anyone to take her? How did you come up with her name? Is it from the Bible? It's Jewish, right? But you aren't Jewish, are you? Not that it matters. But I guess you aren't raising her too religious or whatever? What am I saying? Why not? You can raise her however you like. It's your prerogative, right? Do the Feds know about her, um, condition? Do they help out at all? I mean, don't they have to? I think they should. How did you end up entering data for porn sites anyway? I mean, was the father into that scene? Oh my god did he have a big dick? Don't answer that, but seriously what was he like? Do you ever feel like your life is over? I'm sorry. Don't answer that.

Bobbi felt like the oxygen was being sucked out of the room when Nicole talked, but it also sort of energized her. The lights seemed brighter. It was nice to be the subject of so much interest, but it also sent a fearful tingle, like a burn, up the skin on her arms. Sometimes Bobbi fantasized that Rachel would answer for her.

One day Nicole came home carrying a bag of bright yellow tee shirts she had printed with a photograph of

Rachel's face on them. She said she had only wanted to get one for Bobbi, but there was a deal where you got three shirts for the price of two and she couldn't resist it.

Now all three of us have shirts, she said.

Bobbi tried not to look at Nicole like she had just lit herself on fire. When had she taken the picture? She imagined Rachel snapping at her while she tried to zoom in with her phone.

The man at the print shop thought she was cute, Nicole said. She said it in a way that Bobbi thought was supposed to be reassuring.

Actually, I think he might have thought she was some kind of doll, Nicole went on. I told him it was a bad picture.

Bobbi held up the shirt and looked at the picture. The way Rachel's teeth and gums were exposed made it look almost like she was smiling, but there were thin white maggots erupting from a lump in her cheek. The worms looked like spaghetti, still-captured the way they were in the photograph. Bobbi thought of Play-Doh.

They look great, Bobbi said. She was afraid she sounded like someone evaluating a photographic exhibit of motorcycle accident victims. It was a struggle to appear comfortable, holding the shirt and hiding Rachel's eyes with her forearm at the same time. Rachel wiggled on her lap until her head popped free and she came face-to-face with the tee shirt. She barked at herself and hid her face in Bobbi's breast. She nibbled between whimpers.

Nicole stood over them smiling like someone watching a dear friend open presents.

Web Sharing

The tee shirts ended up being a hit. Bobbi wore hers with reluctance at first but Nicole seemed to wear the shirt all the time, putting it on first thing when she got home, and

Rachel began to grow infatuated with the thing. In the beginning she had been scared but it wasn't long before her face grew animated whenever she was around the tee shirt. She followed Nicole through the apartment with her eyes, transfixed by the image of her own bobbing disembodied head.

The compulsive, instinctual way Nicole moved about her apartment made Bobbi think of an animal tending to a nest or a web. She and Rachel spent the afternoons alone in comfort, watching cartoons on a big, flat television, waiting for Nicole to come home and begin scurrying about. Bobbi tried to imagine what flies felt when they were captured by a spider. She thought being trapped in the soft, sticky web might be comfortable to them as they watched the spider come and go. She imagined a kind of resigned satisfaction at having nowhere to go, no more choices to make. She wondered if an insect's time spent caught in the web was ever the warm, shiny part of its life. Did spiders ever fatten the animals in their webs? She knew they sometimes clothed them in silk to be preserved.

Sainthood for Suckers

I would rather wear a fur coat than a hair shirt, Nicole said out of nowhere one day, as if they had just been talking about either of those things, which they hadn't. Bobbi looked up from the television, confused.

Faux-fur, Nicole said. I'm a vegan.

Bobbi was still confused.

How do you know you want to become a saint? Nicole asked.

Bobbi had not mentioned sainthood to Nicole before. She wondered if Nicole could have been reading the notes she placed in her Bible. She eyed the plastic rosary Nicole was twisting around her finger. She answered anyway.

I just do, Bobbi said.

It sounds like something that ends badly, Nicole said.

Rachel was on the carpet at Bobbi's feet, her face hung slack against the side of a stuffed pig. The pig was wearing a tiny tee shirt with Rachel's face on it. Nicole had apparently made more of them. The soft pig was wet, its plush ragged. Bobbi noticed it was starting to look a bit like Rachel.

I guess I never think about how it ends, she said.

Bad Thoughts

Bobbi first felt a devotion to suicide the same morning she prayed for her daughter to disappear. It was raining and Nicole was at work. Bobbi was alone with Rachel on her lap. She could feel Rachel's chest move softly against her belly. Rachel was pretending to breathe.

She touched Rachel's scalp with a napkin from the take-out Indian food Nicole had ordered the night before. Then she reached for a pen and wrote this note: *I don't know why any of us are pretending to breathe anymore.* She tore off that section of the napkin and flattened it in the leaves of her Bible.

The bad ideas came almost all at once, as if they were being squeezed into her mind by many strong little hands. Prayers of her own death, then prayers begging for forgiveness, images of Rachel alone in a hole somewhere for eternity eating worms, prayers for Rachel's death whatever that meant, to disappear, were all working themselves around her brain at once, so she couldn't even be sure which prayer had come first and which had been a reaction to another prayer. She shook her head. She concentrated on forgiveness, begged for punishment, and pinched each bead of a white plastic rosary on the table, jewelry marked and dented by Nicole's teeth. She breathed.

She calmed down some but she still couldn't help wondering if anyone had ever prayed herself to death before. She knew of many cases where the saints — and maybe even members of other religions, she thought, surprised to be thinking it — had their lives saved by prayer, but she couldn't think of a single story where someone had prayed for death and then, just died. It felt wonderful and terrible because she was afraid she had a new goal in life.

She tried to distract herself with television, but then turned it off. She went online and tried to work at entering dirty video tags for a while, something she had not found herself keeping up with much, the longer they had been staying at Nicole's apartment. It was difficult for Bobbi to remember how they had survived before the storm, even though it had only been — how long? Not long. It was hard to imagine survival in the future. Death also seemed impossible.

Bobbi held Rachel to her chest and breathed. Rachel copied her. She had been silent as a rock all day. Now Bobbi could hear crackling in Rachel's chest. She imagined her breath and her thoughts tied up together, like a thick braid of soft fabric pulled in and out of her body and the body of her daughter, a giant lure pulling their souls somewhere, tugging them into non-existence somehow. It didn't happen. Eventually Nicole came home and switched the television back on.

Bobbi managed a smile at the door as it opened. Nicole said something about a woman's fingernails being like daggers and groaned, then said she was going to take a shower and did a little dance on her way there. Bobbi waited until she heard the water turn on then she took Rachel out to the balcony. It was still raining.

Bobbi stood on the balcony with Rachel in her arms. She wished Rachel would stick her tongue out over the edge to catch a raindrop. Rachel was a toddler now and it seemed like something a toddler would do. Bobbi put her own tongue out and waited until she caught one. She looked down at Rachel, who was getting too large and cumbersome to be carried. Rachel did not copy her or do anything at all. Bobbi looked down over the balcony. She eyed the lines on the concrete, the parking blocks. She was only four-stories up.

Bobbi heard the sound of the screen door grating behind her.

It's only four-stories up, Nicole said.

Bobbi was startled. She looked over her shoulder at Nicole and almost dropped Rachel by accident. She gripped her tight in her fingers. Rachel's body made a noise like tiny bubbles being squeezed from a piece of softened fruit.

If you jumped feet first, you would probably just break your ankles and maybe your knees or hips, Nicole said.

Bobbi held Rachel even tighter. She meant to pull her back from the railing at the edge of the balcony, but she couldn't move. She was still just looking over her shoulder at Nicole.

Nicole nodded at Rachel. I'm not sure what would happen to her. I guess she'd break in pieces or something. After that, who knows? Nothing good though.

Bobbi tried to breathe. She could feel a tiny wind from Rachel's mouth on her neck.

If you tried to belly-flop, you'd break your shoulders and ribs for sure. I guess you'd crush her though. You'd both probably live somehow.

Bobbi tried to swallow but it didn't work.

A nose-dive most would likely break your neck and give you some serious brain damage but I'm not sure you'd get anything more than that. You might die. If you want to do some real hurt, you'd better wear her like a crown when you dive, Nicole said, lighting a cigarette. Drive yourself through her like a stake. Even then…

I was just trying to catch raindrops with her, Bobbi said.

Do you know what you should do? Nicole said. Is get high. And start a blog.

Bobbi had never smoked pot before. Or started a blog. She had never jumped from a building before either. She wanted to do all three at once.

I'll help you, Nicole said. I can help you.

Bobbi smoked pot that night but didn't start a blog or jump from the building.

She ate corn chips and called them wafers, then laughed at the face of the girl in the logo on the bag they came in. She sat Rachel on her lap and they pretended they were an airplane, together in the sky, a fighter jet, while Nicole blasted away at them on the floor with big guns, wearing a yellow tee-shirt with Rachel's face on it. The shirt was stained with ketchup.

Rachel convulsed, laughing, when Nicole pretended to die.

You Deserve A Funeral

Bobbi sometimes felt like a burden on Nicole. She cleaned the house while Nicole was at the salon. She tried to pay her from the little bit left after the last deposit the Experts had made in her account. Nicole refused the money. She said they were paying her back all the time, even if they didn't know it. Bobbi hid cash in her books when she wasn't home.

One afternoon, she logged onto the computer and tried to do some work writing copy. One job was from a live chat room of people who were supposedly in your area and wanting a sexual encounter. She was supposed to write some enticing dialogue for a cartoon to say in a pop-up ad containing a portal to the site. Underneath a flickering animated gif of a white-haired warrior princess with bare breasts and a scepter shaped like a penis, Bobbi wrote: *YOU DESERVE AN ORGY!*

She looked at the screen; it blinked back at her and she imagined the inside was full of candles. Rachel was lying on the cushion next to her with her arms and legs up in the air, like a dead turtle. Bobbi shut the computer and picked up her Bible. On a piece of an envelope, she wrote: *YOU DESERVE A FUNERAL!*

She shut the Bible and sat it on top of the computer.

Video Stars

Sometimes Bobbi caught Nicole videotaping them with her phone. She would shoot them just playing together, or Rachel being cleaned, or Bobbi praying with the television on. Bobbi always covered both of their faces as best she could when she noticed, like they were celebrities leaving a scandalous hearing. Stop, she shrieked and Nicole would just laugh.

Chill, Ladies, Nicole would say and click off the camera. We're just having a little fun. I'll send it to your computer and erase it. Nobody else will see. Unless you want them to. You'll both thank Auntie Nicole one day, for preserving your little lives together.

Social Networking

So tell me about these porn sites, Nicole said, picking up a notepad. I mean how did you get in touch with them?

Bobbi didn't say anything.

Through Craigslist probably, Nicole said and scribbled on her pad.

Bobbi was quiet and tried to look busy chewing her nails.

Do you know any of the guys who run the sites? Like, at least know them on Facebook or whatever? Could you introduce me to them?

I don't use Facebook, Bobbi said.

Nicole looked shocked or at least like she was pretending to be shocked, Bobbi thought.

How do you keep in touch with … you know … people?

Bobbi put her hand back in her mouth and closed her eyes.

Do you want to smoke pot again? Nicole asked.

I don't think that's a good idea, Bobbi said. I need to keep an eye on her.

Bobbi looked to Rachel on the far end of the couch on top of a pile of yellow paper towels. She hadn't blinked in an hour.

What do you think is going to happen to her? Nicole asked, pen ready. I mean, what else…

I worry about all of us, Bobbi mumbled through her fingers.

What? Nicole asked.

Nothing, Bobbi told her. I said Nothing.

Did you ever consider working on camera? Nicole asked with a smile that was both mischievous and sincere.

Best Friends Forever

Weeks turned into months. Bobbi had run out of meat in her cooler long ago and taken to ordering steak subs during the afternoon while Nicole was at work. She would feed Rachel the greasy beef and save the bread and condiments for herself. She had started trying to feed Rachel with a little pink spoon. It was supposed to make them both feel more normal.

Nicole kept asking her questions. Bobbi tried not to answer much, but it was becoming harder not to trust

Nicole. Proximity had made her Bobbi's closest adult friend. Bobbi wasn't sure she was meant to have any friends.

What were your friends like growing up? Nicole asked. Your old friends.

She had just gotten home from a session at the tanning salon. Her eyes looked pale.

I don't know, Bobbi said. She could feel Rachel between her legs, trying to chew through her shoe. Nice?

But what were they like? Nice to you, like the way I am?

Nicole was clicking a pen with her thumb. It made Bobbi nervous.

I moved a lot, she said. People were nice to me sometimes.

Come on. You must have some crazy girl-stories. You were a teenager like yesterday.

Bobbi didn't feel like she had ever been a teenager.

I was quiet, she said.

Now that's a shocker, Nicole told her on the way into the bathroom. I have to pee.

Bobbi felt like a small child and she felt like an old woman, but nothing in between. She didn't inhabit the part of life when you were supposed to have friends.

While Nicole was out of the room, Bobbi removed her sneaker and Rachel put her mouth to her mother's foot. Bobbi wiggled a big toe against her teeth.

Best Friends Forever, she whispered.

She had heard girls say this and seen them write it in each other's notebooks when she was in school.

What was that? Nicole shouted from the other room.

Nothing, Bobbi said, but she didn't mean it.

The Oldest Tree in the World

The oldest tree in the world lives on a white mountain in California and its roots remember a time before pyramids and it is still dying. Bobbi learned this from her computer. The video she watched told her about the tree and how long it had lived for, but didn't mention that it was dying. That was something Bobbi inferred.

Bobbi made silent plans to take Rachel to visit the tree. It was a gnarled bristlecone pine, twisted and dead-looking but still very much alive according to the video. The earth around it was rocky and off-white. It looked like dusty snow. She held Rachel's fingers out to touch the image of the tree on her computer screen. Their hands lingered. Rachel left a smudge like a shadow over the tree and its surroundings.

The Definition of Death

So who was your best fuck? Nicole asked. She had been drinking. She was holding her phone like it was a microphone and she was a television news reporter.

Bobbi blushed. She looked at Rachel, almost expecting her to blush also.

She shook her head.

You're obviously not a virgin, Nicole said. Then she mumbled something. Bobbi thought she said: I think…

I'm not a virgin, Bobbi said. Duh.

Nobody says that anymore, Nicole laughed into her phone.

Bobbi wasn't sure what she meant. Nobody says duh or nobody says they aren't a virgin?

Duh, Nicole said and laughed some more. *No doy.* Now that we've established the shape of the table…

Bobbi fake-chuckled. She knew she sounded fake. She wanted to climb out the window.

It's a weird table, Bobbi admitted.

Nicole seemed to get lost in that thought for a moment. Bobbi hoped Nicole was realizing that her questions made her uncomfortable.

People like weird though, Nicole said finally. She started flicking channels on the television. People eat that shit up. Weird people get famous.

Even famous people die, Bobbi said. She wasn't sure why she said it.

Maybe, Nicole answered. Her tone was absent. She pretended she had become preoccupied with the remote control but Bobbi could tell she was thinking about something.

Depends on how you define Fame, she finally said. Depends on how you define Death.

You don't define Death, Bobbi thought but said nothing.

Reality Television

Bobbi watched Rachel with Nicole. She had originally been afraid for Nicole around her daughter, but now she was worried about something else. She was afraid they would become friends.

Rachel never seemed to connect with Nicole, not in ways that inspired jealousy, unless they were watching reality television. Then Rachel and Nicole would both become transfixed, side-by-side, in front of the television. They didn't seem to notice each other or anything else while the shows were on, but they reacted to the screen in unison like puppets on the same string. During the commercial breaks, Rachel would stare at Nicole and smile. It was like Nicole had just given her a magic potion or showed her a crystal ball.

There were several shows Nicole watched in a religious way and those became Rachel's favorites too.

There was one about a family of dwarves and another about a family whose children were covered with thick black hair from head to toe. They also watched one about people racing across the country in trailers and having adventures, trying to live life faster than one another in order to win a fantastic prize. None of these shows interested Bobbi. She sat on the floor between Rachel and Nicole, and tried to enjoy them, but she couldn't. She ended up behind them on the couch looking over the top of her Bible, watching them sit as a pair.

She tried to understand what her daughter saw in these shows. Was it just the quick moving images and voiceovers that drew her in? Bobbi wondered if Rachel thought she was watching real life. She worried that Rachel was learning how to live from something she herself didn't understand. She also worried that Rachel looked up to Nicole.

She vowed to read the lives of the saints to Rachel, every one she could find. She also vowed to give her a life full of adventures, even as she swore to keep her safe. She prayed and hoped that someone heard her prayer and would help her, or at least hold her to it. She prayed to understand anything at all.

Missed Connections

Bobbi forgave Nicole the night she destroyed her computer. The destruction appeared to be an accident, but Bobbi wasn't so sure. She forgave Nicole anyway. She stayed up all night on the couch in the dark with Rachel nested between her legs, trying to make herself forgive. She prayed. She saw this act of forgiveness as practice for a larger test just as much as she saw it as doing the right thing. More maybe, but she refused to admit it.

She also worried. Her computer was like an umbilical cord that attached her to the rest of world. She worried she would never be able to leave the apartment, work, live on her own again. She ate all of her cuticles thinking she might be with Nicole forever. Then she felt guilty for worrying, because Nicole had provided them so much.

This is how it happened:

Bobbi and Rachel had been eating an extra large meat-lover's pizza all day. They had ordered it at noon for breakfast. Rachel ate the meat and whatever scraps of crust her mother could get her to swallow. Bobbi ate the dough and bits of torn-up cheese. Nicole came home late from work, drunk and wanting to dance.

Bobbi didn't feel like dancing. Bobbi had almost never felt like dancing in her entire life. She watched people dancing and it was like she could not hear the music, like the music had not been made for her ears.

Nicole tugged at Bobbi's wrist but she resisted. Nicole danced on her own for a while. She drank pink wine from a box. She kept offering Bobbi wine. Eventually Bobbi said yes, but only took sips from her glass when Nicole was looking at her. Rachel was licking grease spots off the empty pizza box on the floor.

Sometimes you just gotta dance, you know? Nicole was thrusting her buttocks against the refrigerator. She wore a sideways baseball cap. There was a photograph of Rachel on the front.

Bobbi nodded, as if she knew anything about dancing.

Nicole strutted out onto the balcony and then back inside and across the room, skipping over the mess of wires that crawled from the back of her TV like snakes. She tried to hop on a stool in the kitchen. She stood on the coffee table in front of them and gyrated like an exotic dancer, beckoning with her finger. Bobbi smiled up at her weakly. She was protecting Rachel with one arm and the computer with the other. Nicole laughed. Bobbi was sure she would topple at any moment. Nicole hopped down from the table and started dancing in front of Rachel. She pretended her plastic cup of wine was a microphone. She was lip-synching. A love song. Bobbi didn't recognize the song but she knew it was about love.

Bobbi sat her computer next to her on the couch. She should have closed it.

Rachel was reaching for Nicole. Bobbi put a finger inside the collar of Rachel's shirt and held her back. Rachel continued to reach. Bobbi couldn't tell if she was smiling or straining with her teeth against the air. Nicole bent to pick her up.

She likes me, Nicole said. I'm her biggest fan.

Bobbi smiled but held tight to her daughter's collar.

Nicole kept trying to pick her up.

She was also still holding the wine glass.

She moved closer to the couch. She tugged.

The wine glass tipped onto the computer.

Nicole let go of Rachel, panicked when she saw what happened. Bobbi pulled her shirt off and threw it on the keyboard. She started scrubbing.

Nicole ran around the apartment looking for paper towels, apologizing.

Oh my god, she kept saying.

You keep them in the kitchen, Bobbi screamed. They are always in the kitchen!

Nicole came back with handfuls of paper towels. Bobbi's screen had gone dead.

We'll put it in front of the radiator and dry it off, Nicole said. It's okay. We'll surround it with rice. Do we have any rice? Oh my god. I'm so sorry.

Bobbi crumpled into the couch next to her broken computer. She was topless. She watched Rachel on the floor. Rachel only looked confused.

I forgive you, she told Nicole.

But she hadn't yet. It would take her all night to forgive.

Purgatory

Bobbi spent the week following the destruction of her computer feeling very alone and even more fragile than usual. She blamed herself for the accident now and she felt deeper guilt for even partially blaming Nicole.

Rachel didn't know the computer was no longer in their lives or what that meant, Bobbi thought. She only sought her mother's attention. Bobbi gave it to her. They wrestled in the most gentle way, almost in slow motion, and Bobbi read her stories from the gospels and they rolled a ball back and forth on the carpet. Bobbi loved her daughter, but she felt a dark wire tickling her heart. She knew she was failing her and probably had been all along.

Nicole promised she would buy Bobbi a new computer, a better one, as soon as she could afford it. Any day now, she said. Or at least very soonish.

Bobbi didn't ask for the password to Nicole's computer or even ask to use it. She was being shy and hated herself for it. Nicole offered a few times though. She sat next to Bobbi and watched her, excited to see someone enter captions beneath clips on amateur pornography sites. Bobbi felt uncomfortable with Nicole watching. She didn't look at or do anything on the computer but work and she only used it those few times.

She felt like the apartment was more of a cave than ever, like she and Rachel were hiding from life inside its walls. She thought about it as if they were in purgatory.

Missing Children

It was a pale Sunday morning when Bobbi woke up to find that Rachel was missing and she was alone in the apartment. Bobbi searched everywhere. The bedroom, bathroom, and balcony, in closets and drawers, beneath sinks, cushions, and chairs, as if she was looking for something the size of lost keys or a sock. She looked on the counter and the door for a note from Nicole that would explain everything. She tried to pray the note into existence on a pink Post-It, probably saying something like: *Went for a girl-date!* But Nicole had never taken Rachel out of the apartment before. There was no note.

She went into the bathroom to find some clothes, which were all mixed into a hamper with Nicole's at this point. When she saw herself in the mirror, she stopped. Her face looked weak and yellow. It was as if she had not seen her reflection in a very long time. Her eyes were dark and her hair stood in greasy clumps. Her arms and the sides of her breasts had wrinkles in them from the cushions on the couch. She started to turn on the shower, then thought of Rachel and how she was supposed to be running to find her. She hesitated between the shower, mirror, and door. She stepped under the water. I need to be clean if I am going out there to look for her, she told herself but felt like she was lying.

People will think I am crazy, she shouted at the mirror.

She took a very fast shower and was throwing on clothes from the top of the hamper as she hurried out the door of the apartment. She still had soap in her hair. She only wore socks on her feet.

The hallways were long and empty. Bobbi looked both ways like she was crossing a street in busy traffic. She tried to follow Rachel with her thoughts. She pictured her stumbling through the halls. Why would she leave? It hurt to think about it. Bobbi was almost sure Nicole had taken her. Like a witch in the night, she thought, only it was morning. She imagined Nicole as a spider, taking Rachel off to a nest wrapped in silk.

Bobbi headed for the stairs. They were dirty concrete and only ever used for emergencies.

She climbed down in circles, jumping the last three steps at the bottom of each level. She searched the two floors beneath Nicole's apartment. She pulled on maintenance closet doorknobs and looked behind the leafy plastic plants some people placed outside their entrances. She would search all the hallways and then she would begin knocking on doors. She couldn't imagine herself knocking on stranger's doors, but she knew she would be willing to do it. She entered the lobby and scanned the parking lot, then started back up the steps to search the rest of the floors.

She searched each hallway, in a panic, and moved upward. The roof was calling her.

She imagined her little girl on the roof, floating.

She imagined joining her and being lifted up to heaven.

There was no one in the hallways. Not even a neighbor searching their pockets for keys. It was like she was the only one in the building.

Then she was on the roof. She didn't remember pulling the door handle. She didn't even remember climbing up the ladder on the wall. It was like she had been carried. She was not even out of breath. The roof was empty.

She circled it to make sure. There were fans whirling inside of cages. There were puddles on the roof and tiny pebbles everywhere. She walked over the pebbles in her socks, to the edge of the building, and shielded her eyes from the sun. The parking lot was covered in more black puddles with rainbows inside them. Bobbi knew it was pollution but she thought it was beautiful and looked for

Rachel among them. Her van and her trailer were out there. The parking lot was quiet as a cemetery.

As Bobbi looked into the distance, her fingers went numb. The horizon made her realize she had no idea where she was on the planet. Had never known. The buildings were as unfamiliar as any others she had seen. One of them, only a few blocks away from the apartment, was a small brick square with a sign on it that caught Bobbi's attention. The building was a library.

Bobbi went there in a daze, looking for answers. She peered behind bushes on the way. She felt as if she had died and was entering an afterlife. Her socks were wet and the sun was stinging her eyes.

She walked into the library as though she had been there many times before. Nobody asked her any questions. If anyone was looking at her, she didn't notice. She sat down at a computer and went online.

She looked up missing children first, even though she knew Rachel had only disappeared while she was sleeping. There are a lot of children out there, she thought as she looked through their faces. Just missing.

The Internet suggested things and Bobbi let her thoughts be guided by them until her search had turned from Missing Children to Dead Children, then Dead Child, and finally, Dead Girl.

That's where she found Rachel.

Her daughter had gone viral.

The first thing she saw was a video montage, set to synthesizer music with a funky horror beat that she listened to through a pair clunky headphones held together with duct tape. The video reminded her of something she had seen at a group home, a game that involved a turquoise balloon like a piece of jewelry floating on air. It was a game the other kids had not let her play. The video had no balloons in it. It had only her playing with her daughter, tending to her, living their lives on a couch, hiding their faces from the camera over and over again. But it felt like a game she was not allowed to play in.

There were more videos, with different soundtracks. She watched herself mothering to death metal, Gregorian chant, theme songs to old sitcoms she hardly remembered from reruns.

Then she found the image macros and still shots scattered across the web.

Her daughter was a meme.

THE WORMS GO IN, THE WORMS GO OUT, one said in big white block letters with thin black outlines.

There were hundreds more.

One of them called her a harelip.

She is not a harelip, Bobbi almost screamed.

Another said she should run for president.

Fuck, Bobbi thought.

She worried that Rachel might also think: Fuck.

Bobbi prayed a prayer of thanks every time her daughter was called a hoax.

Being called a fake made Bobbi feel safe but it also hurt her. It made Rachel not real, but an image. Something like Saint Mary burnt into a piece of toast.

It made Bobbi not real, too.

People put Rachel's faces on things.

Rachel's head was on the body of a kitten.

Rachel was a clown with a top hat.

Rachel was popping out of a snail shell.

Rachel's face was at the center of a flower.

Rachel was the baby Jesus on a holy card.

Bobbi saw these things and too much more, clicking on links with a swollen red finger. There was never going to be a deeper answer than FUCK. FUCK. FUCK.

There was an image macro of Rachel holding a melted ice cream cone. I SCREAM it said at the top. At the bottom it said, AND YOU SCREAM AND YOU

SCREAM AND YOU SCREAM AND YOU SCREAM AND YOU SCREAM…

There was another picture of Rachel, a still shot from the video montage, with her drooling something black and full of chunks down her chin. REMEMBER TO EAT YOUR VEGETABLES, it said.

Bobbi slogged back to the apartment in her wet socks and waited, poised on the couch, holding Nicole's computer on her lap as if it were evidence or a ransom.

Nicole came home after dark with Rachel behind her on the leash. The lower half of Rachel's face was wrapped like a bandit's in a black bandanna printed with pot leaves. Bobbi dropped the computer on the table and marched across the room to meet them. She pictured the way it would feel to slap Nicole and watch her neck snap backward but when the door opened and she saw them, all she could do was pick Rachel up and hold her. She removed the bandanna from her face. Rachel was smiling. She smelled like smoked meats.

Relax, Nicole told her. We were just, you know, getting a snack.

Why is my daughter famous?

Bobbi knew she was supposed to be yelling but when she heard her voice it came out weakly, as only a question, like something a child would ask.

She's not famous yet, Nicole said. Internet famous, maybe.

Nicole said she had been waiting to tell her after they had gotten enough hits. Generated some momentum, she said. I wanted you to be surprised *and* impressed with all the work I've done. Not just surprised.

Nicole explained how this was good for them, the start of a better life. For *all* of us, she said. She walked to the sliding glass door and opened it for air.

Nicole used the word: *Career.* She used the word: *Vocation.*

My grandmother always used to say you've got to make use of what the good Lord gave you, she told Bobbi. Actually, my grandmother never said that. But I heard it somewhere on TV and it makes sense, right? This is what the good Lord gave us.

Bobbi did not like being referred to as *Us*. It felt too permanent. *Us* means me and Rachel, she thought. *Us* means nobody else. *Us* means forever.

All your favorite saints were famous, said Nicole. Think of me as your agent. Like John the Baptist was for Jesus. See, she said. I went to Sunday school.

Bobbi had never been to Sunday school.

There's no going back now anyway, Nicole said. People live forever on the Internet. Besides, look at her: she likes it!

Rachel was just sitting there in Bobbi's arms. Her eyes were rolled back in her head. Her mouth was slack.

She's hypnotizing us, Bobbi said in her mind as if Rachel could hear her thoughts.

Sleep on it, Nicole said. Just go to sleep.

Bobbi nodded but did not go to sleep.

She went to the couch and Nicole went to her bedroom. Bobbi lay in the dark holding her daughter to her chest and counted her own heartbeats. We are all just pretending to sleep, Bobbi thought. Everyone in this apartment is pretending we're asleep.

She had counted thousands of heartbeats when she got up from the couch. In the darkness, she started to pack her things. She adjusted the dangling plastic blinds to let in bars of moonlight to see by as she gathered Rachel's toys, clothing, medical equipment into the three duffle bags they had been living out of since they had been in the apartment. Most of her own clothes were mixed up with Nicole's. She wasn't sure what had ever been hers anyway. She stuffed as much stuff as she could find lying on floors and chairs around the apartment into the three bags.

She was about to leave when she heard Nicole moving in the room next to her. Bobbi froze and listened. Nicole was reading something. She could hear pages turning. Bobbi took Nicole's computer off the coffee table and slid it under her arm. Rachel made a croaking sound. Bobbi started to the door. She tripped on an empty wine bottle on the way out. It rolled across the floor and made a loud noise.

She knows we are leaving, Bobbi thought in the hallway. Rachel was next to her on her leash. She stood there for a moment, breathing. The heavy sacks weighed on her shoulders. She was waiting for something.

Why didn't she try to stop us? Bobbi thought as she trudged their belongings to the elevator. Rachel followed right behind her and pressed the button.

A Truck Stop Dumpster

Bobbi had been on the road for a long time with Nicole's computer. It was unopened, locked, in the back seat. It distracted her while she was driving to know it was back there. One evening as the sun pulled behind a group of pine trees planted to block sound from the highway, she pulled into a near empty truck stop and parked the van next to a dumpster at the far end of the lot. It was about to storm. The dumpster was open. She could see a bouquet of roses inside. She opened her trunk and unearthed the computer from beneath Rachel's things. She carried it over to the dumpster, where she closed her eyes and said a prayer.

I am sorry, she said. I'm the worst.

When she opened her eyes, she noticed a yellow bin next to the dumpster. It was there for dropping off donations of clothing and books. Rain clouds were moving overhead. Bobbi hesitated between the dumpster and the bin.

Vitae

Rachel continued growing. Even as a bigger child, her face was newborn. It got longer and leaner and Bobbi was always stitching to keep it together. Her eyes stayed large in their sockets and what there was of her nose remained upturned, like a button holding her expression in place, keeping the whole thing from falling off her head. It was a scrunched up face and sometimes reminded Bobbi of something carved into a very old tree-trunk.

Rachel was old enough for Bobbi to know she needed an education. She read to her from the Bible and any other book that came into their possession. She read from menus and newspapers. It was hard to tell if Rachel understood any of it. Bobbi mostly just sounded out the words for her regardless of what they said. After a while she began to think she was learning more than her daughter from all the reading they did. Especially from things like the newspaper. Bobbi couldn't remember ever reading a newspaper before. The world inside it was different than the one she knew. It was different than the one she had encountered on the Internet, too. Both of them just sort of shimmered and danced around her and Rachel, as if they were living in a glass ball. She remembered something about how Saint Francis of Assisi taught Saint Clare and her Order of Poor Sisters to hate the world. She wondered how many worlds there were and if she was supposed to hate them all.

Bobbi's memory of the *Canon of Saints* book she had gotten from the library as a child was not as strong as it once was. So much has happened since then, she thought. It was sometimes as if her childhood had not existed.

Now Bobbi was sweating and bugs kept landing on her skin. She was in a small town in the southeast somewhere. North Carolina? Georgia already? She gripped the handles of two empty two-gallon jugs in one hand. Her other arm was wrapped around Rachel, holding her close. She tried not to use the leash anymore. Rachel had reached the size of a child too old for a leash. Bobbi thought it attracted stares. She had to hunch slightly to hold her. She sometimes felt like an old witch, guiding a youth back to her cabin.

They were walking down the only large street in the town, which was mostly full of fast food restaurants and tire shops. There were little strip malls here and there and she had seen a bowling alley. She was looking for water. She had already been turned away from a fast food restaurant when she'd gone inside and asked to fill her jugs in the bathroom. She knew she shouldn't have bothered to ask. She should have just done it. And maybe left a note. Now she felt stupid. She thought Rachel might melt on the sidewalk. Her cheek felt squishy against Bobbi's side.

The bookstore was not on the main drag, but right off it down a sidewalk overhanging with Spanish moss, in a small blue house with a battered front porch. There were lots of little places where the paint had chipped away to reveal different colors. It made the house look spotted with confetti. A sandwich board out front said: BOOKS. AIR CONDITIONING. CAT PETTING. COFFEE AVAILABLE UPON REQUEST. There were chimes in the tree above, but they were not moving. There was no wind.

A bookstore, Bobbi pointed out for her daughter. Wanna go inside a bookstore, Rachel? Watch out for kitty.

Bobbi imagined Rachel repeating her.

Watch out for kitty! Rachel would say.

She said nothing.

Inside the front door was a hallway of books and boxes. It was cold. Bobbi could hear air-conditioners humming. The hallway looked much longer than the little house could fit, she thought. On either side of the hallway doors had been removed from their hinges to reveal dimly-lit rooms: small rooms, medium-sized rooms, rooms that looked a little too big for the house, like the hallway. All of them were full of books and boxes and what looked like piles of trash, some with stacks covering the windows so only little slivers of light stabbed through and danced in the center of the room.

Hello? Bobbi said. For some reason she expected to hear an echo, but she didn't.

Customer! she heard a woman's voice call out from somewhere deeper in the house.

It sounded like a frog, but Bobbi could tell the voice belonged to a woman.

Bobbi did not feel like a customer. She felt like a refugee. Now she knew she would have to buy something.

Come in! another voice called. It was a friendly male voice that also sounded like a frog.

I'm in! Bobbi said. She didn't know what else to say. We're in!

Then come further!

Yeah! Come further!

Bobbi guided Rachel further inside. The hallway smelled like cat urine and old pulp. There was sawdust on the hardwood floor. Bobbi could hear footsteps and the shifting of furniture somewhere inside the mess. She sneezed. The air in the house made the inside of her face itch.

Bless you! both voices shouted.

Bobbi was feeling allergic and strange and she didn't know why but she felt like the voices really meant their blessing. Every other time she had heard someone say that, it sounded like they were being polite.

Bless me! Bobbi said. Rachel was holding close to her side. Bobbi patted her on the head. She was wearing a wig that was too small for her and it moved a little.

When Bobbi finally found the couple, they were sitting in a spotless kitchen filled with bright yellow light.

The kitchen made Bobbi think of old movies. There was one fat fly hovering around the room. A black cat eyed it from one of the vinyl floor tiles, tracking the fly with its neck.

They were sitting next to each other, facing the door Bobbi and Rachel had come through, with smiles on their faces like they had been expecting someone. They were both round like eggs with bulges of fat beneath their chins that wiggled when their necks moved. The man had a large bald spot in the middle of his head and thin curly blonde hair that looked like a halo. The woman's hair was dark with grey streaks in it and she had a lollipop in her mouth.

You found us! the man said.

Bobbi felt like she had won something.

This house is deeper than anyone thinks, he said. His wife nodded.

People get lost in here forever.

All the time, she added with the lollipop still in her cheek.

Not all the time, the man corrected. They both laughed so Bobbi did too. Then she put her fingernails in her mouth.

So, the man said. What are those jugs full of air for?

Bobbi looked confused. The couple laughed. Bobbi laughed too.

How about we fill them up with water? he said. Unless you are still attached to the air?

Bobbi looked down at Rachel, hiding her face against Bobbi's butt cheek. Thank you, she said. We don't need air.

She waited for the couple to laugh or say something. At first they just looked at her very seriously, but then they did laugh and she laughed too.

The woman got up from her seat with some trouble and took the empty jugs from Bobbi's hand. She went out through a door into the backyard to fill them with the hose.

The man turned to Rachel. She looked at him and then pressed her face back into Bobbi's side. Would you like to pet the kitty? he asked.

I don't think that's a good idea, Bobbi told him. She had her fingers in her mouth again. Rachel is not used to animals.

The man smiled at her with his lips closed. We are not afraid of her, he said. His mouth looked so wide he could swallow them both.

She listened outside for the sound of the hose but heard nothing.

The cat stepped closer to Rachel.

Bobbi hesitated, but then loosened her arm on Rachel's shoulder.

Rachel reached out and petted the kitty.

So, he asked. What are you looking for? Something for the little one?

I don't know yet, Bobbi said. I think so.

That's not a lot of information, but it may be just enough to work with.

The man got up from his chair and steadied himself against the Formica countertop.

Follow me, he said and led them back into the hallway. He moved with purpose, as if each step were the product of deep effort and focus. Bobbi and Rachel followed him a short way down the hall and then into a dimly lit room that looked like all the others, full of books and videocassettes and milk crates full of trash on the floor.

This room is where I keep books for people who don't know what they are looking for, he said, flipping a switch that lit half the bulbs on a small chandelier above them. Dust hovered in the light. I have a little bit of everything in this room. That's what most people end up here looking for anyway.

Bobbi looked around the room. The bookshelves were tall and messy. Too big. The dust is getting to me, she thought. She wanted to get out of the room before it started spinning.

Do you have anything about the saints? Bobbi said. She had not left the trailer that morning planning to buy anything but now she felt like she had to if she wanted to get out of this place with their water. She had wanted something about the saints for Rachel anyway.

The man grinned and squinted and shook his finger at Bobbi. I had a feeling that was what you were looking for, he said. I can usually tell what books people need within a few minutes of meeting them and for you it was tricky, but I had a hunch…

Bobbi could tell he was waiting for her to laugh, so she did.

The man rooted through the pile of trash in the center of the room. There was a strong odor coming from the pile as he lifted up stained shopping bags and pizza boxes and towels with brown, molded spots eating holes in them and tossed it all back to the floor at his feet.

Here it is! the man said. Right where I left it!

He was holding a thick book with padded white covers and a red tassel with a small magnifying glass at the end. It looked ancient. The cover had gold lettering on it and reminded Bobbi of a wedding album. The lettering said:

VITAE,

And More.

This is the book you've come looking for, the man said. This is the book for you. You can flip through some of it here if you like, but I am almost sure you'll want to buy it.

He handed Bobbi the book. It was not as heavy as it looked. The pages were very thin. She could see through them if she held them up to the light. The writing was tiny. Dots on a page. Footnotes in the margins were even smaller. Bobbi was squinting. The text looked like a glitch on a computer screen.

That's what the eyeglass is for, the man told her. It comes with the book free-of-charge.

Bobbi could feel him watching her so she laughed and he did too and Rachel made a gurgling sound.

Back in the kitchen, the man's wife was cradling the jugs of water in her arms like they were babies. Thirsty? she asked.

Bobbi nodded. She took the jug and knelt down to pour some into Rachel's mouth. Then she drank from it herself.

So did you find her book? the woman asked her husband.

Right where I left it, he said and Bobbi felt them looking at her so she swallowed her water and looked back at them and everyone laughed on cue.

It's not a cheap book, the man said. But well worth your sacrifice. And since you figured out what you needed so quickly, I can cut you a deal.

Bobbi had her mouth full of water again. Gulp.

It is so clean in here, Bobbi said. She was looking around the kitchen like it was the first time she'd seen it.

Not like the rest of our lives, the woman said.

Don't you want to hear my deal? the man asked.

Bobbi wasn't sure.

You two just pose for a few pictures with my wife and the kitty out in front of the house, he said. Maybe holding up your book. Something we can use to promote the store. And the book is yours. I won't take no for an answer.

Bobbi looked to the man's wife. She was nodding. Her smile was large enough to eat the house.

Outside, Bobbi thought their collective weight was going to sink the front porch. She imagined falling through and then falling through a brittle skin of earth and then falling forever into a pit lined with crushed houses and dead animals and roots and bones. The sun was bright and a light breeze had picked up. The wind chimes in the tree were playing a song now. Shadows danced beneath their leaves. The woman gave Bobbi a dandelion and told her to put it behind Rachel's ear. The neighbor's dogs were barking.

Smile, the man burped from the lawn in front of them. And hold up your book!

Bobbi held up her book and they all spread their cheeks wide as he captured their image with a Polaroid camera. Bobbi thanked them and began to leave.

Aren't you going to wait and see how your picture turned out? the woman asked.

Bobbi waited. The man stood in front, smiling at them and shaking the photograph in his hand.

Minutes passed. Time slowed down until it became awkward.

The image was still black when Bobbi said goodbye.

Hagiography

Vitae was very different than the slim *Canon of Saints* book Bobbi had read at the library as a girl. *Vitae* was endless. There were only so many saints in the *Canon of Saints* and each one with not more than a short chapter describing the events in their lives: the lessons they had learned and taught, the miracles, their death, and usually some more miracles afterward. *Vitae* had many more saints, ones she had never heard of. The chapters were long and detailed and horrifying. Instead of just saying what happened, the book described it until it was painful to hear any more. Pages devoted to the color of blood in a puddle somewhere. Bobbi read aloud in the trailer, with Rachel next to her. She felt invisible hands touching her chest or moving down her spine sometimes when she read and she had to shut the book like she capturing something inside.

Bobbi looked for the names of the authors but the front pages had been torn out. When she first noticed this on the front porch of the bookstore the woman just said that was standard procedure in the book business. Bookstores tear the front pages from lots of books, she said. It's what you do if the book is damaged or nobody wants it. You tear part of it off and send it on its way.

Bobbi continued to check the front of the book while she was reading, as if the pages might have grown back.

She suspected there was more than one author. The voice shifted and contradicted itself, even within the chapters, as if the book had been written and revised over a very long period of time. Maybe forever, she thought. She liked thinking of the book as something ancient, but there were modern saints included in the book so it couldn't have been. She thought of the pages like they were treasure maps she knew she would never understand but enjoyed holding anyway. She ran her fingers across the paper in her trailer at night.

I don't want treasure, she thought. I just want to follow a map.

Sometimes she couldn't read all the details to Rachel. There were too many or they hurt her to read aloud. Her tears rolled off the thin paper as if it were coated with wax.

Instead she just told Rachel what happened. It wouldn't teach her how to read, Bobbi knew that, but she told the stories anyway, often at night before they went to sleep. She liked telling the stories about young girls most. She knew children liked to imagine themselves as characters in the stories they heard. She grew used to telling the saints' lives, sometimes making up little details of her own.

Saint Maria Gorretti was a crushed lily born to a peasant farmer. She lived in a room in an old cheese factory on a count's plantation and her family's greatest possession was a painting of the Virgin. Maria was a modest young girl who spent her time doing housework with her mother. She was called "the little old lady" by her neighbors in the factory, whose oldest son, Allesandro Serenelli, raped and pounded her eleven year-old body like he was breaking wood with his fists, then stabbed her eleven times in the abdomen with a sharpened file and went to sleep in a nearby room, leaving her for dead. Half an hour later, he heard her opening the latch to her door. He stabbed her three more times through her heart and lungs and went back to sleep, certain she was dead. Three hours after that, her whimpering was mistaken for her baby sister's and her mother came to her aid.

She spent six hours in an ambulance on bumpy roads on her way to the hospital and offered up her thirst as a sacrifice to God when told drinking water would give her peritonitis. She pardoned her attacker before she died and requested his presence in heaven. A medal was placed on her chest. From the first day she was interred, miracle seekers visited her grave for cures and received them.

Allesandro pleaded insanity but was found guilty and sentenced to twenty-seven years in solitary confinement in Sicily. Maria appeared to him in a dream in his cell, dressed in white and gathering lilies that turned into fourteen glowing white candles, one for each time he stabbed her. He confessed and upon his release, he visited Maria's mother to ask for forgiveness. She led him through town, past a statue of her daughter, to receive communion.

Saint Agnes was a lamb of twelve when, in the name of her Lord, she rejected the advances of a group of young Roman men who admired her beauty and wanted to put themselves inside her. The men were bitter and reported her to the local Prefect who had her whipped and dragged by her hair, naked and bloody through the streets to a brothel. As her body was broken against the cobbled roadway, men in the surrounding crowd tried to rape her but were struck blind and fumbled, lost and erect, over one another as she was dragged away.

Another man pitied her and wanted to save her. He bent his knee and proposed marriage as the small girl was hauled past.

"I am already married to God," said Agnes. "This is our wedding party."

She blessed the man with the sign of the cross and he felt God's long, gnarled finger touch him and he converted there on the street, kneeling in Agnes' blood. Agnes was tied to a stake outside the brothel to be burned but the wood did not catch fire no matter how much it was stoked. A soldier tore her down from the stake and stabbed her through the throat. She prayed for him, gargling. Christians collected her blood in rags along the path she was pulled. They saved her tiny bones as relics. Many who prayed in front of the bones were healed. People still pray to the bones.

Saint Eulalia was a little dove who wanted death so badly that her mother moved her to their country estate to keep her from joining the martyrs in town. Eulalia ran away from her mother's home and interrupted the morning session of the local court to protest the persecution of the faithful that had blood filling the city's gutters and fountains. The judge spared her because she was from a noble family but Eulalia did not give up her protest. She spat and hissed at the judge. She smashed their gods and offerings. She was given one more chance, but refused to kneel. Soldiers stripped her naked before the court. Hooks for catching large fish pierced her sides. The lines were tugged slowly. Torches of burning oil were held to her newly formed breasts until they melted down her ribs.

Eulalia laughed at the judge. The courtroom watched terrified of her and for her at the same time. She was put in a barrel lined with nails and rolled down the steps of the courthouse. Her eyelids were removed. Eulalia begged the court to repent for their crime. Her skin was peeled off with knives. Her teeth were twisted and pulled. She was tormented until the men grew bored with her.

The judge ruled that Eulalia should die by fire and decapitation. People had gathered to watch as she was mounted to a small cross above a pile of broken wood. The flames swallowed her legs and a heavy sword was held over her head. As she spoke the name of God, a white bird flew out of her mouth and over the audience. Her head came off and rolled to a stop on the ground, smiling. Her bones and ashes were collected and stored in a silver casket.

Bobbi repeated these stories often, and many others, until it became as if she was telling Rachel of their own family history. She felt connected to these saints like she had inherited something from them and it was holding her up but she also felt separate, the way a bird's nest is part of a tree.

Good night, Rachel, she whispered.

Mommy loves you.

Rare Bacon at the Diner

Bobbi was at a diner peering into her new book with the magnifying glass. It was dark out in the parking lot. She and Rachel were sharing one side of a booth. The other side was empty. Bobbi sat this way whenever she could, using her body as a kind of wall between Rachel and the restaurant. If Rachel sat across from her, Bobbi felt out of control and could not eat anything but her fingernails.

There was a miniature jukebox at each booth in the restaurant. Bobbi gave Rachel quarters to pick something out. Rachel only stared at her. A quarter fell onto the table and spun. Bobbi held Rachel's hand in hers and pushed the coins through the slot one-by-one with Rachel's small fingers. She took Rachel's hand and pressed a few buttons without looking. Music came on. The soundtrack to an old western gunfight.

Good choice, Bobbi said. Mommy's little Deejay.

Bobbi ordered rare bacon for Rachel, toast and iced water for herself. A man in a grey suit pushed through the door, making a little bell ring. The noise made Bobbi jump. The man walked to their booth, sat down across from them and took off his hat like he was supposed to meet them for dinner and had been running late. His face was friendly but pale and blank. When Bobbi looked at him, all she could think of was a snowman. The waitress came over and took his order. The man ordered coffee and rare bacon.

You haven't come to visit us, he told Bobbi. We've missed you both.

The man wiggled his fingers at Rachel, then held his hand out.

High five, he said.

Rachel slapped his hand and made a noise like laughter. Bobbi felt sick. Her fingers were tingling. She wanted to push the heavy book into his chest and make a run for the door.

Visiting us was part of the deal, he said. He was doing something with his paper placemat, folding it into something. Not that we were worried, he said. We never worry. What's the point? No one has that much time to waste.

Bobbi had not even said hello. She just looked at the man's face. Nothing about him felt real.

Your daughter's famous now, he said. Semi-famous. Internet famous. We've been trying to handle that for you.

The man shrugged.

It was inevitable, he said.

Just another thing to watch, he said.

Where is the waitress with that coffee? he said.

Bobbi watched him fold his placemat. His hands were steady. He was folding it into a flower. Rachel was licking grease off her plate.

People are always saying life is short. He looked back and forth between them. But if they knew how short life was, they wouldn't even take the time to say it.

When the waitress arrived, the man in the suit thanked her. He finished his folding and placed the white paper rose on top of the pink bacon, then slid it across to Rachel. He held his mug up to his face and inhaled deeply.

Bobbi watched him do this several times. He picked up his hat and stood next to the booth.

I just like to smell it, he said. I try to stay away from the caffeine.

He handed Bobbi a business card, printed on thin, almost translucent paper. The address was the clinic in the mini-mall where Rachel had first been examined as an infant. There was nothing on the card but an address.

The man smiled at Bobbi.

Hold onto that. *Use* it.

Bobbi nodded. Rachel copied her mother.

Good book, the man said. He pointed at *Vitae* with his hat, then he turned and walked out the door. Bobbi watched for taillights to pull out of the parking lot.

Travel

It was late in the summer and the sky was dark at noon, about to crack open and soak the pavement. Bobbi was filling her tank at a gas station. Rachel always sat in the front seat now, like a big girl. Bobbi still had to fasten the seatbelt for her. Rachel seemed to like wearing the seatbelt. It held her in place. It was like a hug.

Bobbi was feeling restless, antsy. She thought of places she needed to see, places she wanted Rachel to see. She thought about what the man at the diner, the Expert, had said about life, how short it was. The ocean, she thought. A rainforest. The moon. Disneyland. The world's oldest tree. Everywhere in between, she said to herself, not even sure what she meant.

Go.

There was a billboard and a wall of bamboo behind the gas station and a neighborhood of small houses behind that and then she thought there were probably some more towns and then mountains and valleys and mountains and valleys and plains and deserts and mountains and valleys and mountains and valleys and the ocean and islands and faraway places and then outer space and who knows what beyond that.

The billboard was for a time-share vacation property. Bobbi didn't even know what a time-share was. DON'T BE SCARED, the billboard said. IT'S JUST LIFE.

Go, Bobbi thought.

She imagined getting back in the car after the gas had pumped and holding Rachel's hand in the air and squeezing it once then pushing her weight against the gas pedal. They would surge forward, leaving the gas station in a cloud of smoke that would hang around for years. They would bust through the billboard and the bamboo would separate before them and they would drive on in a straight line around the world, crush through houses and tunnel through mountains and forge new highways with their tires burning a scar through the planet's face. They would soar off a cliff into the Pacific Ocean, only to find out that their mini-van and trailer floated, in fact made an excellent boat, and they would keep on that straight line over reefs and through lagoons, cutting giant waves in the sea on either side of them, waves that threw whales into the air, waves that broke clouds in pieces like puffs of smoke. Over more landmasses and oceans faster and faster until day and night were like the flicking of a light switch and everyone in the world was so dizzy they toppled over and died happy to have been witnesses to the travels of Bobbi and Rachel.

She needed to take a deep breath just thinking about it. The air was wet. The gas had stopped pumping a long time ago. The rain had started to fall.

The Church With No Name

That vulture has been following the car for days, Bobbi thought.

It probably hasn't, she told herself.

There are so many vultures. At least one for every day.

When she woke up after sunrise in the Visitor Center parking lot, she could hear something pecking at the roof of her trailer. She got back on the highway with nowhere to go.

Bobbi heard the singing from the overpass. At first she thought it was in her head. It sounded like birds whispering to god. She got off at the next exit and turned around. She tried to follow the sound of the music, although it seemed to be coming from all places at once.

She was headed up a wooded hill. There was a stream running somewhere below and it almost drowned out the singing but she could still hear it. She felt like she was getting closer. The leaves swayed in the trees around her. Rachel hung her face out the window and got bugs caught in her teeth.

The road wound around the hill and grew narrower, then turned to dirt. At one point, there was a small wooden bridge, painted red. Bobbi could hear clapping now. The singing grew louder and made the hair on her arms tickle. Around the bend Bobbi came to an opening, a field of dry grass with a white church and a gravel parking lot in the middle. There was a readerboard with replaceable letters behind a sheet of stained plastic. The letters said:

> OUT WITH THE OLD: "Rachel is crying. She refuses to be comforted for her children,
> because they are no longer alive."
>
> —Jeremiah 31:15

IN WITH THE NEW: GOD KILLED HIS ONLY SON SO WE WON'T HAVE TO DIE

Bobbi looked for the name of the church but there was nothing.

She parked the van and helped Rachel down from her seat. Rachel was not crying. Rachel would never have children, Bobbi thought. It was a sad feeling but also comforting in a way, like giving your kid a toy to play with that is already broken so you don't have to replace it when it starts falling apart.

The music was loud in the clearing. Bobbi could hear people screaming inside the church. She and Rachel stood outside and listened to the clapping and singing and screams. There were large black birds cutting back and forth, high over the white building. The sky looked like an ocean. The doors and shutters of the church were painted red.

Bobbi expected the doors to be heavy, but they almost flew open when she touched the handle, like a wind was pushing or sucking them inside.

A hot breeze inside rushed through the open windows. There are more people in here than fit in the cars and trucks outside, Bobbi thought. White and black people sweating, with deep stains underneath their outstretched arms. Dancers in the aisles. Babies were being held up in the air or were just on the floor crawling, naked among the dancers' feet. Everyone's lips were moving or their mouths were open. Bobbi couldn't tell who was singing and who was just making noises. Who was screaming like murder. The sound was so enormous it felt like it would blow the sides off the building. Bobbi held her hands over Rachel's ears and winced, but stayed to hear the singing. Nobody had even noticed her come in.

A man's voice came over a microphone, even louder than the song. Bobbi had no idea where the man was.

Somewhere lost in the crowd. The man's voice was like a flame overtaking a candle. The music seemed to calm for a minute, but Bobbi wasn't sure it had. The voice started talking about death.

First you're dead, then you're born, then you're dead again, the voice said. Why do we do this? We don't have to!

People were egging the voice on with amens and yessirs and other praises. The whole room, Bobbi thought, had a single idea among them. She wasn't sure it mattered what that idea was. There was a woman next to her in the back, humming louder and louder like something about to explode.

We are born from death but we don't need to go back there. I don't have to die and you don't have to either. We can live forever if we want. The Lord is not a fountain of youth but a river, an ocean, a tidal wave that has come to smash the world to bits and all we have to do is let the water inside our pores, our blood, our meat, our hearts until we become part of that wave and smother death and the world death calls home! There will be foam in our wake, he said. There will be foam!

Bobbi was rocking back and forth on her feet, only vaguely aware that she was doing it.

Rachel also rocked back and forth.

Some religions talk about a Satan, the voice said. And some just talk of death but I testify to you in this nameless house of the Lord today that Satan and death are one and the same! Satan has his own Trinity. An unholy threesome made up of the devil, death, and this very world we live in and are a part of everyday! Make no mistake, these three things are the same! Turn away from one and you will rid yourself of all three!

Bobbi was sweating now. She thought of her sweat and the rest of the congregation's sweat evaporating and rising up to the ceiling to form a small cloud over their heads and rain down on them in salty drops.

Underneath where she pictured the cloud, a bony young man with a crew cut rose up out of the assembly. Bobbi couldn't see his feet through all the praying and dancing bodies. He was pink in the face and wearing a black suit that hung in soggy wrinkles from his thin body. His microphone was painted red. In his other hand, he was holding a glass bottle with a rubber pot-stopper top. He must be standing on a stool, Bobbi thought. He looked like he was floating.

Serpent poison, cyanide, flaming water from your poisoned wells. You've seen me drink of these. Scorpions, spiders, the congealed blood of diseased men. You've seen me eat of these.

Bobbi watched the man pop the top of his bottle. The scent of formaldehyde filled the room. Fetal pig, Bobbi thought. Death. My daughter.

She kept dancing.

She was holding Rachel's hand. She squeezed it hard without knowing it.

Rachel was wiggling, smooshed between Bobbi and the fat woman humming next to her.

Why do I ingest these terrible things? Am I showing off? Yes! I am showing off the careless faith, the reckless grace we receive through this religion we are practicing here today. I am not already dead. I have always been dead. I don't need to be re-born. I need to be born. If I am wrong about any of this, then let the poison have me. I don't want to be alive if our God did not create my soul for something holier than this world of death and sin. *We* don't want to be alive if this is all He gave us! Give us death, if not true life. It is our God-given right and our only freedom!

More praise was shouted. There were whistles and noises like birdcalls. The preacher could not have been much older than Bobbi. Maybe younger, she thought.

Formaldehyde eats a man's intestines, the preacher said and drank. He wiped his face and grinned.

The crowd kept clapping and singing. Bobbi stopped dancing to watch. The humming next to her had turned into a growl. The fat woman was screaming through mucus deep in her throat. Noises like someone full of demons. Bobbi was afraid. She picked Rachel up off the ground. It was hard. Rachel was getting too big to hold.

The preacher saw Rachel held up in the crowd and pointed, his eyes lit as if he had just found something shiny.

There will be a resurrection, he said.

The Red Cabin

The young preacher — he still had acne, which made him look like he was blushing — lived in a red cabin in a valley behind the hill that the church was built on. Bobbi and Rachel stayed with him six days. The preacher lived with his wife, Sarah, who was even younger than he was, and a girl they had taken in, who was just slightly younger than that. The girl was named Eliza and she had a baby, named Lu. All of them lived in the three-room cabin together. The preacher's name was Oral.

Oral made sure that Rachel and the baby were never in the same room, which didn't seem like a bad idea to Bobbi. Since there were only three rooms, Sarah and Eliza were always calling out: Baby Lu! Coming through! whenever they had to do anything with the baby. That meant Bobbi and Rachel had to switch rooms or go out on the front porch. Because of this arrangement, Bobbi spent most of her time on the porch. That was where Oral spent most of his time, too.

Oral didn't go out onto the porch to drink or smoke or chew tobacco. He just sat out there in a white tee shirt on a straight-backed chair and stared at the trees like they had done something to him or he thought they were about to. There was no other furniture on the porch, so Bobbi just sat on the floor and Rachel sat between her legs.

I own this whole mountain, Oral told her. He closed his eyes and put his head back. Somebody gave it to me. They're dead now. I don't need a mountain though. What is a mountain but a zit on the earth's face? Tell me that.

When Oral wasn't preaching, he was always saying, Tell me that. Bobbi never knew how to answer him, but she liked the conversation. Oral sounded like a much older man than he was, like someone used to speaking with authority. Before the end of the first night, Bobbi had already started telling him all about the saints.

Oral closed his eyes while she talked. He looked thoughtful, if not confused. When Bobbi was finished, he kept his eyes closed a minute or so before speaking.

Don't let trying to be something special in the here-and-now trip you up or trick you into believing life means more than it means when you and that daughter of yours right there know it means exactly nothing. Waiting time. Death comes before life, he said. People have got it the other way around.

He asked Bobbi what saints were her favorites. The way he asked it made Bobbi feel like he was asking who were her favorite dolls.

Bobbi found herself telling him the things she didn't understand about the saints instead.

I don't understand Saint Christopher, she told him.

He nodded as if he knew all about it, but didn't say anything. He always nodded that way. Bobbi told him anyway.

Well, Saint Christopher lived all alone in the woods beside this river, Bobbi started. She could hear the stream running in the background and smiled. Oral winked at her.

Bobbi went on.

And he made it his job to help travelers across the river so they could get where they were going. So one day a baby shows up all alone and wants to cross the river. Saint Christopher picks the baby up and starts to carry him across. The baby begins to grow very heavy and they both start to sink in the mud but Saint Christopher keeps on going. The baby is like an anchor. The current picks up and it's pulling him downstream and giant waves are rising all around him and he and the baby are drowning.

Bobbi paused to touch Rachel's shoulder. Oral just waited for her to finish. Bobbi was pretty sure he had never heard the story before.

But they make it. And when Saint Christopher gets to the other side, he catches his breath and the river calms. Saint Christopher asks the baby who he is and the baby tells him Jesus.

Oral stared at the trees.

But why would a baby need to get across a river? Bobbi asked. And why does picking up a baby in the woods and helping it make you a saint? Even the worst people wouldn't just leave a baby in the woods.

It was a test, Oral told her.

But why would God want to test anyone like that? Especially someone who is just living in the woods alone, praying and helping people cross the river?

God doesn't make all the trials we go through in this world, he said. He looked very serious now. This world belongs to the devil. The devil is the one that teaches lessons here. Do you think a God who promises life would leave a baby alone in the woods? Tell me that. For a test? If those girls in there take their hands off that baby for more than ten minutes she starts wailing.

All those saints you hear about are just normal folks who got famous being tested by the devil. Now why would you and your daughter want to court anything along those lines? Tell me that.

The stream was almost singing in the background.

They lived good lives, Bobbi said quietly.

Lots of people live good lives, he said. Anyone who lives a good life is going to be tested by the devil. That doesn't make them special. It just means they belong to the devil like everyone else. Their lives still happen here on the devil's dead planet. There is no way of getting around that until you're gone. You have been tested lots of times already, I bet. He nodded at Rachel. You are probably being tested right now.

But at least it doesn't hurt anyone, Bobbi said. Living like a saint.

Oral sucked on his lips.

Might not, he said.

Inside the Red Cabin

There were no pictures on the walls. They were covered in red paint. Bobbi was glad to be outside.

The Week Before Resurrection

Bobbi and Rachel sat on the porch with Oral, who didn't work except to sit in his chair and stare hatefully at the nature around him, then put it all into his sermon each Sunday. When either Sarah or Eliza called for him, he hollered back that he was busy. Then he would continue staring or talking to Bobbi.

How are you going to interrupt a man while he is doing the only work he knows how? He asked Bobbi. Tell me that.

Then one of them would usually bring him a red apple. Oral ate a lot of apples.

Bobbi noticed that he had grown a small moustache during the week. She wondered if he would shave it off on Sunday.

She kept Rachel on the porch unless she was right by her side. Black vultures floated over the woods. She knew Rachel was too big to be carried away by a bird, but she always remained cautious.

It was in the middle of the afternoon and the sun was in their eyes when Oral told Bobbi, I can see her growing.

I can see everyone growing, he said. Growing, shrinking, dying, being dead.

Bobbi listened to the woods. Rachel hissed at a squirrel in a tree.

I can see it in myself, he said. We are all just marching along, in all the wrong directions, but we end up in the same exact place. What kind of world do we live in? he said. Tell me that.

Bobbi didn't know.

I don't know either. I don't guess we get to learn about the part we are stuck in until we get to the next part and look back.

Bobbi did not like looking back. Sometimes she couldn't help it.

Bobbi asked Oral to tell her how he knew he was supposed to be a preacher. She was afraid to ask him, but she did it anyway.

Oral chewed his apple a minute and swallowed.

It didn't happen the way it must have for you, he said.

Bobbi thought that despite everything in her life, it probably hadn't happened yet. She had never felt called to do anything but be a mother and not even that until she already was one. She started to say something but Oral kept talking.

With me there was no fireworks or anything as telling as, you know, a child like yours. I just always knew there was a God up there waiting for me. People say life is short but that's only because they have no faith that there's anything better. I think life is endless, he said. Just like death.

I didn't have any fireworks either, Bobbi said. She could feel Rachel sucking on her hair. Bobbi thought there might be a bug in it. That had happened before.

On the third night, Eliza and Sarah made apple pie. The apples were sour, but nobody seemed to notice except Bobbi. They offered Rachel pie but Bobbi declined for her. My daughter hasn't developed a taste for fruit yet, she explained.

Later that night on the porch, Bobbi read to Rachel quietly in the corner from *Vitae*. Oral sat on the other side of the porch in his chair, eating apples.

What are your plans? he asked her. Bobbi stopped reading. For after the resurrection?

Bobbi wasn't sure she even knew what that meant. He pointed at Rachel, who was picking at a rotten piece of the floorboard.

None of us can know until it happens, he said. I know what resurrection has meant in the past though.

What? Bobbi asked.

It means you have to keep on living.

That Thursday Bobbi took Rachel for a walk in the woods. There was a trail that led behind the house and down toward the river. Rachel held tight to Bobbi's side. Bobbi could feel the rhythm of Rachel's footsteps trying to match her own.

The stream was narrow and windy with little beaches around each meander. Bobbi walked slowly on the trail alongside it. She wondered if the water from the stream would ever end up in the ocean. Didn't all water join the ocean at some point? She imagined floating on a log with Rachel, all the way to the ocean and ending up on a beach somewhere nice, secluded, somewhere they would never have to leave. But first she would stay for the resurrection. How could it make anything worse?

When Bobbi got back to the cabin, Oral was sitting on the porch in his tee shirt. He was holding a knife with blood on it. Bobbi stopped and held Rachel back with her hand.

Oral laughed. It's just red paint, he said. We inherited buckets of it.

Bobbi relaxed and came up onto the porch.

He wiped the blade on his shirt. It was only a paint scraper.

I was making a sign for down by the roadway, he said.

What does it say? Bobbi asked.

He pointed to a piece of plywood with red lettering.

It says BEAT DEATH THE EASY WAY WITH GOD, Oral told her.

That's nice, Bobbi said.

Look at the other side. He hopped down off the porch and went to flip the sign. WITNESS A RESSURECTION! the sign said.

The fifth night, Bobbi massaged and stretched Rachel's muscles on the front porch and picked little bits of dirt from her wounds. Oral watched her, nodding. I can't believe she doesn't eat apples, he said.

On Saturday night, Bobbi and Rachel slept in the trailer. The women insisted she stay on the couch but Bobbi said they had some stuff packed away they needed to get to and they thought they could use some time alone anyway.

She's got to do what she's called to do, Oral told Sarah and Eliza.

Bobbi nodded even though she didn't understand what he meant.

Tomorrow is a big day for these ladies, he told the women. Let them be alone to pray to their God in whatever ways they know how.

Oral turned to Bobbi and Rachel.

If He is listening, tell him I am still saying Hi.

He sunk his teeth into an apple and juice squirted out the sides of his mouth.

It rained that night. Bobbi stayed inside the trailer with Rachel, trying to pray. Every time she started to pray, it only felt like she was thinking to herself. Just another stream of thoughts running nowhere in her head.

Bobbi considered driving down the dark hill and getting on the highway but she didn't.

Do you ever feel as alone as I do? she asked Rachel.

Rachel looked like she was nodding in agreement but she was actually falling forward, unbalanced. She fell until her forehead pressed against Bobbi's. She bit the air between them and gas came out her mouth. Bobbi had to hold her breath for a second.

We're not alone, Bobbi said. No more than anyone else.

Sunday Service

The congregation was larger than it had been the previous week. Bobbi could already hear them singing in the church when she woke up.

She led Rachel across the gravel parking lot in the clothes they had gone to bed in. The sun was already high. She covered her eyes and turned Rachel's face into her side for protection. She walked quickly. She was late. She worried the resurrection might somehow start without them.

The doors were heavier this time, like they had swollen with water.

The last time she had been in the church, the inside smelled of formaldehyde and sweat and incense. Now it smelled like someone had left the windows open during the storm. Like moss and fungus and root vegetables. The air smelled alive, as if she had buried her face in the earth. Bobbi hadn't noticed it the last time, but there were kudzu vines climbing in through the windows in the back of the church.

The room was packed with strangers in white tee shirts. They were having ecstatic trances. Bobbi was beginning to suspect that she had made a mistake. The crowd parted slightly in the middle of the aisle, just enough to let Bobbi pick Rachel up and carry her to the front of the church where there was no altar, only a workbench painted red.

Oral was standing behind the altar, face shaven, holding the microphone. His eyes looked excited. Hopeful, Bobbi thought. Uncertain, as if something was about to happen. Sarah was off to the side with Eliza and Baby Lu near a small, beige amplifier. The speaker gave Oral's voice a slight echo that rolled over the congregation like waves of syrup. The noise sounded unnatural coming out of so small a speaker. Bobbi had the opposite of déjà vu. She felt like she had never been anywhere before. Like she was in someone else's body living someone else's life, watching someone else's daughter be laid across the workbench.

The crowd folded in behind her. The dancing had never stopped. People were making noises. Some were crying. Bobbi felt like she had woken up too quickly, like maybe she was still in a dream. She rubbed crumbs away from her tear ducts.

This child bears no more the mark of death than any of you, Oral said into the microphone. Bobbi watched his lips move. Sarah and Eliza doted on their baby. Rachel was limp. Everyone else just danced. She wears it on the outside, he said. We hide from death, look away from it in ourselves. We make death come after us.

This little girl is braver than the whole human race.

This little girl will live forever.

Bobbi could hear humming behind her. The rafters were vibrating. Rachel was looking up at her from the table with terrified eyes. Her body was still limp. Oral focused on the crowd. He didn't bother to look down at the girl he was preaching about. He seemed to be conducting the congregation with his voice, guiding the energy in the room with soft touches and bits of emphasis.

Amen, people said. Some of them looked like they were going to faint.

Bobbi watched as Oral laid his hand on Rachel's forehead. Be still, Bobbi said with her eyes. Everything will happen the way it is supposed to.

She had no idea what was supposed to happen.

She imagined Rachel as a living girl on the edge of a green field, smelling flowers; but it was not Rachel, it was some other girl. Rachel was not a living girl.

This girl who has brought us together today is a pure symbol of our religion! But our religion doesn't rely on names or symbols. This girl is more than a symbol to us. This girl is life fighting death. Divorcing death. For you are a fool if you do not believe life and death are married. Death won't sign the papers! Death wants custody!

Bobbi was careful to manage her hopes.

She wasn't sure what her hopes were yet.

Oral was pouring snake venom on Rachel's forehead.

He was calling everyone devils.

Bobbi was dizzy. She thought she was going to pass out.

It was hot in the church. She felt like mushrooms were growing on her skin. Someone handed her a glass of water; at least she thought it was water. Anything liquid felt nice. She poured it down her face. She imagined a plant, a small tree, growing out of her daughter's forehead. She saw the tree sprouting fruit, apples.

We have to get out of here, she said. Her lips were moving but no one could hear her voice over the singing and clapping and screams.

Oral was praying.

Take this child and lift her up to a heaven beyond this world, beyond this foul universe, resurrect her in a more perfect place as a more perfect being! If you have truly made us in your image, then let us — let this girl — live in your kingdom! Do not segregate us until our hearts have stopped beating! Do not keep this girl in limbo! We have had enough death and disease! Give us the eternal life we deserve!

Bobbi needed to get out of there.

Rachel's tongue was hanging out. Her wig had slipped off the back of her head.

Bobbi imagined her own stomach swelling up like a planet. She imagined it bursting open and a race of tiny humans crawling out. Tiny infants covered in slime crawling next to old people with skin like paper, both so close to not even existing, sliding over one another like insects from her belly.

She thought she saw Rachel flinch on the table, but it was Bobbi herself who was flinching.

It's time to go, Bobbi said.

Oral was dancing now with his women and the baby. Everyone's arms were spread out and upturned toward the ceiling. Bobbi stepped forward and took Rachel's hand.

It's time to go, she shouted. No one could hear except Rachel.

Rachel sat up and slid off the edge of the table. She staggered through the parting crowd, one fist gripping Bobbi's hand, the other her pajamas. They looked like a sad two-person conga-line.

She has risen! Oral kept saying. She is dancing!

She has risen! She is dancing!

She has risen! She is dancing!

He was chanting it as they pushed through the doors.

Bobbi thought he sounded like a child.

She sat in the mini-van and rolled down the window. She was breathing heavily. Rachel copied her mother's breath. Bobbi took Rachel's hand and held it against her chest. She wanted her daughter to feel her heartbeat. She wanted her to know what a heartbeat was.

The people in the church kept singing. Bobbi thought they would sing until their heads fell off. She imagined Oral preaching into their necks.

I bet you're hungry, she said once they were a few exits down the highway and her pulse had slowed down. She hadn't noticed how hungry she was until now.

Let's keep our eyes peeled for a Waffle House or something, she said. I bet you must be starved.

Rachel stared through the windshield. There was a giant black bird cutting across the sky in front of them. Bobbi kept driving towards it.

Tween Dream

Bobbi wanted Rachel's teenage years to be special. Normal was special enough for Rachel, she thought. Normal was special for her too. Sometimes they would be driving through a town and they would see other kids Rachel's age out the window of the car. The kids were usually in groups. Rachel would watch them on the other side of the glass. Bobbi would try to distract her, get her to turn away from the window. She was afraid they would point. Teenagers always looked like they knew nothing but bliss to Bobbi; like they were having so much fun they forgot they were alive. Bobbi knew this wasn't really the way it was. She had once been a teen. Sort of, she thought. Bobbi remembered watching other kids out of car windows also.

When other girls her age were going through puberty Rachel only grew larger, not more physically mature. Her eggs did not drop. Any coarse hairs that grew on her skin were coincidental.

Bobbi wanted to buy her new, fashionable clothes. She wanted her to feel cool. Bobbi had never felt cool.

It was not that she believed Rachel would ever be a popular girl or have a boyfriend or go to prom. She just wanted her daughter to brush against the illusion of that life. Even though Rachel couldn't say it, Bobbi was pretty sure she did not feel good about herself. Bobbi didn't understand how anyone did. Sometimes she wondered if the whole world was silently pretending not to hate themselves completely. Everyone hoping no one else would notice what was inside their heads.

She read about Blessed Margaret of Castello. She repeated the story to Rachel. She repeated it several times in a row.

Margaret was born blind and partially crippled, a dwarf with a spine that curved until she was forced to stare at the floor. Her right leg was too short. Her left arm was malformed and crooked at the wrist, with a tiny hand. Her forehead bulged and dominated her face. Her teeth were small and serrated. When her body was exhumed, the cloth covering had rotted to dust but she remained preserved as if she had only just passed. No embalming chemicals were found in her body but three little pearls were found inside her heart.

From birth Margaret was kept hidden by her family, who were ashamed of her condition. They prayed for a miracle to heal her, but none came. As she became a young lady, her deformities only grew more intense, her spine more curved. Her mother and father were desperate. They shrouded her and placed her in a box with holes drilled into the sides to let air through. They took her on a pilgrimage to a shrine in the nearby city of Castello. They stood before the shrine and opened the box, then removed the shroud as if the child inside were an offering. The couple knelt beside the box and prayed but there was no miracle. They stayed all night praying. In the morning they returned home without Margaret.

Margaret was left at the shrine, unwrapped. A blind pile of misassembled human parts in a box.

The box did not end up her coffin. Some local women found her and took care of her while they searched for a family to adopt her. A husband and wife who had not been able to have a child learned of the young girl and took her as their daughter.

Margaret did not let her disabilities ruin her life. She grew into a kind woman, generous and sympathetic to the sick and poor, men and women gripped by demons, the imprisoned. She became one of the most popular women in her adopted city of Castello. Packs of citizens led her through tow, seeking out those in need so Margaret could help them or talk to them or listen or pray at their side. She saw her suffering as a blessing. She thanked God daily for being able to share His pain.

Margaret's disabilities ensured her life would not be a long one.

The city amassed at her funeral service. The crowd insisted she be buried inside the church, with other significant local persons of faith, instead of in the cemetery where a plot had already been dug. The priest resisted until a small girl with lame feet, who idolized Margaret, dragged herself to the coffin. She touched the box with a finger and was healed.

When Bobbi and Rachel would have been driving in silence — or with Bobbi talking for both of them — they now listened to pop music on the radio. Bobbi danced in her seat, self-consciously at first, and encouraged Rachel to at least bob her head. She parked at night and read to Rachel from *Vitae* and the Bible, but now she began to supplement it with gossip magazines and novels about handsome vampires that she picked up at truck stops and gas stations. Rachel started wearing make-up. Bobbi applied thick eye-shadow, lipstick, and rouge to her daughter's face several times a day. Bobbi started wearing it too.

They spent a lot of time trying on cheap sunglasses.

People are going to mistake us for sisters, Bobbi joked. Rachel's make-up was smeared from pressing her face against the car window. Bobbi gave her a piece of bubble gum, which she swallowed like a pill.

She pretended Rachel was a cool kid and she was her cool older friend. Rachel did not look like a cool kid. Sometimes she thought that if Nicole (or even Tayana) were there they would probably be able to assist in the illusion. Thoughts like those only made her try harder on her own. Bobbi was willing to live any illusion at this point, so long as it felt like a positive one. Giving Rachel a pretend life was the purest gesture she could think of. Living her own pretend life, she told herself, was an unintentional bonus.

Nicole was not around to encourage them or dream up things to do or tell them what was cool. There was nothing to rebel against except reality.

Bobbi needed the Imaginary Mother to administer discipline, give guidance, and hold them in her arms when they were scared, lie to them and say that life wasn't the saddest thing that ever existed. Bobbi wrote a note on a receipt and slipped it into the leaves of her Bible. *All great things are sad*, the note said. Bobbi looked at it for a while. She wished the Imaginary Mother would see the words over her shoulder and shoot wind through her teeth in disapproval, reach down and scratch out the note with a firm stroke of her wrist.

The Imaginary Mother Returns

The Imaginary Mother visited Bobbi in her thoughts as she zig-zagged west across the plains. Bobbi pictured her in the rearview mirror: a loose skeleton slouched in the backseat, surrounded by clutter. Bobbi also thought of her against the enormous blue sky they were always driving further into. She soared over the van like an angel. She wished the Imaginary Mother would make an incision in her skin, climb inside and replace her bones. She imagined that would make her a better mother.

Landscapes

Bobbi drove through landscapes with her eyes widened, absorbing them like they were still images painted on a wall. The size of the horizon grew as she drove west through the middle of the country. The roads grew longer. The sky pushed away from the earth.

The world is too big for any one life to feel significant in this landscape, she thought. In a world this size, everything must be a mistake.

Oklahoma

Bobbi met an Indian in Oklahoma named Jeff. At least Jeff told her he was an Indian; Bobbi didn't think he looked very much like one. She and Rachel were sitting outside their trailer, trying to smoke cigarettes. The trailer was parked at a Wal-Mart, in the back of the lot.

The cigarettes were a new thing. Rachel was fourteen-years-old now. Bobbi saw smoking as a rite of passage, something normal teenagers tried when they wanted to sample adulthood. She thought it was time for both of them to experiment with smoking. Bobbi did not enjoy cigarettes, but she tried to. They burned her throat, left her woozy, made her brain hot. It felt like there was life exiting her mouth with the smoke when she exhaled.

To Rachel, cigarettes became a new toy. She learned to hold them in her hand. It made Bobbi glow with pride to see her use something in a human way, but Rachel barely remembered to inhale any smoke. She just stared into the embers, hypnotized as if by a candle lit for someone important she had once lost.

Bobbi was kneeling next to a beach chair, adjusting the training bra she'd bought for Rachel that morning. The bra was sticking to her skin and it was too big, but Rachel didn't squirm. She sat still as if Bobbi were only applying a bandage to her shoulder. A shadow landed on her face and stayed there. Bobbi looked up to see what caused the shadow. Jeff was standing in the sun, watching them from under the brim of a black cowboy hat. He had a baby pool under his left arm, deflated inside a cardboard box.

Summer is over, Bobbi thought. Leaves are already starting to fall.

She threw her cigarette on the ground.

Can I help you? she asked.

I'm sorry, he said. I couldn't help but notice you and your daughter. Just sitting out here…

It's not her, Bobbi interrupted. She was already lifting Rachel to her feet and picking up the beach chair to load into the van.

Excuse me? he said.

From the web, she said. It's not her. It's a skin condition. Or a hoax or whatever. It's not her. I'm sorry. Thank you. We're fine.

He held his palms out in front of him, like he was trying to calm a horse.

I was just going to say I saw you all were traveling through and thought maybe you could use directions or some local pointers on the scenery or what-have-you, he explained. I assume you're in town for the sulphur springs? On account of the, uh, skin condition you just mentioned?

Yes, Bobbi said. We're here for the springs.

Bobbi had no idea any springs existed. She was only there in a parking lot outside a megastore in Oklahoma because she was not in some other spot on the globe. She hadn't even known she was in Oklahoma.

Jeff had a kind face, young but wrinkled around his eyes, which were set deep behind his cheekbones. It felt good to be offered an agenda.

Would you like company? he asked.

Bobbi felt herself nodding. She looked at Rachel. Rachel was nodding along beside her.

The sulphur springs were only twenty minutes away. They drove in Jeff's truck. He took his hat off when they got inside. His dark hair was matted down, dented in a circle above his ears like he had been wearing a heavy crown. Bobbi sat in the middle between them. Rachel hung her head out the window. Her make-up was a mess. Bobbi wondered how her own make-up looked. She wanted her make-up to look good. She pictured herself at the foot of the Imaginary Mother's large canopy bed asking for advice about boys. A pink nightgown hanging like curtains off the Imaginary Mother's bones. Her teeth chattered as she laughed. The laughter was meant to soothe Bobbi, but it didn't.

Jeff was quiet in a polite way, but friendly. He asked Bobbi how much of Oklahoma she had seen. Bobbi said she wasn't sure how much there was to see. Jeff smiled like he thought his state wasn't great to look at.

Oh no, Bobbi said. I'm sorry. I didn't mean it like that. I just meant I'm not sure how big the state is. We've kind of been driving all over for a while now. We don't pay much attention to the borders or maps anymore.

Jeff nodded like he knew what she meant all along.

Bobbi was embarrassed. She bit a sliver of cuticle and tugged it from her finger. A speck of blood appeared. She squeezed her hand in her shirttail so Rachel wouldn't notice and think the blood was for her.

People come to these springs from all over, Jeff said. They drink the water, take baths, fill up milk jugs to bring back home. I've heard there are doctors who still prescribe the stuff.

At the red light he turned and gave her a soft smile. His eyes looked very sincere for a moment, like the eyes of a deer. The light changed and he turned back to the road.

Is that what brought you here? he asked after they had started moving again. A prescription? From a specialist? For water?

Bobbi nodded. It felt no more or less true than anything else he could have asked. He was easy to agree with.

Sulphur made Bobbi think of fireworks. She pictured the springs as pools of white twinkling light. She thought of drinking the light with Rachel. Then she imagined they were both drinking from Jeff's hands. She had to stop. She did not like the thoughts she was having about Jeff.

The first springs they went to were not more than twenty yards from the parking lot. The milky water bubbled up through a pipe and emptied into a round concrete basin surrounded by a stone and mortar ledge. Bobbi thought they looked like any other fountains she had seen, even less spectacular than most.

She sniffed the air. She thought of eggs rotting in hot garbage. Rachel didn't seem to notice the smell. Jeff was apparently used to it. Bobbi wondered if he welcomed the odor after being in the truck with Rachel. Rachel's scent had become part of her own years ago. She barely noticed it.

Bobbi had expected a line of crippled and bandaged pilgrims holding mason jars and buckets based on the way Jeff had described the place, but the three of them were the only ones there. She looked around. She saw no other tourists, no kids, no dogs straining their leashes in Rachel's direction. They were alone, except for a few empty cars parked in the lot. Bobbi assumed there were some rangers inside the little building nearby.

The grass beside the path to the fountain was a lifeless golden color. She took a deep breath of the mineral breeze coming over the springs until it made her gag. She expected to see steam rising from the fountains, but the water was cool.

Bobbi showed Rachel how to bend over and touch the water with her fingers. She pretended to shiver. Rachel pretended too. Jeff stood on top of the ledge, watching them. Bobbi looked up at him. She could feel the blood in her cheeks.

The water is supposed to be great medicine for your skin, he said. Your doctor probably already told you this, but it's got the same stuff in it that you use to grow fingernails and toenails and hair. I forget what it's called. The sulphur makes you produce collagen too, which makes your skin elastic and your face look young. It's what rich women put in their lips. Plus it's supposed to be good for arthritis and hemorrhoids, I think. All the chemicals eat away at parasites too, if you've got them. It smells like rotten eggs though.

Bobbi acted very impressed with all the information he had just given her. She rolled up her jeans and helped Rachel step into the fountain.

Jeff just watched them. He cast a wide shadow with his hat.

Maybe the fountain of youth is in Oklahoma, he said. Maybe we'll all live forever.

Bobbi liked the sound of that, but she also found it a little terrifying.

The water in the basin was not deep enough to bathe in. She considered leaning over the spouting geyser with Rachel, but didn't. She worried the force of the water might damage Rachel's body.

There was a section in *Vitae* about Saint Bernadette of Lourdes. Bobbi remembered most of it.

Bernadette was a weak, asthmatic child playing by a cave when she was visited by an apparition of the Virgin as a young lady wreathed in yellow light. The spirit appeared to Bernadette eighteen times over the next several weeks. Her reports of the visions drew large audiences to the cave to watch. The Virgin appeared to her a final time and told her to get on her hands and knees and dig. Bernadette scratched into the earth with her fingers, pulled at it with her hands. She was in a trance. It was as if all the people around her had disappeared. After hours of digging, water seeped through her fingers and a spring began to bubble. The spring turned into a flowing stream that cut through the crowd, who were cheering. Many years later when asked about the miracles of her youth and if the Virgin still spoke to her, Bernadette told an interviewer she was like a broom tucked behind a door when the Blessed Mother was finished with her.

Bobbi wanted to be a broom, but just visiting the sulphur springs was nice too. It is nice to be taken anywhere, she thought.

She splashed around a little bit. Rachel looked confused then splashed her back. Jeff clapped from the sideline.

Bobbi began to sing a poem she had read in *Vitae* and in singing it she was surprised she remembered the words. This was the poem she sang:

In the little town of Lourdes one day
Our Blessed Lady came
To a little peasant girl at play.
Bernadette was her name.

Chosen by God, she suffered much
In many ways and yet,
The world is a better place
For the life of Saint Bernadette.

Did your mother teach you that song? Jeff asked, clapping.

No, Bobbi said. She was still surprised. I didn't even think I knew the words.

It's a miracle! Jeff said. His voice sounded so light that Bobbi pictured the words flying out of his mouth like three little birds.

Rachel had her hands in the water. She was scratching at the concrete. She was trying to dig.

I know a deeper spring, Jeff said. Where we can swim. It's a little drive and we have to hike a bit once we get there, but it's a lot prettier than this. It's away from parking lots and all that.

Bobbi again felt herself nodding against better judgment. She had just met this guy and she already felt like she might do anything he said. It felt dangerous. The way he spoke, the shadow his hat cut across his cheekbones in the sun. She hoped he would only say nice things to her. She didn't want to ruin the image she had so quickly created. Another part of her thought that image was something that needed to be shattered and she would go through any Hell to let him do it.

The other springs were in a more natural setting, tucked in a range of scruffy green hills with pale rocks jutting out of them like bones. There was garbage here and there along the trail: wrappers, cans, cigarette filters, a diaper. They passed several other hikers on the way. She hoped they would be more alone at the pool in the woods, but she was also nervous. Rachel humped along at the back of Bobbi's feet, holding onto her shirt, almost burning her with the tip of a cigarette.

It felt like they had been walking a long time. The spring Jeff was taking them to was always just a little further than the last one they passed. The pools were beginning to look more natural now, filling actual holes and grooves in the earth instead of concrete basins. The springs were colors Bobbi had never seen before. Blues and turquoise and greens shining like laser beams, dyed glass, with creamy white marbling underneath that reminded her of Rachel's eyes. Some pools were just light brown, the color of a diluted soft drink.

Jeff was pretty far up ahead of them. Every now and then Bobbi lost sight of him around a curve in the trail and her nerves tightened up. Rachel tugged on her shirttail.

He was already in the spring when they came around the bend. Bobbi couldn't see his body through the thick teal water, chalky and clouded in places, but she could tell he was naked because all of his clothes were hanging neatly in a row across the limb of a black walnut tree near the low waterfall that dumped into the pool.

He was treading water in his black hat and grinning at the opening of the trail as if he had been waiting for them awhile. Bobbi waved at him. It felt awkward. She let her arm fall to her side. She was waiting for him to invite her in the water. She wasn't sure what she would do if he did.

She took off Rachel's shoes and then she took off her own. They sat on a flat rock and dipped their feet in the spring. A beetle ran up Rachel's leg when her toes hit the water.

Mister beetle doesn't want to drown, Bobbi told Rachel.

They sat like that for a long time and were quiet. Jeff watched them from the water. Bobbi peeled the bark off a stick. Rachel put the bark in her mouth but then spit it out in the spring.

I can get out and put my clothes on, Jeff said. If you want to bathe now and don't feel comfortable. I got overheated walking through the hills, is all. Even Indians can feel the sun.

You don't need to do that, Bobbi said. It's a big enough pool for everyone. We'll get in when we want to.

Rachel was already sliding herself down the rock, into the water. Bobbi didn't reach after her. She wondered if Rachel understood what it meant to be healed. Healing the dead, she thought. Bobbi didn't understand it herself, but she knew enough not to get her hopes up.

Bobbi splashed in wearing all of her clothes. She pulled Rachel close to her and held her up above the water as if she might drown. The water that dripped off Rachel's arms left little flakes in the pool. Bobbi held her hand over Rachel's mouth and they both slipped under together. The smell of sulphur filled her face underwater. A burst of bubbles, tiny pearls, raced from her nose.

She looked at Rachel before pushing back up. Rachel's eyes were wide open and she was smiling up at the surface. The surface was a glass window constructed of milk. Rachel was staring at it like they might plunge back through to another world.

They stayed under the water until they couldn't. When they came up, Jeff had moved closer but not too close. He was still naked and had a worried smile on his face.

We weren't drowning or anything, she told him. Water poured from Rachel's neck like her throat was a watering can. We don't need to be saved.

Later that night, they sat in front of Jeff's trailer home for several hours after sunset and drank light beer from cans. Bobbi's teardrop was parked nearby in the driveway behind Jeff's truck, poking slightly out into a small gravel road. Rachel was inside. Bobbi had laid her down to rest. Rest felt like the right thing after their mineral bath.

Jeff told her she could park in the spot outside his trailer for as long as she wanted. There is a fold out couch inside, he said. If you two don't want to sleep in that little pod of yours.

Bobbi did not normally drink beer but it tasted good now, after the bath. Her skin felt smooth, too. Like it had been scrubbed with strong, grainy soap. Maybe Oklahoma *is* the fountain of youth, she said, and burped a little. Excuse me, she said.

There is no fountain of youth. Jeff sighed into the top of his bottle. The bottle made a faint whistle. I was only joking before, he said. Make believe. You aren't old enough to need a fountain yet anyhow.

Bobbi did feel old. She was thirty-one years old. She remembered most of her life thinking that anyone over thirty was old, but now it had come and passed like a day and a night and she had barely even noticed. Rachel was almost as old as she was when she got pregnant. She thought Jeff was probably a couple of years younger than her. A few years seemed like nothing to her now.

You'll be pretty when you're old, Jeff said. Just as pretty as you are now.

Bobbi wasn't looking at him. She pretended he had said something else.

Maybe it is all just make believe, she said.

It definitely is, he said and laughed a little. There's no fountain like that I ever heard of. Are you all right?

If it is just make believe then we can drink from it every day. We just have to pretend.

Heavy, he said. Do you want another beer? I'm going inside for more beer. The empty bottles dangling from his fingers clanked like a bell as he walked.

Bobbi went to the trailer to check on Rachel. Once inside, she stayed there. She poked her head out the door and told Jeff goodnight when he came back out.

Don't go to bed yet, Jeff said. His words hung in the air. I mean, don't forget the fold-out couch. Both of you, he said. I just want you to be comfortable.

She peeked back inside the trailer at Rachel's body lying in the dark.

Maybe tomorrow night, Bobbi told him. My angel has already gotten comfortable.

Jeff waved to her. She waved back and tucked her head inside the trailer.

Rachel's eyes were open. She was looking at stars in the sky. The bedding was damp. Rachel's skin was slightly waterlogged and seeping. Bobbi lay next to her. There was a bright star blinking above them. It looked like it was coming closer, like it was a meteor headed for Sulphur Springs, Oklahoma, the trailer, their faces. Probably just a satellite, Bobbi said. Part of her thought they would be lucky if it landed on them and splashed their bodies out into the universe. She felt like Rachel thought it too, like that was her reason for looking in the first place. She thought about going back inside Jeff's trailer for the night but she didn't. Instead she waited for the star to come crush her. She watched it getting closer and closer until she fell asleep.

In her sleep, she had a dream.

In her dream, she saw Death.

The Imaginary Mother had left her in a supermarket with tall shelves and long aisles. All of the products were different than the products she was used to. They had different names and faces on their labels. Bobbi was shivering. She tucked her arms inside her sleeves and hugged herself. She knew she had been left behind and that her mother was speeding away from her as fast as she could, but she searched through the aisles for her anyway. She could feel something searching for her too, but it was not her mother. Even though she hadn't seen it, she knew the produce section was rotten because it gave off a sweet must that filled the air in the store like a cloud. There were rows of still-eyed fish nestled in ice at the back of the store. She had not seen those yet either, but she knew they were there.

If her mother would not have her then she would take a stranger, she thought. She would take anyone, if anyone would take her.

The butcher shop was empty. The ground meat looked like earthworms. There were pink chicken feet with nerves and veins like wires poking out at the ankles.

Then she saw the fishmonger's stand and Death was sitting on a high counter. His feet were soaking in the lobster tank beneath him. The lobsters were pulling soggy flesh from his calves, which looked dead. His face was as she remembered it: pale, cracked like old plaster, yellow teeth, little moustache. Bobbi thought he winked at her.

She was not looking for her mother anymore. She was looking for her own child.

She needed help.

But she refused to ask Death. Death had already given her all he could. He smiled at her and drew smoke from a cigarette. She thought he was proud to watch her realize something, anything, especially this. To discover that every living animal is always all alone. She tried not to feel proud, herself. The way he looked at her, she couldn't help it.

In the middle of the night, Bobbi woke up sweating and stared at Jeff's trailer through the teardrop's porthole window. The dirty water collected between the glass made the trailer look as if it was floating, Bobbi thought. A houseboat, an arc.

She felt like a miracle had happened but she didn't know what it was exactly. Just a special feeling, she thought. The best way to ruin that feeling was to stick around and learn about it.

She stepped out of the teardrop and climbed into the driver's seat. She started the engine. In her side-view mirror, she saw the light outside the trailer turn on as they pulled away. She watched the sky in front of her. The stars were never getting any closer. They were not crashing. She wouldn't let them.

The Kindness of Strangers

Bobbi met special people all the time. Sometimes people touched her heart and the same day were gone from her life forever. People she thought of as part of her life story, but who just barely were. Others she might want remembered if her story were ever told.

In other accounts of her journey, some of these characters might be in the forefront of the narrative. In this book, they exist in brief or not at all but are no less important. All life is equally important to this story. All lives are worth being remembered, if only to acknowledge that life exists.

The Alphabet Song

Bobbi still sang The Alphabet Song to her teenage daughter. It was a secret code they shared. Bobbi couldn't be sure how much of the code Rachel understood, but she was almost sure she was aware of its secrecy. The melody was also a set of living messages between them, like the sounds of the insects at night in the darkness that folded over their little trailer.

Watery Eyes

Sometimes when Bobbi was driving along the highways, she would feel hypnotized like life didn't even exist and she was just a speck of dust floating through the world on autopilot. During these times, she wasn't happy or unhappy but content. Still she would often find tears running down her face. This happened even when she was not driving. Tears pooled on the ridges of her lower eyelid. They slipped down her cheeks in small rivers. Sometimes it made her laugh because she didn't know why she was crying.

My eyes are just saltwater factories, she said out loud, to herself as much as her daughter.

She saw herself walking around the planet, carrying oceans in her eyes.

Nosebleeds

In addition to watering eyes, from time to time Bobbi's nose would begin to bleed without warning. Gushing, she called it. Mommy is gushing. The blood filled her nose. It smelled like rust. She held her head back. She coughed. She clogged her nostrils with tissue papers printed with little padded roses, with shirtsleeves, with her fingers. The blood collected in the light hairs above her upper lip, in her teeth. It covered her chin and neck like a red beard. If the bleeding persisted long enough it made her dizzy, drunk. Her teeth felt loose in her gums. Her head rolled around on her neck.

Give mommy a kiss, she said. Sometimes she said it laughing, her head thrown back. Other times she was like a bird feeding a chick in its nest.

When the blood dried it left red rings of delicate crust around her nostrils.

The Amusement Park

They had been in the van for a long stretch. They only stopped a few times so Bobbi could sleep in her seat. They were about to stop again when they drove past the sign for the amusement park. The park's theme was mining for precious metals. There were silver and gold coins and bars on the billboard, as well as crystals from deep in the earth. The billboard advertised rides and old west shows, as well as electronic slot machines.

I think this means we better stop to stretch our legs, she told Rachel.

The sign had said the park was twenty miles off the exit. Follow The Golden Coins, it said, but Bobbi didn't see any other signs with gold coins or any mention of an amusement park. She saw a couple of vacant gas stations and a couple of operating ones and a few rundown homes in between, but nothing indicating there was an attraction or anything but shrub and desert further along the stretch of road until a large tan lump separated itself from the hot landscape in the distance.

It was a mountain that looked made of plastic, with crags and paths with ramps and steps cut into the artificial cliffs and boulders. The fake mountain was surrounded by a chain-link fence of barbed-wire frosted with rust.

The parking lot was giant and totally empty except for broken streetlights and white dust collected in patches on the ground. Bobbi parked the van up close, near the entrance. She did not park in a handicapped space. She parked right next to one. She was careful, as if someone was watching.

Bobbi stretched in the parking lot first and then twirled around with her arms spread out like wings. She shook her legs like they were rubber. Rachel copied her, turning in a slow circle, but stopping halfway like she had forgotten what she was doing. Bobbi took her by the hand and they tried to dance.

We have the whole park to ourselves! Bobbi screamed. These mines are open for business!

Rachel's head bobbed.

She knows she is supposed to be excited about something, Bobbi thought.

They bobbed their heads together.

The gateway to the Old Mine Road, a paved walkway that cut through the park, was an enormous silver horseshoe. The actual gate was locked shut but the bars had been bent in several places so trespassers could fit inside. A gold nugget the size of a car confronted them as they entered the park. God's Booger was painted on its flank. There were fiberglass cactuses everywhere. Graffiti. Bobbi did not think the pretend desert inside the park looked very much like the real one surrounding it. She pointed out one of the cactuses for Rachel. Look at the cactus! she said.

The entire park was dead. Occasionally a gust of hot wind would shake the machinery and it felt as though the place might jump to life. Swings rattled on their chains.

There were wooden cutouts of prospectors and cowboys and mustached saloon men knocked over and scattered on the ground. *You must be this tall to ride, Pardner,* a figure with an eye patch told her. There was a robotic Madame that was supposed to tell your fortune through a speaker in her cleavage, where clusters of frayed wire protruded. There were large silver tumbleweeds on concrete blocks in the middle of Old Mine Road, as well as crystals made of cut-glass. Real tumbleweeds had gotten into the park and were pushed around them by the breeze. Rachel reached for the broken rides, their control boxes, loose wires.

The path had interior corners filled with sand where the wind had built little mounds that Bobbi told Rachel were gold dust. The bumper cars were painted like small covered wagons, only large enough for one person to ride west inside. She imagined a country full of single people heading west. Cracks in the floor grew bits of weed. One of the wagons had crashed through the wall containing the others. It sat on Old Mine Road like it had been marauded by bandits, its only passenger killed.

Bobbi wondered if there was a patron saint of abandoned places. She almost went back to the van to look in her book.

The Flooded Mine was a log-flume ride that went under a tunnel cut into the plastic mountain at the center of the park. There was no more water. Bobbi and Rachel walked through, unsure what was on the other side of the mountain. There were several turns that cut off the light completely.

When they came out on the other side, there was a carousel full of donkeys and oxen. Some of them were dragging small carts with seats buried in yellow plastic to make it look from the outside like the rider was sitting in a pile of gold. A number of the gold and silver light bulbs around the exterior were shattered and made the ride look crowned with thorns. The mirror that wrapped the inside cylinder was broken. The pieces were covered in dust.

They sat in a pile of gold and waited for the sun to go down through the chain-link fence. Bobbi could see real mountains faraway in the background. Large black birds floated over the desert. Bobbi wondered if wolves or coyotes came into the park at night.

Let them, she thought.

Rachel was chewing on her own hand. Bobbi took it and held tightly.

When the sun disappeared, the park became almost as dark as an actual mine. The nearest streetlight was down the road from the huge parking lot out front. Above them were so many stars it was impossible to not be aware she was looking at space. There were also several dots that could be seen on the ground in the distance. Bobbi imagined gas stations or fast food restaurants. They seemed so far away they might as well be in space. The ground was black beneath the carousel. They were on a pedestal atop a deep pit, surrounded by galloping mules.

Rachel stood up and shambled forward. Before Bobbi could get a hand on her. She was lost among the livestock.

Bobbi followed her. She thought she could hear the sound of clawing on the other side of the ride. Scratching. Gnashing. She imagined Rachel devouring the neck of a fiberglass ox. That's when the lights went on. And music. The world began spinning around her.

A whole section of the park lit up wherever the bulbs were not broken. Victorian-style streetlamps glowed white in the area around the carousel. The music coming from the speakers was missing notes, like it was only half of a song plunked out one string at a time on a lonely banjo somewhere in the plastic mountain.

Bobbi tried to navigate her way around the swirling carousel one step at a time. She held onto the poles. Rachel had gotten off the ride somehow. Bobbi thought she saw her hunched over an electrical box nearby but the carousel was still spinning. She was afraid to jump off but she did anyway. Her hands and knees scraped the ground. Her bones ached.

Bobbi sat on the dirt, bleeding, and watched the colored lights on the carousel spin. Rachel came and collapsed to sit at her mother's side. Bobbi held her. The lights are a miracle, Bobbi said. She thought about it. A miracle for no one but themselves and to no end but to provide a moment of beauty in their lives. A miracle like secret jewelry, she said.

Bobbi saw Rachel watching the lights. She recognized something in her face. They watched together.

Our faces are alike, Bobbi said. The whole world's faces are alike.

She thought of cavemen around bonfires staring into the flames. She thought of children in backyards pointing at shooting stars. Time slowed down as she watched the ride spin. Rachel leaned against her side. We are all taken by the light, she told the empty park.

Let there be light.

Jesus and Friends

Bobbi did not know Jesus. She had read the gospels but felt like she knew less about Him than most of the saints, even the most mysterious ones. She knew people talked about building a personal relationship with Jesus, but she could hardly learn to have a personal relationship with other living humans, how was she going to bond with a god, a *thing*, she thought, like Jesus? The more she learned about the Trinity, the less she understood. She read about Saint Patrick and the clover. She still had questions. If the Father, Son, and Holy Ghost were all part of the same *thing* — again it was the only word that seemed to fit — then what was that thing anyway? A team? Why had the team selected her to live this life? And how come they never checked in to see how things were going?

Bobbi looked toward heaven. She saw airplanes as crosses circling the globe.

She was waiting for something to intervene.

She sat in a lawn chair outside the trailer as the sun rose one morning. There was dried blood over her lip from waking up with a nosebleed. She had first gone outside to bleed in the dirt, but she brought Rachel out when she couldn't get back to sleep. She was putting mascara on Rachel's eyelids, which had no lashes. The sun looked like an egg yolk low in the sky.

We want to look nice when we meet Him, she told her daughter. All three of them, whatever. We want to look like normal girls.

The Rubber Snake

The teardrop trailer was covered in a slurry of bird waste and dust. So was the van. Bobbi took Rachel to a drive-thru car wash. They both loved being pulled through the wet, foamy tunnel on a conveyer belt. It felt like they were passing through the internal system of an enormous beast. A whale, Bobbi thought. It was refreshing even though they were not getting wet. It felt like their whole life was being dipped in water. There was R&B playing on the radio and Bobbi was dancing in her seat.

Before she pulled away, Bobbi rolled down her window to thank the attendant. We are smiling so hard, she thought, it must look like we have rainbows shooting out of our faces.

You're welcome, the attendant told her. You should get a snake for your roof.

Bobbi didn't understand.

A rubber one. Put it up there and it might scare some of these birds away. Less shit on your vehicle, he told her.

Bobbi purchased a rubber snake from Wal-Mart and glued it to the top of her trailer.

She told Rachel it was their new pet. She told her the snake was there to protect her. It was.

They cooked cans of corn beef hash outside the trailer that afternoon. She was still thinking of a name for their pet, when a large raven landed on the roof and pecked at the snake, then flew away with the tail end in its beak.

Bobbi chipped the diamond-shaped head off the roof with a fork and put it in a trashcan near the truck stop's vending machines. She was afraid the severed head alone would look like an advertisement for dead meat.

Tiny Acts

Bobbi and Rachel performed tiny acts of charity everywhere they went. Bobbi scrubbed dust off the hoods of cars with her sleeve as she walked past. She fed parking meters. She left notes under windshield wipers. I LOVE YOU, the notes said. YOU DESERVE TO FEEL LOVE WHILE YOU ARE ALIVE.

She let car after car pass her on the highway. During heavy traffic, she pulled over. She didn't want to contribute to anyone's stress. She picked up garbage. She gave cigarettes to homeless people. Sometimes she bought a candy bar from the truck stop vending machine and just left it there in the slot to be found — she hoped — by a child's hand.

She said prayers for people who smiled at her and prayed even harder for those who didn't. She wondered whether God only responded to other people's prayers and if anyone had ever said a prayer for her and Rachel. Maybe those prayers have already been answered, she thought, without us ever noticing.

The Road

The road never ended. It just went on forever and forked into other roads that looped back around and turned into more roads again, going everywhere. Even a dead end was just a place to turn around.

It is impossible to be lost when you are homeless, she thought. She felt a sense of comfort. The world was a giant hammock, too big to ever fall off. Sometimes she thought the road was built just for her. An infinite track and she was the long-awaited train it had been designed for.

Bobbi prayed to St. Christopher as she drove, even though she still did not understand his story. She also prayed to the moon in her skylight after dark. She knew it was blasphemy but she didn't care. Any God who would place something like the moon in the sky must want people praying to it, she said.

Bobbi occasionally passed through cities like throbbing ulcers on the earth's surface but mostly she saw their lights and skylines from the highway. She saw dead animals in the thousands along the roadside. Rachel watched them go past on the other side of the window. She liked to think Rachel was counting, keeping track of all the other dead things in the world.

Bobbi had stopped keeping track of life a long time back. She remembered how long each day seemed when she was a child. Now the days just blended together. She began to think in terms of lives, not days or years. One was the biggest number there was.

The World Is Infested With Life You Can Visit

Bobbi visited many places.

There was the town next to the lake where Rachel battled the goose, eventually biting its neck while Bobbi stood nearby wringing her hands. The used car dealership where she asked to use the restroom and was talked into taking a Cadillac out for a test drive; the look on the salesman's face when he saw Rachel climbing into the backseat, only half-hidden by a deep purple hood. The dirt mountain road they climbed to reach the sun and how even though they never got to the sun, they knew they had come close — close enough to feel the hot rays brushing against her fingers when they reached for the sky. There was the cave in Arkansas where Bobbi drew a heart on the wall in lipstick and wrote Rachel's name inside, next to a little dot. There were churches, laundromats, campsites, bridges, banks, butchers, barnyards, and everything else. Bobbi drove through the world. She couldn't believe she existed at the same time as any of it.

She turned the knob on the radio. She bit her fingernails. She turned the knob again.

There was so much out there for them to hear. She banged her head with the music. She listened to political talk radio and learned about the huge, over-arching systems humans had created to guard themselves or take advantage of themselves or both. She drove fast and rolled down all her windows. The world blew past and filled the car like something so loud it had gone blurry, like a wave of fuzz hitting her in the ear. Her head sometimes ached and she had to pull over. Sometimes it felt like her face was pulsing and blood was coming out her ears. She would touch them and they would be dry.

The Fruit Stand

The road they drove was long and thin and hot like a black snake in the desert, dotted with color in spots where natives sold drums and pipes and other bits of craft and junk for the tourists that drove past what seemed like every couple of hours. Bobbi had not seen another car in a long while when she came upon the fruit stand. She felt a deep urge to stop and buy some fruit.

Her cells first demanded it, then begged for it. She couldn't remember the last piece of fruit she'd eaten. She worried. Can normal people remember the last fruit they have eaten? She pulled onto the shoulder a little ways past the stand. She was almost too weak to walk. She needed to eat one piece now, she thought, before she could make it to the others.

Mommy is going to buy some fruit, she said. Rachel wasn't interested. She was busy watching birds out the window and picking at a stain on the dashboard.

The fruit stand reminded Bobbi of the stable in nativity scenes she had seen at Christmas; only inside there was a Mexican woman with buckets of red and green chilies, chili powder, and dried corn instead of a baby in a manger. Behind her, filling the area where the shepherds and wise men would have been sitting, were cantaloupes, plums, peaches, onions, and nectarines. Black flies filled the air above the produce. The woman didn't seem to notice. She let the flies crawl on her forehead. Just like a cow, Bobbi thought, admiring her.

Bobbi was filling a plastic bag with nectarines and peaches when she heard another car pull up next to the stand. A door opened and closed. She didn't bother to look. She was too busy squeezing fruit. She had already bitten into a plum. Its juice was running down her chin.

I'm going to pay for that! she said over her shoulder, mouth full.

She heard a man's voice. It was cheery and familiar.

I'll be happy to take care of her fruit, the voice said.

Bobbi turned and there he was, smiling in his grey suit and hat, the man who had visited them in the diner, the man who had given her his calling card. In one hand, he was holding a melon the shape of his head. Even in the desert, she thought, he still looks like a snowman.

I can pay for it, Bobbi told the Mexican woman.

The man deflected her words with a smile. On us, he said and handed over a few bills. What's the difference? All comes from the same pot anyway.

He carried Bobbi's fruit back to the trailer. She tried to carry it herself but he wouldn't hear it. He handed her a nectarine. Eat this, he said. It's an excellent source of Vitamin C.

Bobbi bit into the fruit. Her face was still sticky from the plum she had just devoured. Her mouth tasted fresh, alive, like she was eating the essential stuff life was made of, all of it contained in this juicy orange ball. Tiny bubbles danced on her lips.

Thank you, she said.

They stood outside the van. The man waved over Bobbi's shoulder at Rachel in the passenger seat. She was touching the window as if she wanted to reach through it and hold his hand.

The three of us should talk, the man said. In the trailer.

Bobbi was startled, confused. Nobody else had ever been in the trailer. She wasn't even sure they would all fit. She made a string of empty vowel sounds. She looked at Rachel.

It's okay, the man said. She should hear some of this.

Bobbi wasn't sure Rachel could hear anything. Part of her knew she had always just been pretending to believe her daughter was listening.

He was already opening the door and climbing inside the trailer as if he had done it hundreds of times before. He looked over his shoulder and nodded at Rachel in the passenger-side window. Bobbi opened the door and helped Rachel down from the van.

Bobbi was still making vowel sounds.

Come on in, the man said. He was kind of scrunched into a ball on the tiny bed, trying to keep the bottom of his shoes off the sheets. It's nice in here, he said.

Bobbi just looked at him.

Come on!

He was obviously trying to appear optimistic.

Let's eat some fruit!

He nodded his head like fruit was the answer to everything. He patted the mattress and then put the fruit down in front of him like it was a bag of Halloween candy. Rachel climbed in and sat down but she avoided the plums, peaches, and nectarines nesting in her bed.

High five, the man said and Rachel gently touched her hand to his.

Bobbi stood hunched at the foot of the bed with her arms crossed. She held half a nectarine in her hand and felt uncomfortable, chewing.

You are missed, the man told her. Every day, you are missed.

I've been, Bobbi started. She trailed off into nothing.

Missing? he asked.

Missed, she said.

We know you haven't been feeling well, Bobbi.

Bobbi was genuinely surprised. Her body felt numb like scab tissue, like a ghost sometimes, but not *unwell.* She touched her nose to see if it was bleeding.

You don't even know how you are feeling anymore, do you?

He looked concerned. He offered her another piece of fruit.

I'm still chewing, she said.

We can help you, he said. I mean, more than we already have. Frankly, I'm here to tell you it would be easier with a little more cooperation on your part.

He held his hand up and Rachel gave him another high five.

Bobbi bit her lip.

Love the make-up by the way, he told her. He shot Rachel a wink.

The air in the room felt thick. Bobbi opened the skylight.

We're worried about you, he said.

I thought you told me that you guys never worry? The last time we met you said no one had time to worry.

He shrugged his shoulders.

Well, sometimes we do.

Bobbi heard a sharp birdcall through the opened skylight.

I'm not telling you we have all the answers, he said. Or even all the questions at this point, but I think we have the right group trying to figure out what to ask at least. Am I confusing you?

Bobbi nodded.

We ask questions, he said.

The man sighed. Look, if anything, please come in because you are getting sick and you know it. Or come in because you said you would, but do come. I promise I'm your friend.

He held out a peach and then made it disappear for Rachel. Bobbi could see the peach the whole time but Rachel was stunned. He showed her the peach and she started laughing.

See, he said. She knows what I'm talking about.

She doesn't know anything, Bobbi said, and then she felt bad for saying it. You know what I mean…

It's hard to tell what your daughter knows until we get a better look at her. I wouldn't be surprised if she knows a lot more than even you think, he said. He was maneuvering himself off the bed toward the trailer door. He was being careful not to kick Rachel as he turned around to stand up. The more we learn about her, the more you do, he said. We can improve your lives.

He handed Bobbi another card with the same address on it.

Think about us. That's all. Meanwhile, I'm going to get out of here and stretch my limbs. Let you ladies hit the road. Need any recommendations? I've travelled everywhere you have and a whole lot more too, he said, climbing backwards down from the trailer door. That's why I can't blame you for not wanting to be tied down. Here's a hint: It's all worth seeing while you can see it. But it's worth making sure you stick around to see more of, too.

Bobbi watched him through the porthole as he walked back to his car. He was stretching, reaching for the sky. She looked around at all the fruit on their bed. She had no idea what to do with any of it.

Mommy is going to take you for a hot dog, she said.

Faith

Bobbi was looking at pamphlets she had collected from truck stops. The pamphlets contained photographs and information about National Parks and other attractions: mountains, caves, waterfalls, whatever was out there that people had decided was special. She had hundreds of them. Some of the places, she'd visited. Most she never got around to but it was nice to know they were there. It was also a reminder: there were even more special places that still didn't have pamphlets. She tore the back page off one and wrote on it, then slipped the note between the leaves of her Bible. This is what the note said: *Living just to live is the great daily act of faith. Anything more than that is extra, bonus faith.*

She turned on the engine. She felt the van come alive.

Taking Care

Bobbi was pumping Rachel with embalming fluid behind the trailer, which was parked under a tree on the side of a small road. She had the fluid all over her shirt. The landscape had changed on them again and Bobbi didn't know where she was. Somewhere in California, but the state was enormous. Maybe we are not even in California, she thought. Maybe we are in some other state.

Bobbi was also tending to herself. Her brain felt like it was being squeezed and released, pushing blood and water from her face. She took a small handful of Tylenol but the pain didn't go away. She took some more. She stuffed wet tissues in her nostrils. She looked at Rachel, who was expressionless but shaking a little in her lawn chair. Bobbi held a wet rag to her forehead then to Rachel's. She let a deep breath slip from her lips.

Hippies

Call me when all the flowers start talking like puppets again, she told Peter. But make sure they have something to say this time. I'm working.

Bobbi had been working in the organic chicken farm for at least three months. She used a wide broom to herd chickens from their walking area to their feeding and waste area and sometimes, at least in the last week, to be killed. The farm was a co-operative owned by people Bobbi recognized as hippies. They were trying to be nice to the chickens but they were bad at it. They were not that good at selling the chickens either. Chickens were not the only product that funded their communal living. Drugs mostly, Bobbi figured, but also soap.

When Bobbi went to work, Rachel stayed on the far end of the property near the trailer after one of the hippies said she gave off bad vibes. The others had invited her down many times, but Rachel stayed up on the hill by the trailer, pacing a tiny square of dirt and burning cigarettes. Bobbi left the trailer door open so she could move in and out. Bobbi could see her through the window from the dining hall when she was eating.

The man on Bobbi's walkie-talkie was Peter. Peter was the one who had found her in a parking lot and brought her home. Peter brought a lot of people to the farm. Apparently, he was a sort of Admissions Director.

I bring home the human resources, he liked to say. I bring the human resources *home*.

Peter was always on mushrooms. Bobbi was afraid of what she might see if she ate them. But she was agitated a lot of the time at the farm, so she thought about it a lot.

Herding chickens made her feel jaded even though she liked them. Their short lives made her sad. The way they jumped and skipped like little dinosaurs, unsure of what they wanted from one moment to the next. They were born to die, she thought.

The hippies collected healing crystals and glass marbles. Bobbi had them placed all around the inside of the trailer. They weren't working.

Peter said they were.

Bobbi went up to the trailer at night after dinner and singing. She slept there with Rachel, despite Peter and the others' near constant invitations to bunk at camp.

You'll have better dreams if you sleep around the rest of us, Peter told her. We all go to sleep in a pile of good energy.

Thank you, she said. I'll pass. I've got a kid up there that needs me.

It was in that and other small ways — like kneeling for daily prayer alone with Rachel on the hilltop each morning, where everyone could look up and see — that Bobbi kept a distance between herself and the rest of the group. She didn't feel comfortable dancing at the drum circle. She often spoke of her plans to move on, visit Alaska maybe or Mexico. Nobody was interested. People just pretend they don't hear things in this place, she thought, and then it is like they never happened.

Despite all this, they remained there for months. Nobody had been anything but friendly, she thought. Except for the one bad vibes remark, which was rude but not out of the ordinary given Rachel's appearance. She found it easy enough to forgive. The hippy that said it was long gone anyway.

Yet somehow she couldn't get with the program. She blamed herself. Living around this many other people, socializing, being a part of something. It all felt like it was supposed to be good for her, but it wasn't. It felt like her body was slowly rejecting the other humans' proximity.

She pushed the chickens around with her broom. I am like God to them, Bobbi thought. And still they don't notice me until I am pushing them. Even then they forget about me or ignore me or fight as I shove them back through the barn doors in a clump.

The chickens chattered in a near constant stream. Bobbi thought it sounded like they were talking to themselves. Not like they were interrupting each other but like they couldn't hear anything but the sound of their own voices.

Bobbi wore a cloth on her head while she worked. A lot of the women wore cloths on their heads but it wasn't mandatory. Nothing was mandatory at the farm. They kept telling her that. Nothing except tending the chickens.

Rachel wore a poncho and love-beads. They were a gift that Peter had given to Bobbi and she had passed on to her daughter.

Make-up was another thing that Bobbi used to keep them separate from the group. Nobody else on the farm wore make-up except her and Rachel. Bobbi first applied it in the morning before they said their prayers. Afterward she fed Rachel chicken meat, tuned the radio to a pop music station and headed down to the barn for work.

She hoped physical labor would change her somehow. It would make her better, more grateful to be a part of the universe. She took on extra tasks as they came up during group meetings or at meal times. She lugged bags of corn and oats on her shoulder when they arrived on the truck. She sprayed vegetables with organic insect repellent made of garlic, onions, and hot peppers. She composted. She collected herbs. She scrubbed the walls of the indoor and outdoor shower stalls. She sometimes helped dig a large hole that the hippies had been working on since the day she arrived on the farm. Her nose bled. She coughed and her blood mixed with the dirt.

Bobbi looked up at Rachel on the hillside as she worked. She was checking on her. Rachel looked like a scarecrow made of meat.

There were times when Rachel disappeared and Bobbi felt a rush of panic. There were woods at the top of the hill. Bobbi always feared Rachel had wandered inside. She hoped she was just in the trailer but she imagined her stuck in thorn bushes or attacked by owls or broken in pieces and struggling at the bottom of a ditch. Bobbi imagined her shot in the head by hunters, then shot several more times to make sure. Then maybe shot again. But after a while Rachel always returned to her spot by the trailer at the top of the hill to wait for her mother.

Peter brought in several new people while Bobbi was there — mostly women; some stayed, some didn't —

but Bobbi could tell he paid special attention to her. Part of her enjoyed that. Unless she was just imagining it, she thought. Then she asked God's forgiveness for caring one way or the other.

Nothing happened when she prayed.

Rachel prayed along with her. Only God knows what she prays for, Bobbi thought. Maybe everything she has prayed for is still coming true. Maybe it already has.

But Bobbi kept praying and reading about the saints at night in the trailer. The pages of *Vitae* were wrinkled and stained with brown-red spots. Her Bible was bloated with all her thoughts on napkins and tiny scraps of paper. Some of her words were illegible. Some of them were so faded it was like even the idea they represented had never even existed. Some looked like hieroglyphs.

One time Bobbi looked up to find Rachel missing and instead of praying to God, she asked the Imaginary Mother to go into the forest and find her. Bobbi's cheeks felt hot as she prayed because she knew deep inside the Imaginary Mother wasn't real. Rachel turned up soon after anyway. Bobbi felt bad for doubting.

The hippies gathered together to play games. They told Bobbi the games were not mandatory, but somehow the way they said it always made her feel like they were. One of the games involved bouncing glowsticks in many colors on a rainbow parachute spread out in a giant circle between them. The pale lights shot across the circle in soft arcs. They crossed paths for an instant before falling back down into the glowing parachute. The fabric splashed like they were landing in electric soup. Bobbi thought the game was beautiful. She liked that there were no winners or losers. She felt herself smile as the parachute threw a gust of wind toward her face and she thought of Rachel above, watching alone on the hill. She slinked away from the group to join her.

This happened night after night.

After the hole was dug, the hippies planed the inside so it was smooth. The hole was deep. A ladder was needed to get inside with tools. As they planed the surface, earthworms retreated into the dirt to hide from their trowels. Bobbi helped when she was not with the chickens or Rachel. Bobbi was willing to help with anything. She didn't ask questions. Regular work was the best thing about living on the farm.

Bobbi enjoyed being given directions. She liked feeling useful. She wanted to feel all used up at the end of her life. She wanted her brain to be like a raisin at the end, her skin a dry, transparent husk. She didn't want to die with anything left to give of herself. Motherhood had so far been an excellent guarantee of that, but digging a hole didn't hurt either.

She felt sorry for not loving life with the hippies. Everyone she saw looked so happy, or at least content, like it was their natural state. She assumed they all must have other lives, dramatic moments, tragedy, but they had each made a conscious decision to leave as much of that stuff somewhere else as they could. They had made a choice to enjoy their time on the planet and for now at least that choice looked like it was working.

Bobbi sometimes felt like she had never had any choices but then she saw herself as spoiled and rotten for having such thoughts and realized she had a world full of choices to make everyday. She knew that thought should make her happy but it didn't. It made her feel worse and then she felt even worse for being ungrateful.

Some people call life short and cheap, Peter told her. I prefer mine fat and absolutely free.

The dead will never die, Bobbi said. It just popped into her head.

I need to go write that on a napkin, she thought.

Peter was sitting with Bobbi on the edge of the hole. They were dangling their feet. It had just gotten dark and everyone else was inside eating dinner. Bobbi had taken her dinner outside to eat alone where it was quiet. A few minutes later he joined her, holding a bowl of noodles with fruit and seaweed on top. Bright stars dotted the sky. Bobbi stared into the hole beneath their feet.

Life is a big joke, Peter said after awhile. You just got to get in on it, understand?

I don't always get it, Bobbi said.

Don't get it. *Get in on it*, he said, as if the difference was profound.

Okay, Bobbi said. She was trying to remember her own thought about death so she could write it down.

Do you want to know what we are digging this hole for? Peter asked.

No, Bobbi said. She meant it.

Peter was quiet. He had not expected her to say no.

She looked at the stars and then down at the hole again.

Thank you for offering, she told him. The quiet grew between them.

She would miss the chickens.

The Oceans of the World

Bobbi liked to drive along the Pacific Coast. She told Rachel about animals that lived underwater. The ocean was the biggest landmark on the planet, a void. She liked to ride the edge of it. The trailer sometimes felt like it would pull them off the cliff on a sharp turn.

She knew there was only one ocean in the world. She knew the same water flooded the planet everywhere. It lived in the clouds above her. When their van wobbled or got close to the guardrail, she saw her and Rachel disappear into the ocean. They got lost in the current. They dissolved. They circled the earth in water molecules like tears. She dreamt of becoming a cloud.

Nature Speaks

There were times when Bobbi thought the natural world was speaking to her. She would be watching a tree or a rock — not doing anything, just existing — and then Nature would be telling her: *No one knows whether we are enjoying any of this.*

The Accident

Bobbi was the first to come upon a red sports car flipped on a curved stretch of mountain road surrounded by tall pines. The wheels were up in the air like little black feet and there was dark smoke coming from its belly. She stopped her van and ran toward the accident with Rachel still in the passenger seat.

The roof was not collapsed and she couldn't see any flames yet so Bobbi expected to find anyone inside still alive or close to it. As she got nearer she saw glass and bits of plastic all over the road. Candy-coated red paint was in chips everywhere. The side of the car looked clawed by giant fingers, swatted across the road. There were no other vehicles nearby.

The man and woman inside were beautiful, even with blood on their faces and broken teeth. They looked ageless to Bobbi, like actors on a screen. They were upside down, hair full of glass from the broken sunroof and windshield. The man's arm was snapped below the elbow, the woman's collarbone had been crushed. Bones stuck through the skin above her breasts. Bobbi was scared to move them.

They were both dressed in white. White dust from the airbags was settling in the interior of the car, illuminated by sunlight. The man was barely awake. His eyelids were fluttering. The woman looked unconscious but she was moving — her legs kicked like a sleeping dog's — and she made a sucking sound with her lips. Bobbi hesitated at the driver's side door, which had popped open. These people were something fragile, like glass figurines or a rare insect. She pictured their bodies coming apart in her hands as she tried to save them.

She unclipped the man's safety belt and his body clumped against the roof. Bobbi ran around to the other side of the car and undid the woman's belt. The way her torso crumpled toward his shoulder made Bobbi cringe. She pulled the bodies from the car and piled them alongside the road. She turned her head toward the mini-van. Rachel was hanging out the window. She looked hungry.

Bobbi hadn't even thought of praying yet, but now she prayed. She sat next to the bodies, in pine needles wet with blood. The first thing she prayed for was forgiveness for not praying sooner. She could hear their breaths, raspy and struggling in the direction of a rhythm. Bobbi had seen CPR on TV and knew it was a thing people did to the dying, but she didn't know anything more than that. She opened her eyes and looked at the couple's faces. Their noses were almost touching.

Kiss, Bobbi said.

She didn't know why she said it, she just did. She wanted to see these two beautiful people kiss. She prayed to watch them give each other CPR.

Please live, Bobbi said. She already felt like it was her fault if they died.

The car was burning now. It did not explode or burst into flames. It was a gentle burning, like a campfire.

Rachel appeared at Bobbi's side and put a hand on her shoulder. Bobbi wasn't sure if she was trying to comfort her or just keep herself standing. She had wet pine needles stuck to her lips.

The couple kept breathing. Their breath was like wind through brambles full of trashed paper and plastic wrappers. They were breathing though and Bobbi didn't want to hear sirens. She didn't want the sirens to interrupt her prayers or the sound of their breaths in her head. She didn't want to give a statement either. She had nothing to say.

Even imagining the sirens was a distraction from her miracle.

Saint Patrick

Vitae had much to say about the life of Saint Patrick: his capture as a boy, his escape, attacks by boars and Druid lords, the banishing of snakes, his letters, his walking stick grown into a tree, a bell that he once owned.

But Bobbi was still most interested in the part of the story where Saint Patrick said God was divided into three parts like the leaves on a clover. The image didn't make sense to Bobbi. It was easier for her to picture God as a whole field of clovers, green and rolling into the distance on all sides.

She had to spin in circles to see.

The Old Woman With Bones in Her Yard

The old woman was actually a man dressed as a woman. She lived alone down a long road in the middle of nowhere in the far northwest of the country, where there are still eagles. Bobbi thought it was funny that she bothered wearing anything but sweatpants, all alone and in such a remote location. Even real women wouldn't bother to wear dresses out here, Bobbi thought but said nothing. She didn't want to hurt anyone's feelings.

They first met in a thrift store operated in the basement of a small brown church. Bobbi was there buying sweatpants and old washcloths for cleaning up after Rachel, as well as for cleaning Rachel herself. Bobbi liked the washcloths that had been worn down and softened against people's skin, the ones with frayed edges.

The old woman wore a large red wig. She approached Bobbi in the housegoods aisle and said her name was Leslie. She seemed like she hadn't spoken to anyone in a long time and was driven by a need to say something. Bobbi appreciated that. She liked her immediately and they left the store talking. When Leslie saw the teardrop trailer she let out a gentle gasp and held her hand to her mouth. She was just like what Bobbi had always imagined a grandmother would be like.

I used to have a trailer like that, Leslie said.

Her voice was trembling. Bobbi thought she might cry.

I took my family inside it, she said. We used to go camping.

Bobbi couldn't imagine refusing when she invited them to make camp in her driveway. She pointed to Rachel in the window and they both waved at her. Rachel's eyeballs were rolled back in her head.

The house was at the foot of a mountain with snow on it. It was the only house nearby, down a long beat-up driveway lined with big trees. It was always raining, or about to rain. Leslie had no pets of her own, but she drew the local wildlife to her backyard by feeding them rank or freezer-burned fish and scraps of roadkill that she threw off her porch. Her backyard was full of bones. They were scattered like wildflowers throughout the grass and clover. Eagles came in the mornings, foxes, cats, wolves, an owl, a badger, and whatever else was out there. Bears, Leslie said, but Bobbi had not seen one. The yard was full of eyes at night.

Leslie loved nature and magic and with Bobbi and Rachel around, she enjoyed the chance to go on and on about them. She repeated herself a lot.

There is no magic in life, Leslie would say. Only illusions. And there isn't even that.

Nature isn't trying to hide what we can't see. The best stuff is just invisible, like time or love.

Animals have brains. They are all out there with electric signals dancing around their skulls, just like us. And we're all magic.

I'd try to understand the universe but I can't even make sense of how my television works. I only sort of pretend to understand but it all just feels supernatural. What feels the most magic is that any and all of this is plain real.

Magic is only real things you don't understand, you know.

The less you understand, the more magic there is in the universe.

Bobbi mostly just nodded. Leslie was a sweet person who loved to feed her animals, even if she was hard to understand sometimes. Bobbi thought talking in circles like that worked to reaffirm her convictions. Like she had been feeling all these things in her heart but she needed to say them out loud to make them real. Like a spell, Bobbi thought.

Bobbi enjoyed being a kind of mirror for Leslie to look at herself in.

The more Leslie talked, the more she had to say.

Leslie sometimes encouraged Bobbi to wear less make up, which Bobbi thought was funny advice coming from a man dressed as a woman. You don't need it, Leslie said. Neither of you. Your faces are miracles the way they are.

Bobbi nodded, coughing. She felt like she was always coughing now. She didn't know when the coughing started. It was like she had been coughing forever.

She went outside in the mornings while Leslie fed the eagles. They kept Rachel in the sun porch. She stood by the sliding door and watched.

First one or two eagles arrived and landed on the edge of the deck. They stretched their wings. Leslie tossed them pieces of fish from a bucket. Then more and more came until there were many of them in the lawn, multiple rows back, and Leslie had to switch to an overarm throw. The throw was a man's throw, the throw of an old guy who had grown up playing catch with his dad and then with a son of his own. It made Bobbi laugh inside to watch her throwing fish meat in this giant red wig, but it also made her feel sad. She wondered where Leslie's family had gone.

Rachel pressed her face against the window to watch the giant birds feed. She left thick stains that Bobbi scrubbed everyday, even though Leslie told her they were fine. The stains had a sour odor.

Once Leslie came home from a trip to the store with a roadkill deer on the hood of her truck. It was half gone rancid, but Leslie said the birds liked it that way. The next morning she heaved the carcass out into the yard as the sun rose and the birds flew in over the trees.

The eagles stepped carefully around the animal, as if it might come back to life. They tore into the meat, pulled off stringy hunks of it in their yellow beaks. They snapped their necks back to swallow. Their throats bulged. Foxes slipped in to snatch bits and run off. At the end of the day there was a deer skeleton in the grass, which the other animals probed for gristle and marrow. Beetles ate what was left of the hide.

Bobbi could tell Leslie liked her being interested.

Eagles have a hole in their tongue, Leslie told her.

Their tongues looked sharp, like spearheads. Bobbi hadn't noticed any holes yet.

It is the opening of their respiratory system, Leslie said. That's how they breathe.

Bobbi hadn't considered the eagles breathing before. They had almost seemed to be made of the air itself. Eagle's breath. She wasn't sure what to do with that information.

Rachel has holes in her tongue, she thought, but not for breathing.

Leslie slipped her a handful of fish guts, which she threw into the yard.

There are a lot more of them up in Alaska, Leslie told her. The fishermen leave their nets out and the birds come to pick them clean.

Bobbi couldn't imagine more eagles anywhere else in the world. Any more, she thought, and they might become mutinous. Tear the house apart. Pluck out our eyes. She was surprised they hadn't done it already. These were powerful birds. Bobbi thought the other animals in the vicinity must be grateful Leslie kept the eagles' bellies full.

Rachel was pressed against the window, her face smeared like it had been blurred out. She was wearing a pink sweatshirt that said: Born To Babysit!

Bobbi sneezed. She wiped her nose and there was blood in the gook on her hand. An eagle bent down and shot its tongue at a gob stuck to the railing.

She looked back at Rachel's face. She had pulled it away from the window and was staring with dark eyes.

What did Rachel think of when she watched her mother bleed?

The Orcas of the Hills

Bobbi kept on the lookout for bears. She had never seen a bear before, or any animal that large, and she wanted to share the experience with Rachel. As a girl, Bobbi had read a story about a bear that lived on a mountain by the sea and ever since, she had associated bears with the ocean and the hills. They were large and mysterious and Bobbi wanted to see one.

She told Leslie about the bear and the ocean and the mountain.

They aren't marine mammals but they do live in families and are very smart, Leslie said. So they are a bit like whales, I guess. The Furry Orcas of the Hills.

Bobbi didn't know what an orca was but she liked the way it sounded.

Leslie promised she would see bears if she hung around long enough. Bobbi told her she would stay until she saw a bear and then she would know it was time to move on.

Leslie seemed to like that.

That sounds magic, she said.

Bringing the Family Back

She wanted to do something nice for Leslie but, as it had been so often in her life when Bobbi met people she wanted to help, she wasn't sure how. She had very little to give in terms of material goods. She knew Leslie was lonely, so she listened. She knew she missed her family but there was nothing Bobbi could do.

Rachel stayed by the window most of the time, near the door, watching the bones in the yard.

Leslie kept offering to make them sandwiches and hot tea. Bobbi only ate when it felt impolite not to. She wasn't hungry and felt guilty eating more than a small share of Leslie's food. Rachel didn't want the sandwiches. Bobbi fed Rachel what the eagles ate. Rachel held it in her hand and chewed. She tossed her head back. She swallowed the hunks of meat just like the birds.

Bobbi clapped. She could feel Leslie's eyes watching her as she fed Rachel. She wondered when the last time Leslie had seen her own children was, but she thought better than to ask. She will tell me what she wants when she wants and I will listen, Bobbi thought. I will do what I can.

She knew she would never be able to do very much.

Bobbi invited Leslie to join them on walks over trails she had shown them in the wooded area around the house. Leslie always declined to follow past the entrance. You two go along, she told them. No one can spend enough quality time with her child. I'll just talk too much and get in the way.

Leslie turned to Rachel. Same goes for spending time with Mom, she said. Take every second you can get. You two young ladies don't want an old hag like me following after you anyway. There's no telling what you will run into in those woods. Bears, she said. A prince maybe.

Leslie snapped her knobby fingers together.

Just like magic, she said.

She snapped them again.

Bobbi prayed Leslie would find her family or at least an imaginary one she could love. She looked for them in the woods. She didn't know what they looked like or how old they were or their names but she believed she would recognize them if she saw them, even the imaginary versions. Rachel walked next to her and they held hands. Bobbi could feel maggots moving under the skin on Rachel's palm. She thought of them as their own large family in a way she had never done before. She wondered if the worms being inside Rachel meant they were all related, an extended family, and that she was distantly one of them.

The forest was old, mature. Bobbi thought of all the life started and finished in the shadow of the trees, how much was in some stage of the process right now. She had to pee. She stopped and pulled off the trail to find a tree to squat against. She told Rachel to sit on the trail and not move until she came back. She placed her hands on Rachel's shoulders when she said it. She pointed at the ground. When she got back only a couple minutes later Rachel was not where she had left her.

Bobbi called her name. She expected to hear an echo but heard nothing. She called it again, running forward and then backward on the trail. When she was out of breath, lightheaded, she paused with her hands on her knees and listened. No echo; but she thought she heard a scratching sound like something digging nearby off the trail somewhere. She followed the scratching. The floor of the forest was thick and soft under her feet.

Bobbi peered through the trees. She saw a small brown bear alone in the woods. She froze. She thought the twigs under her feet must sound like firecrackers and the mother was probably nearby.

The little bear was preoccupied, rooting in a dead log on the ground, curious. He still had not noticed Bobbi when he lifted up his head and made a sad, hooting sound. She thought he might be crying. She backed away, taking slow careful steps toward the path.

Okay. I have seen a bear, she thought. Now where is my daughter?

Rachel was not far away, in the bush only a few yards off the trail from where Bobbi had first stopped to pee. Bobbi saw her and almost shouted her name, until she remembered the bear. Rachel was also on the ground rooting through something. Bobbi felt like a mother bear. It made her smile. She walked over to see what her daughter had found.

It was a nest of some kind, a mess of mud and plant matter near the base of a tree. It was kept from Rachel by fallen branches that poked into her skin as she reached through them. There were leaves in her hair and dirt collected in a wound on her neck. Bobbi pulled her off the branches and tried to brush her clean. She almost scolded her, but hugged her instead. Then she placed her hands on Rachel's shoulders again and she pointed at the ground right next to her. She lit a cigarette and put it in Rachel's hand before turning to get a better look at the nest.

Bobbi expected to find birds, but the little pink animals resting there were not birds. Bobbi didn't know what they were. She could see internal organs through their soft, pink skin. Their bodies were barely formed, just dull outlines rolled in clay. Their eyes were closed. Bobbi wondered if they had ever opened them before. The nest, or whatever it was, looked broken. She thought it maybe had fallen from the tree or else it had been built under the branches but abandoned to nature, which had broken it. She reached in with care and picked up the animals. There were five maybe six, clumped together like gummy bears. She pulled them to her belly and kept them warm in her sweatshirt. She looked like she was carrying fruit she had gathered from a field. Rachel leaned into her side as they walked. Bobbi used her elbow to protect the baby animals from Rachel's reach.

No, Bobbi said. These animals are still living.

Rachel was curious.

Bobbi showed them to her with care. They were miniature and barely moving, each about the size of a thumb.

We're going to take these babies back to Leslie and find them some milk, she said. Maybe with sugar in it.

Rachel stared down into the sweatshirt. The little pink bodies were shivering.

Babies are our friends, Bobbi reminded her. We don't eat our friends.

The sun had moved across the sky while they were in the woods. All the shadows had shifted, making places Bobbi had just been earlier in the afternoon look altogether different. Familiar trees looked new, as if they had just appeared alongside the trail fully grown. It was disorienting. Bobbi touched the animals with her palm. She could feel a small pump, baby blood pushed through tiny veins. She hurried along the path.

Just as she thought she was getting closer to the trailhead, Bobbi became aware of more hooting sounds, deeper now and accompanied by grunts. She picked up her pace. When they came around a bend in the trail, they saw a huge brown bear on its side amid the trees. Darkness was gathering against its flank. Bobbi started to run, then stopped, then started and stopped again.

The bear was sick.

She looked again.

The bear was not alone.

There was a hiker in a black hooded sweatshirt kneeling beside the mother bear's head. The bear's mouth was open and it kept swallowing as if it was trying to drink the air. The man in the black sweatshirt looked up at Bobbi and waved, as if noticing her for the first time. Bobbi held the baby animals tight against her body.

Bobbi knew Death when he was this close. She watched him pet the thick brown fur on the bear's giant neck. He kneaded the skin as if he was giving it a massage. He smiled at her and his teeth looked small and rounded, like baby teeth, like pearls.

Bobbi clutched the baby animals close. She was afraid she would kill them if she held any tighter.

It was as if Death's smile was talking to her.

Worry about yourself, the smile said. I am always here for you. We all meet up in the end.

The mother bear was spitting blood from her face. What was killing her?

Bobbi thought about the little bear, alone in the woods with no mother.

I have enough time for everybody, Death's smile was saying. The smile had a tone of voice. The tone was mocking and confident. Think of yourself first, it said.

Her toes curled in her shoes. She was nodding. The mother bear moaned and Death massaged her neck and the side of her face. She made another hooting sound. She was calling for her child. Bobbi squeezed the baby animals tighter in her sweatshirt and backed away from the mother bear, holding onto Rachel's shirt collar with her other arm.

They went on down the trail with the mother's cries echoing in Bobbi's head.

You didn't see that, she told Rachel as they walked. None of that really happened.

They paused near the back of Leslie's yard. Bobbi scratched her mouth and saw that her nose was bleeding. There were tears in her eyes.

Rachel was just staring at her.

Bobbi looked in her flat eyes then put an arm on her shoulder. Rachel's tongue was hanging out.

I'm fine, Bobbi told her. Mommy is going to be okay.

Rachel stared right through her. Bobbi took her stare for doubt.

I will always be in your heart, she said. She thought of the yellow diary her mother had left her, the heart with the little dot drawn inside. She had no idea what any of it actually meant.

Pictures, words.

She was afraid to look at the ball of baby animals in her sweatshirt. She took them to Leslie so she could give them names, whatever condition they were in.

Lessons From *Vitae*

Bobbi knew there were infinite lessons to be learned from reading the lives of the saints, but she was looking for something in her own life to boil it all down into one lesson that made sense. A crystal of truth. She worried she was looking for meaning in a universe where the only thing she needed to know was that there was no meaning. She kept reading out loud and in her head. She kept living out loud and in her head too.

Pressure

A lot of the time Bobbi felt like someone was inflating a basketball inside her skull. She took headache medicine in handfuls. She blamed it on stress. I am taking everything too seriously, she thought. Life is killing me. She couldn't remember the last time she had been looked at by a doctor. Meanwhile Rachel was as old as Bobbi had been when she gave birth, but she needed as much care as ever. Bobbi thought they were starting to look more alike everyday. Sometimes it made her smile.

Being a mother never ends, she said, lying back in the trailer. She allowed the needle and thread she was holding to fall to the bed beside her. She let out a giant sigh.

The sigh was a prayer, a mix of exhaustion and thanks.

Rachel lay next to her and forced a sigh of her own.

Laughing and Crying

More and more Bobbi found herself breaking into laughter when the world wasn't funny and tears when she didn't feel sad. She found herself weeping at rainbows and cackling as she tried to order fast food. The fits came on like a blip of energy had bubbled down from her brain and exploded pop! out of her face. They were uncontrollable, involuntary. She often felt itchiness, a twitch in her nose seconds before, but otherwise there was no warning. Several times it happened when she was driving and she almost lost control of the van. She had to pull over until the wave had passed.

Sometimes the laughter was unpleasant sounding, harsh and cutting to her ear. She always apologized to Rachel as she was doing it, or right after. She didn't want her to feel responsible for causing these emotions in her mother, outbursts that didn't fit what Bobbi was feeling inside. Sometimes a burst of genuine laughter or tears followed the original fit. It was both desperate and hilarious to realize how little she was in control.

The Claw Machine

Bobbi leaned on the counter of the Taco Bell, trying to convince the manager to let her purchase an entire pastry tube of the ground beef product they used to fill their tacos. The pastry tube was for Rachel. She had already ordered a Mexican pizza for herself. Rachel was in front of the claw machine near the truck stop's automatic sliding doors. Bobbi kept looking over her shoulder to make sure she hadn't gone anywhere.

She hadn't. She was staring down at the pile of plush animals trapped in the glass box, as if she were waiting for one to move. Bobbi waved off the manager. She had given up on the tube of meat. She took her Mexican pizza over to join Rachel at the machine. She was going to win her daughter a new stuffed pet.

She sat her food on top of the machine and gently nudged Rachel aside. She put a dollar inside and surveyed the prizes. She realized that if Rachel were different, she might point out which prize she wanted. On the one hand, she would probably be too old to care about a stuffed animal, Bobbi thought, unless her boyfriend was winning it for her.

Bobbi wished she could be that boyfriend.

She looked at Rachel again. Rachel was reaching for something. Bobbi got excited.

Which prize do you want Mommy to win for you? she asked.

But Rachel was only reaching for the Mexican pizza.

On The Library Steps

The library was in a small white building, formerly a church, on the edge of a town in the northern plains. The town did not look like it would even have a library, Bobbi thought; but it did. The steps outside were concrete, painted dark red, and there were potted wildflowers on the sidewalk. The library called to her like a roadside attraction. It had been years since she had seen a public library. She left Rachel in the trailer while she went inside.

Bobbi wanted information on home remedies or at least self-diagnosis but she was afraid to look for it online or in any of the books on the shelves. She was afraid to learn about her health. She spoke to her symptoms like they were ghosts. If I don't think about you, you will go away. If you don't go away, I will say a prayer. If the prayer doesn't work, I will say another.

She browsed the library in an aimless, nervy way, poking her nose into books about herb gardening, marine animals, baseball, and other unrelated topics. She had always been scared to receive bad news from a doctor and now she was too scared to guess at it on her own. She picked up a book on the lives of hummingbirds and flipped through it without reading anything. It felt good just to know how much information was out there that had absolutely nothing to do with her life. Hummingbirds don't care about me, she thought, even though I could read a whole book about them if I wanted to. This knowledge provided her some comfort or at least distraction. She left the library after only a short while, remembering nothing of what she had read.

Outside on the steps sat a young girl with a blonde bowl cut like an army helmet. She was picking a flower apart with her fingers, plucking the petals from the stem. There were dead flower petals clinging to the leg of her sweatsuit like lint. The girl was alone, perhaps waiting for somebody.

The girl paid no attention to her but Bobbi needed to linger. She wished she had a cigarette or something to explain her presence but she had left them in the trailer with Rachel. She guessed the girl was in her early teens, maybe older or younger than that. It was hard for Bobbi to remember what children other than Rachel were supposed to look like. The girl was glaring down at a blank page inside a little notebook. She was squeezing a red pen.

Bobbi asked her a question, but as soon as she asked it she forgot what she said.

What? the girl asked.

Who are you waiting for? Bobbi said. She was not sure that had been her original question but she was curious.

The girl said nothing. She just nodded.

Bobbi asked again.

What? the girl said. Bobbi noticed for the first time that she was wearing headphones.

She felt stupid. She didn't know what she was doing there but she kept the conversation open. She wanted to talk. The girl took her headphones off.

What is it? she said, looking agitated. I'm not waiting for anybody.

Bobbi felt the wings of the world flapping against her. She was confused.

Do you need help? Bobbi offered.

The girl looked at her like she had a worm crawling from the center of her forehead.

From you? she asked.

Yes, Bobbi said. If I can help, I would like to.

The girl put her headphones in the pocket of her sweatpants.

Bobbi kept watching her.

What? The girl used a sharp tone.

Bobbi had no clue how to answer her. What? she asked back. Then, What are you writing about?

The girl showed Bobbi the page. The page was empty.

Oh, Bobbi said. Nothing, I guess.

The girl smiled like she was eating a sour candy.

I thought it was a diary maybe, Bobbi said. What would you write if it was?

The girl scribbled on the page. No writing, just a quick scribble. She showed Bobbi the scribble. She underlined it.

Bobbi nodded, as if in agreement. Her eyes were becoming watery. She was afraid to cry in front of this little girl.

The girl watched her from underneath a tightly hooked eyebrow. Are you okay, Lady? she asked. Because I can go inside and get somebody?

A wave came over Bobbi. It was a wave of feeling very old, but not at all adult.

I'm fine, she whispered, but she knew that wasn't altogether true. She was dizzy. She felt as if she might turn and sprint back to the van at any moment, even though she wanted so badly to stay and talk to this girl, make her feel kindness, pass her some piece of useful wisdom, form a connection with her, win her respect.

Instead, she saw the young girl pitied her.

Dumpster Babies

Bobbi had heard stories of women leaving their babies in Dumpsters or fast food bathrooms. Even older stories where the babies had been left for wolves. Usually the women were younger than she was, or at least she imagined them to be. The complicated reasons women abandoned their children were often forgotten or left out of the stories. It was only the act and what happened afterward that mattered.

Bobbi thought about what her life would have been like if instead of baptizing Rachel, she had left her in the garbage somewhere or given her to the Experts forever. She couldn't even remember if they had asked to keep her. There was a lot that was hard to remember now.

She remembered first holding Rachel to her chest. She could feel her lips wrapped a sentence. She was calling her daughter an angel.

The life she dreamt up included a lot of images from billboards and television commercials. She saw herself riding a horse or talking to well-dressed people with cocktails at a party. She was on a sailboat with an older man who had a sweater wrapped around his neck. She was meeting the girls for Book Club. She struggled to picture what they might read but she couldn't think of anything except *Vitae* or maybe a newspaper. She started laughing. She didn't know whether she thought something was funny or not. Rachel copied her in the passenger seat. That they were laughing together was what felt important.

Later as she pulled into a visitor's center to park for the night, Bobbi started to think about the Dumpster babies again. It is never too late, she thought. She felt a pang of guilt for thinking it, but she couldn't help herself. She kept thinking.

That night as they lay back-to-back in their tiny bed, Bobbi imagined walking Rachel out to the trash bins in the back corner of the lot. Birds and dogs and other scavengers were poised just outside the scene, waiting. She held Rachel's hand as they walked. The sun was threatening to rise. She stopped halfway there and looked at Rachel, tried to send a message with her eyes, but there was nothing or too much to say, even for eyes. She climbed into the Dumpster with Rachel and held her one last time, and breathed the rank air into her lungs. Wait right here, she said. Mommy will be back soon. But this time she didn't come back. She kept driving and it hurt so bad but then she drove some more. It hurt less and less every day and she remembered less and less of her life until it was like the years she'd spent with Rachel had never happened or were only a dream.

She stayed up all night, lying next to Rachel, her head full of thoughts like these. She wondered what would happen to Rachel after she was left in the Dumpster. It would be black inside except where light crawled in the cracks. Every so often someone would lift the roof to reveal a flash of sky before dumping their waste over her shoulders. First she would eat rotting leftover food and love it. Time would pass and she would be alone except for rats and insects, which she would also eat at the same time they were eating her. Eventually the Dumpster would be turned upside down and she would be dropped into a truck on its way to a landfill. There she would be compacted with all the other things that had been thrown away. They would be buried in the earth or pumped into the sea or burned.

And then what? What if her life improved without me? Bobbi asked no one in particular, not sure that it even mattered. Nobody can be sure what an improvement is, she thought. Not until long after it has come and gone.

The Meaning of Useless

The beach stretched around the side of the lake like a sliver of fingernail. The sand was thick and brown, mixed with dirt and large rocks. There were trees growing in the back. In a cove across the water was a population of geese. The geese made distant honking noises that Bobbi told Rachel was music. There was another sliver of beach in the cove and two tiny people like lumps of grey clay.

They are feeding the geese, Bobbi told Rachel and pointed. They throw out the bread and the geese fight each other for it.

She lay down on their blanket and gently pulled Rachel back alongside her. They looked at clouds in the sky. The clouds did not look like anything but clouds. Bobbi chewed on blades of grass. When she sat up again the people across the lake were gone, but the geese were still there honking, waiting for someone else to come with bread. Bobbi chewed her nails and watched them. Their long necks made their heads look like they were up on pedestals. It made Bobbi feel strange to think of all their little brains floating around, perched above the water, pulsing with blood and thinking about torn bits of white bread. They are not that different from the rest of us, she thought. That's basically all there is.

Bobbi closed her eyes. Time passed. She was very tired.

She was startled when the men walked around in front of her on both sides. She had been almost asleep and their black dress shoes were silent in the sand. One of them she knew, but the other one, in a very similar grey suit except with pinstripes, she had never seen before. His face looked stern, muscled around the eyes and jaw, like he had spent many years holding a purposeful frown.

Your nose is bleeding, said her old friend, who had gained weight and looked more like a snowman than ever. He reached forward and handed her a handkerchief. He tipped his hat to Rachel, who was still flat on her back. Hi, Rachel, he said. Watch out for sand crabs.

Bobbi put her arm around her daughter.

Just kidding, he said. They don't live in this environment. And they're not really a threat to her anyway. Unless she stays still for a very long time, of course.

The other man stood back and watched them with knowledge and authority, like he had seen them many times before. Bobbi wanted his gaze to feel fatherly, but it wasn't that. It was more like the gaze of a man revisiting the site of an atrocity he had some small hand in creating.

The Snowman wiggled his fingers in front of her face and pointed at the handkerchief. Aren't you going to use that? he asked. You're a mess.

Bobbi wiped her face. The blood on the cloth looked brown. She heard geese honking across the lake.

The other man stared at her. She thought of him as the Other Man now.

The Snowman gently smiled. You look exhausted, he said. Here, you want some bread?

The Other Man dug his toe into the dirt.

Why don't you come with us this time? The Snowman asked. He turned and skipped a rock across the water. It hit three times and sunk. What else is there to do at this point?

Rachel made a noise. A deep sucking sound like someone unclogging a whole city's sewer followed by the sound of a bubble popping. Geese flew into the air.

Excuse us, Bobbi said. She made the sign of the cross over her chest and left her right hand hanging over her stomach, as if she herself had belched. The air smelled like it was burning.

We can help you, Bobbi.

The Other Man nodded. She thought he did at least. She wasn't sure if he had moved at all. It felt like he owned the clothes she was wearing but he was having trouble recognizing them. He was a man who was used to being owed great debts.

Bobbi looked at the sky. The clouds still looked just like clouds.

She knew the men wouldn't take her anywhere by force. She had to make this decision herself and she was not ready to confront the sacrifice involved.

We can help her too, the Snowman said. In a way.

In what *way*? Bobbi asked. She had been waiting to ask this question forever, to yell it across a lake with her daughter on the sand next to her.

We can make her ... useful, he said. He scratched his chin. Haven't you always wanted to feel useful?

Bobbi looked at the Other Man. His expression was still. He put his hat back on. There were shadows coming out of his eyes.

I don't even know what useful means, Bobbi said. She buried her face in her knees and cried until she started to laugh.

The Priest

Bobbi tried to look at the world as if she were capturing it with her eyes. She stopped the van more often. She wanted to know something, to store it in her mind before she died. This strategy sometimes didn't make sense to her. Why bother saving memories for after you're gone? She felt selfish or at least deluded. She stopped the van anyway.

One time she stopped the van on a small bridge over a creek because she saw a man with a shopping cart full of bottles and cans and balls of stripped wire. He was holding a fishing rod. From behind she could see he was wearing a bucket hat, which made his head resemble a church bell.

Bobbi had no reason to stop except she wanted to show Rachel the creek and have a few words with a stranger. She was surprised to see the man was dressed in a black shirt with a white priest's collar around his neck. The collar had a smudge on it, a black fingerprint right in the middle. He also had a beard. Bobbi had always pictured the clergy clean-shaven. She was excited enough to put that aside. She reminded herself to call him Father.

She held out a piece of beef jerky for the man. Father, would you like something to eat? she asked.

No thank you, he said calmly, as if she had been standing beside him all day. I'm fasting.

Bobbi looked at the fishing pole in his hands, the line hanging down into the water. He let a soft whistle through a gap where he was missing teeth.

They like it if you whistle to them a little, he said.

I don't understand, Bobbi told him. Rachel was hanging her head over the side of the bridge, biting at the water. Bobbi petted her on the neck. Is there no hook on the end of that line? she asked.

There's a hook, the man said. He kicked a painter's bucket near his feet. And there's a worm on it. The bucket is full of worms. I feed the worms, then I use them to catch the fish, then I feed the fish another, extra worm once I've caught him. Then I throw him back in the water. I use fish turds in the mud down by the creek to feed the worms. It's the circle of life, he said.

Bobbi was still confused.

So you are trying to feed the fish? Why not just dump the worms in the water? Why put the fish through all that just to eat?

The Lord works in mysterious ways, he said. Try not eating for a while and you start to understand them.

If this man really was a priest — and Bobbi was starting to suspect that he wasn't — she was afraid to ask him questions about God. Either way, she was afraid of what he might tell her. She offered him the jerky again. When he shook his head, she broke it into three pieces and threw them over the bridge. She stood next to Rachel and pointed at each little splash as the dried meat was snapped off the surface of the water.

One, two, three.

Okay, Bobbi said. We'll try.

Fasting

Instead of eating, Bobbi read stories in *Vitae* about people refusing to eat, men and woman who had offered up their nutrition as a gift. She read aloud to Rachel about how fragile they had made themselves for God.

Bobbi felt their bodies shrink as she read. She knew the universe was an impossible size, something that hurt to think about, and she dreamt of them disappearing against it. They were hungry. Rachel licked stains on the car's interior for sustenance. Bobbi had thrown out all their food.

She read about Saint Simeon the Stylite who climbed a pillar and stood on top of it for thirty-seven years. Simeon tried to escape the world vertically. He devoted his time to prayers, fasting and offering guidance to the visitors who came to the foot of his pillar each day. The meager bits of bread and goat's milk he accepted, he shared with maggots that he allowed to live in his open wounds. They were crusted with sand, brought on by exposure to the desert heat and winds. The small white worms were blind. Simeon called them his children.

Bobbi thought of the trailer as a pillar on wheels, a cell only feet above the pavement. Rachel looked out the window more than ever as they fasted.

She read about women who walled themselves into cloistered rooms surrounded by cold wet stone. She read how fasting was not only a penance, but a prayer. Every bite she did not take was an offering. Bobbi was praying for Rachel because Rachel couldn't pray on her own. She simply did not feed her.

She read about how fasting raised men up on wings to peek at heaven. She also read stories about the devil, who visited Jesus during the desperate moments of his fast in the desert. She read about young girls living for years on communion wafers, fighting off demons that came to their cots at night. She took comfort in the stories but she worried her reading was only making Rachel more hungry, like watching a commercial for French fries that you know you will never eat. French fries. French fries. Waffles. The billboards she passed were making Bobbi hungry too. She stared into them as they drove by. She tried to think of the giant burgers and fried chicken tenders as gifts to strangers. Someone else will eat that, she thought. Every time she saw a billboard she told herself she was driving closer to heaven.

Her vision often grew blurry as she drove. She saw little spots like tadpoles squirming away into the corners of her sight. Shadows tricked her. Trees leaned into the road. They walked across it from both sides, passing each other in the middle as if they were pedestrians at an intersection. Bobbi rubbed her eyes with her fists.

Moments of clarity also came from fasting. Times like when Bobbi was stuck in a traffic jam in the rain and she felt so linked to the lives of everyone around her and everyone who had lived before her that she had to open her window and yell, I LOVE BEING MADE OF THE SAME STUFF AS ALL OF YOU FINE PEOPLE!

The history of not eating was as old as the history of eating, she thought. She was a part of life; even objects as dead as rocks were part of the same giant organism as her. Bobbi tried to imagine what part of the organism she was — the eye, perhaps? — but the moment of clarity passed and they were still in traffic and everyone was alone.

Death by starvation was not something Bobbi fully understood. Did the cells actually die? Bobbi imagined her body disappearing, growing small and thin until it was like it had never even existed in the first place. Or did the heart just slow down until it gave up? She saw the dead muscle like a gym sock in her chest. Causes of death were weird to think about. She had never understood what it meant to die of old age either. What happened to a body when it had just been alive too long? What was the final cause of death? Why does an organ make the decision to quit living? She continued to drink water, but only in small sips when her tongue turned to clay and she worried she could no longer open her mouth. She smoked Rachel's cigarettes. She filled her empty insides with smoke. She grew older and thinner every second that ticked past. She kept looking forward to the next one passing.

Bobbi had no idea how long it took for a human to starve. It felt like a long time.

She thought maybe if she kept fasting and never learned the answer it would mean a miracle had occurred. Until you are dead, she thought, there is always the chance you will live forever.

Meanwhile, Rachel was chewing on herself.

Stop that. Bobbi swatted her hand away.

Rachel's eyes asked a million questions.

Bobbi lit a cigarette and put it in her hand. Rachel was distracted by the glowing tip.

The days grow thinner too, Bobbi thought, when you do not eat. More of the day was spent in the dark of the trailer, curled up beneath a blanket. Time lost meaning, if it ever had any to begin with. Bobbi drove fewer hours. As she drove, she opened her mouth and inhaled as deep as she could. She pretended she was eating air. She pretended the earth's air alone was enough to live on. She prayed the whole world would learn to live off eating air. How much easier would life be? she thought. The real mystery was why God would build a living situation his creations would find so difficult. She lay in the trailer and hugged Rachel close. She held Rachel's hands to prevent her from putting them in her mouth.

Bobbi knew her own body was eating itself on the inside. Her muscles were disappearing. Her bones wanted to push through her skin until they replaced it completely. Her heart beat off-rhythm like it was in the process of forgetting how to do its only job.

One night as she was holding Rachel, she had the sensation of falling into a deep red pit. As they fell she felt like gravity pushed them closer than ever.

The Girl With The Pet Dog

Bobbi was sitting on a bench outside a Visitor's Center on the highway, basking in the sun. She had remembered hearing the body absorbed some kind of vitamins through sunlight. At first she worried she was cheating on her fast, but her skin enjoyed it too much to go back in the trailer. Her head lolled behind her and she felt the sensation of floating in warm water. She lifted her arms up to the sun as if she were worshipping its rays. She could feel a slight breeze on the sores in her nostrils. The van was parked in a space in front of her. Rachel sat on the sidewalk at her feet, wearing a hood and big aviator sunglasses. Bobbi saw big black birds circling above them. She almost gave them the finger, but she was too weak to bother.

A girl in running shoes and tights with palm trees on them came by, walking a Yorkshire terrier with a pale blue bow in its hair. Both the girl and the dog moved with a sense of excess energy that Bobbi could feel as much as she could see. She prayed the girl and her dog would disappear. Bobbi closed her eyes and pretended to be asleep, which she almost was. She would have made snoring sounds if she didn't feel so spent.

The girl sat down on the bench and started bouncing her knee. Bobbi could feel her leg vibrating against the wood, hear her talking about the weather, telling Rachel she could pet her dog if she wanted. Bobbi couldn't figure out why any stranger, much less someone so *active*, would seek them out for companionship. She knew how they must look at this point. She was surprised no one had called the police.

She tried to make a loud snoring sound but instead found herself saying, Thank you. I'm sorry.

As soon as the words slipped out she could no longer pretend to be asleep.

Don't be sorry, the girl chirped. We all close our eyes. Otherwise they get dry and tired from looking at the world. That's why we have eyelids.

The girl was not much older than Rachel. Bobbi thought she was probably in college. It seemed like an appropriate thing to ask her and Bobbi had nothing else to say. The girl said she was. I knew it, Bobbi said. Or at least I thought so.

The girl just smiled and told Bobbi about her calf muscles. How they got tense driving on long trips so she needed to get out and stretch. Run around a little bit, she said.

The sun is nice, Bobbi said.

The girl agreed with her about the sun. Then she asked if Bobbi and Rachel were sisters.

Bobbi started laughing then. She was just trying to clarify, tell the girl no, she was Rachel's mother, but she couldn't stop laughing to speak. At first it started out spidery, like needles in a glass jar but then it grew bloated. It was a painful noise, a cackle. It hurt the inside of her chest and sounded hot with anger. The girl was still smiling, but she looked concerned.

I'm sorry. It's not funny, Bobbi said but she was still laughing and her voice came out garbled. I'm her mother, she kept saying. I'm her mother.

Panic ran through Bobbi's bones but she was unable to stop laughing. She lurched forward and looked down at Rachel with the tiny dog. Rachel was only playing with it. She had her hands jammed into her pockets and was nudging it with her elbows. Bobbi was proud of her daughter's restraint but nervous it wouldn't last. Bobbi was able to catch her breath and stop laughing as she thought about the future.

Don't worry. Daisy likes people, the girl said. She can warm up to anybody.

Even the girl's sweat smelled happy. Bobbi was starting to feel hot. The sun was getting to her.

They like each other, the girl said.

That is not what Bobbi pictured when she watched her daughter and the miniature dog with the bow in its hair. Bobbi saw Rachel's small yellow teeth in close-up slow motion, stretching the skin on the dog's belly just enough to create tiny wrinkles, waves, before puncturing the soft dark membrane. She saw red, yellow, blue organs emerging, brown blood, black bile, heat exploding like a jelly donut against her daughter's chin. The dog sounded like a crying infant in her fantasy. Rachel sounded like a small pig eating the bones of its sibling.

See, the girl said. They are friends.

Rachel still had her hands in her pockets. She was chewing on the hood of her sweatshirt, eyes averted, nudging the dog away with her elbow.

Bobbi saw her digging into the dog's spinal cord with her cold fingers. She started laughing again. She was confused and horrified.

The dog pawed at Rachel. Rachel nudged it again, buried her face in her shoulder.

The sun burned like dry ice against Bobbi's skin.

It's wonderful out, the girl said. A great day to be alive.

Bobbi looked at Rachel. She saw her chewing a pearly wad of the dog's cartilage like gum. Bobbi hated herself for seeing these things in her daughter as much as she hated herself for creating a life to begin with.

Rachel kept her hands in her pockets. She chewed on her sweatshirt. The little dog pawed at her.

That's when Bobbi screamed. Her scream was loud. Trees bent. Clouds parted in far away places. Somewhere a school bus flipped over on a highway. Stars exploded and died.

The word Bobbi screamed was Fuck.

She held the word in her mouth so long it became unrecognizable. It became her own word. A word no one had ever screamed before. It was a high-pitched, metallic shriek like an airplane sliding across a runway. Time stopped while she was screaming and she was afraid to open her eyes or close her mouth because she knew it would start again if she did.

When the inside of her mouth was a husk and her ears had popped and she could feel the blood from her nose reaching her lips, she stopped screaming. The girl was holding her little dog on the edge of the bench trembling, frozen as if they were afraid to move or a ghost might see them.

I'm sorry, Bobbi said. Her breath was heavy. Rachel was squeezing her leg.

She said it again. She had trouble standing up. Rachel tried to help her. They were both having trouble. Bobbi got them back in the car and looked through the windshield. The girl was still on the bench, shocked. The dog had snapped out of it and was yipping at the van. She backed out of her parking space and drove away.

The radio was playing a rock song about runaway children. Bobbi felt old and doomed and her scream had left her deflated. She almost liked it. She knew she was supposed to be thankful for being alive but she was thankful she no longer cared. She looked in the mirror as she merged into traffic. She saw the blood in her teeth. She drove until the sun turned pink. It was easy to imagine the blood as spilled by an enemy during battle. It was easy to imagine fighting herself and losing. Rachel slumped in the corner and looked for dead animals on the side of the road.

Bus Ride

Bobbi left the van and the trailer in a parking lot near a gas station and a graveyard. She drove around for hours as the sun set, looking for the right place to leave it. It was dark when she found it. She took a trash bag full of Rachel's things and left the rest, except her Bible full of notes and *Vitae.* She tore a page from a magazine, a picture of a woman washing her hands, and wrote a note on it in lipstick. *Still a good home*, the note said. She left it on the windshield and took Rachel to the gas station and bought five hot dogs, no buns. She was feeling more sick than hungry herself.

Bobbi waited a moment near the pumps, half-expecting someone to come by and pick her up. It was as if she had reached a finish line to find that the crowd had just disappeared. She hoofed it up to the highway and held out her thumb.

The first ride to stop agreed to take them to the bus station. It was a work van full of Mexican men who sat with them on the floor in the back. They did not look at Bobbi or Rachel. They kept their faces turned toward their sneakers or their chests like they were saying silent prayers. Bobbi cradled Rachel's head in her lap. I am always in your heart, she whispered and rubbed a hand gently over her eyelids. She thought of the Imaginary Mother crammed in beside them. The Imaginary Mother looked sad. She was shaking her head and humming to herself.

Everything about the bus was grey and so was the sky they drove under. The ride began early in the morning, after a night spent on the floor next to a row of vending machines where Bobbi drank soda and fed Rachel pork rinds and Slim-Jims. The inside of the bus was cold. Bobbi sat the trash bag on her lap for warmth. Rachel was in the window seat. Bobbi wished she could open the window up. She was as worried about her own odor as she was about

Rachel's. The bus was full except for a couple rows on either side of them, which the other passengers had left empty. The blowing of the air-conditioner ducts made Bobbi feel as if they were flying in an airplane or on the wings of a bird. She was looking down at the earth below them and she could almost touch it.

She watched farms and billboards and off-ramps pass and she wondered if she had seen them before. She tore off the white margin of a bus schedule and wrote on it: *I think this is what leaving summer camp must be like.* She waved goodbye to exit signs on the highway. She waved to a broken deer carcass and a billboard with a photo of a beach that said, in white letters: Get Lost. She was saying farewell to things she might not see again. She took Rachel's hand and pressed it softly to the glass. Say goodbye to the road, she told her. A beetle crawled out of Rachel's scalp and marched across her forehead.

Test Subjects

I'm sorry, was the first thing Bobbi said when she and Rachel showed up at the Experts' door. Bobbi looked frail. The trash bag had ripped and Rachel's things were falling out onto the ground. A cab sat idling in the parking lot, waiting for someone to come pay the bill. A clump of Experts were standing together in the small waiting room, wearing grey suits or white lab coats. The old woman with the jaw like a snake was somehow still alive and wearing the same black cardigan. The strip mall the laboratory was located in remained as vacant as the week Rachel was born.

Don't be sorry. We knew you would come back, they seemed to coo all at once, like a chorus of doves.

How did you know? Bobbi asked, trembling.

You have nowhere else to go, one of them told her.

And when we let you go, said another, we know we will see you again.

One of the Experts was bent over smiling at Rachel and reaching for her hand. He was wearing latex gloves. They all were. Bobbi could smell the rubber.

I guess that's why I think of you as the Experts, she said. Her skull felt full of air. Her forehead was wet.

We *are* experts, they cooed. As much as anyone can be.

I'm sorry, Bobbi repeated.

There is no reason for anyone to be sorry, one said. For anything.

The old woman put a blanket over Bobbi's shoulder and gave her a small paper cup with water inside. Several of the experts took great care as they led Rachel to a stretcher and pushed her through a set of doors, down a long white hallway. Rachel did not struggle. Bobbi's face turned pink and crumpled as she watched her wheeled away. She began to cry.

In The Yellow Room

The bed was adjustable and bent in several places to accommodate her. It cupped her bones. Bobbi laid there for what felt like many days. Time had taken on the consistency of soup. Events and conversations were hunks of meat breaking down in the broth. She never got up. She used a bedpan. The old woman came in from time to time and washed her with a sponge.

There were tubes in her arms that she was afraid to touch. She knew they were drugs but she didn't know what kind. One of the Experts told her it was what made everything so soupy. She told him things had gone soupy long before that.

Bobbi kept her eyes closed mostly. She heard distant voices: in the hall, on the television, in her head, sometimes right over her or next to her bed. She did not often open her eyes to see who was speaking. She was in a womb, sloshing gently about. The voices were past the womb on the other side of a pink wall, her eyelids. Even slightly awake, she was never far enough from a dream to care about what they said.

This must be what heaven is like. Why bother dying if you can find it right here on earth?

The old woman brought Jell-O, which she helped feed her with a spoon. Bobbi smiled at her like they couldn't speak the same language. The woman smiled back like they could. Men came in with clipboards and little touch-screen computers. They smiled at her the same way. There was a plant in the corner of the room. Bobbi felt like it was smiling too.

Bobbi thought about Rachel but forgot about her also. She talked out loud to her in her sleep, then she lost the image of her face again, then saw her. It was easy to forget important things about her life.

My life is easy to forget, she thought.

In addition to voices, she heard noises sometimes. The noises sounded like she was hearing them through water. Industrial machines. Gadgets beeping. Animals growling. Music. A soft chant. A giant heart beating through the walls. She heard vacuums and the sound of heavy liquids like syrup dripping into a basin. She heard the sounds of her dreams when she was awake and she heard the sounds of life in the building while she dreamt. She ate the Jell-O with her eyes closed and felt it slide down her throat. She let her body be turned over and washed with the damp sponge.

When they first brought Rachel in to see her, Bobbi thought she was a ghost from her dreams. Rachel looked cleaner than she had ever looked before. Bobbi was glowing and held her arms out as Rachel dove toward the bed. Inside she felt a small hook of failure in her spine as she held her daughter. She had never made it possible for Rachel to feel this clean.

As time went on, they began to bring Rachel in to visit regularly in the afternoons. Each afternoon she looked different. Different stitching patterns crossed her face, arms and scalp. Bulges like fruit hidden under gauze patches that moved around on her body during the week. There were always new odors coming off her. Anise, rose, the smell of moist dirt after a rain. It was as if they were pumping her veins full of perfume.

They're turning my baby into a flower, Bobbi said and started laughing. There was a thick fog in her eyes. The old woman only shook her head as if turning Rachel into a flower was out of their capabilities. Or maybe as if Rachel had always been one, Bobbi thought. She couldn't stop laughing long enough to ask.

Rachel climbed onto the bed with her mother, who drifted in and out of sleep. They wore matching hospital gowns, patterned with blue birds and tiny pink hearts. A pair of men stood in the doorway watching. One of them mumbled into a recording device. The old woman came and went with paper cups of purple Kool-Aid. More men came and looked at Bobbi. She felt like her hospital room was a television set that she was inside of and the Experts came to watch. Opening the door to her room was like pressing the power button. When she tried to tell them this, it didn't come out making as much sense as it had in her head.

Days passed. Weeks. She couldn't be sure.

She never saw the agents who had visited her on the road. The Snowman or the Other Man who had been with him the last time by the lake. They don't work at this location, the old woman told her.

Bobbi nodded and closed her eyes. She had thought they might visit her. We all work everywhere, she said and smiled as if she knew something secret and important. She drifted into sleep having forgotten whatever it was. The world might as well have not existed outside her yellow room.

Death Sentence

One day when Bobbi was feeling a little more lucid than she had gotten used to being, the old woman led a pair of Experts in and they sat on stools beside her bed. They told Bobbi she was dying. Bobbi said that everyone was dying.

Not as fast as you, one said.

Cancer, said the other.

It started in the nasal cavity. From there it has spread to the brain.

I'm sorry, they said.

Bobbi heard the sound of a machine turning on in another room. It made a beeping sound. The old woman stood in the doorway behind them and looked at the floor.

Why? I mean how? I mean are you sure?

These were normal things to ask. These were the questions anyone might ask.

The Experts took turns explaining what they didn't know.

Bobbi could be genetically predisposed to nasal cancer. Or she could be predisposed to not get nasal cancer and she just beat the odds. It could have come from carcinogens in embalming fluid, exhaust, gasoline, cigarettes, the air. Or it could have been something else, some other factor they would never identify, anything at all. Cancer doesn't need a reason to exist, they told her. It only needs a place to live.

Our bodies create it within themselves. And it is not always a response to something obvious.

Sometimes it isn't even a response at all.

Cancer is a living thing. That is important to remember.

It replicates like wild. Cancer cells are very good at living.

Successful.

Until they kill the host.

Cancer doesn't need a reason to exist, Bobbi said.

Laughter Pushes Against the Brain

Bobbi learned that the inappropriate laughter she had been experiencing was the result of a tumor pressing against her brain. It made her question whether anyone's laughter was real. Life was just our brains reacting to stimulation. The idea that the same reaction could be caused by both joy and cancer was difficult to grasp.

A tumor was more tangible than joy.

Enjoy Breathing

Rachel visited and she was a shadowy purple color. The next day she was grey. Then she had no lips. Then her lips were full and cauliflowered. One day Rachel was wheeled in on a table wrapped in blankets because her lower half was missing. The next day she walked in spotted with electrodes attached to a machine on squeaky wheels. Rachel was in a cast. Rachel had no eyes. Bobbi never knew what to expect except love and love is all she got from her daughter.

Sometimes Rachel helped the old woman clean Bobbi. The old woman didn't need any help but Rachel put her hand on the warm sponge and moaned quietly. The old woman began bringing two sponges. Rachel only washed one spot on Bobbi's body at a time, rubbing her hand across the same few inches of skin over and over until the woman reached over and moved it to a new location. Rachel kept rubbing.

Bobbi learned not to worry about Rachel when she wasn't there. At least not the way she thought she would worry. Even distorted by the experiments, she thought Rachel looked better than she had ever seen her. Rachel was calm when she visited, in a way she had never looked before. She isn't lost in dead thoughts, Bobbi informed the Experts. She looked at peace. Bobbi often asked what they were feeding her.

Only good stuff, the old woman told her. No junk. I wish you would eat more. Being hungry is a good sign.

When Bobbi was alone, she often slept. Sometimes the Imaginary Mother came to visit her. She sat in a chair by the plant and said nothing because there was nothing else to say. When she was awake, Bobbi breathed. It is remarkable that air exists! she told her empty room. She felt lucky. Breathing had become more difficult — or maybe it had always been difficult — and now Bobbi enjoyed it more than anything.

Late Stages

Bobbi avoided discussions of treatment. She changed the subject. She pretended she was asleep. She put her hands over her ears and hummed.

The Experts all carried the same resigned look when they came to check on her, like treatment had only been a kind gesture in the first place.

What Bobbi needed was a miracle.

Praying With The TV On

Bobbi opened a prayer with Dear God and then never closed it again. If I don't say Amen, she thought, then the prayer has never ended. I will always have God on the line. She didn't know why she hadn't thought of this earlier in life. She prayed when she watched television and she prayed when she ate Jell-O. She prayed in her sleep and on the toilet. She prayed while the Experts asked her questions. Just sharing the small moments of your life is worship to someone who loves you. She had learned that from Rachel.

Defining A Miracle

Bobbi did not define the word miracle. The dictionary told her what it meant: *A surprising and welcome event inexplicable by natural or scientific laws, therefore considered the work of divine agency.*

That definition seemed murky to Bobbi. Surprising and welcome to who or what? Inexplicable how? If everything that could not be explained was a miracle, then miracles were not as special as they had been made out to be. Miracles were commonplace. All events are miracles if you welcome them, she thought. As long as you are unable to explain why they are happening.

She did not pray for a cure to cancer but she did not pray to die either. She only prayed and welcomed each new moment as it came. They were all inexplicable. She wanted each strange second of life to be the definition of a miracle.

Lawnchairs in the Parking Lot

Bobbi began to feel a little bit stronger. When she was up to it, the Experts allowed her to go outside where she would sit on a lawn chair in the strip mall's empty parking lot. There were weeds growing out of cracks in the asphalt. Bobbi sat next to an empty chair most of the time, but sometimes Rachel was brought out to visit. Rachel would not wander the parking lot or dig for worms. There was no trailer to go in and out of. The two of them would just sit there in the late afternoon and watch the light breeze make the trees come alive. Bobbi would reach for Rachel's hand and it would be there, waiting to be held.

A Birthday Party For No Birthday

A pound cake with icing was prepared for Bobbi the day before she was to leave for a cottage by the ocean, which was located on the property of a small funeral home that the Experts were affiliated with. Bobbi heard waves in her head when they told her she was moving. It could have been the air-conditioner or a machine somewhere, but it sounded like waves.

We have a very long relationship with them, one of the Experts explained.

We use them often, the old woman reassured her. They're family. You will like it there. Rachel will like it too.

Bobbi wanted to know if she could help out at the funeral home. She knew how to take care of a body. I would like to be useful, she said.

The party was held in the lobby. There was not enough room and some of the Experts had to stand together in the hallway. People took turns coming in for cake. It was not a farewell party and nobody said goodbye or mentioned anyone leaving. It was not a get well party either. It felt like a birthday party but it wasn't anyone's birthday. It was only a party, with cake and paper hats. There was a banner that said nothing. The banner just had pictures of confetti and balloons and a space in the middle where it had been filled in with only her name and an exclamation point: BOBBI!

Bobbi and Rachel sat in a brown corduroy loveseat and wore hats. The rest of the room kind of rotated and shuffled around one another so everyone could get a chance to pay the guests of honor their respects. They were careful not to bump into each other and spill their tiny paper cups of grape soda. Bobbi's cheeks warmed as they greeted her, told her she looked beautiful in the blue dress they had given her to replace her hospital gown. Bobbi grinned a lot and acted as if she could tell everyone apart. She avoided saying anyone's name. She was clueless, but nobody expected her to remember anything. It was sufficient to only pretend.

Bobbi looked around for her road agents but they were not there. She wondered if they knew about the party or if they had moved on to following someone else. She felt less than special, but that was okay. Either we are all special or no one is special, she thought. It all means the same thing.

There was one fat candle in the cake for Bobbi to blow out, as if it were her first birthday. Bobbi did not have a lot of breath. Rachel helped her. The flame fluttered, off then on again. They kept blowing at it. The fire went out. The fire came back to life. It was either a miracle or a trick candle. Several of the Experts finally lent her their breath. The flame was extinguished but the wick was still glowing orange when the old woman took the candle from the cake and dropped it in a cup of soda. It made a sizzling sound. Bobbi wasn't hungry but she said Thank you and nibbled at a piece of cake to be polite. The old woman hooked Rachel up to an IV with a pink mush travelling through it. Bobbi nearly reached for the hose — she had never seen someone else feed Rachel before and it triggered something in her wrist — but she caught herself. The soft look on Rachel's face told Bobbi she was having a good time.

What was your wish? the roomful of Experts begged.

Bobbi had forgotten to make one, which meant it was possible the wish had already come true.

The Bay Bridge

The cottage was located on the Eastern Shore, across the Chesapeake Bay. Bobbi and Rachel had to be driven across a long bridge to get there. They sat in the backseat of a black SUV with tinted windows. The seats were made of leather. Rachel scratched at the upholstery with her incisors and left little marks. Bobbi watched sailboats like toys in the blue bay below them. She dreamt each vessel was setting off on a long journey into waters they had never seen before. They were leaving something behind. Her chest tightened. She was honored to be so close to the boats, a secret part of the scene, passing overhead as the wind pushed them out to sea. Her eyes welled slightly. She could feel salt on the rim of her eyelids. Have a nice trip, she whispered and touched her fingers to the tinted glass.

Funeral Home By The Water

The funeral home was in a large grey beach house. There was an embalming facility in a Quonset hut attached to the backdoor by a short hallway. The driveway was paved with oyster shells. A family called Hurtt operated the business. The old couple was still alive, the Experts told Bobbi, but they never left the building. Their adult children ran the place now and had continued their professional relationship with the laboratory. They are good people, she was told. They will take care of you and give you privacy.

The man at the wheel spoke over his shoulder as they pulled up the drive. And you know we will never be far away, he said.

Bobbi wondered why she had spent so much time feeling lonely if it was true they had never been truly alone.

Thank you, she said. I'm sorry if I don't tell you guys that more often.

You're welcome, he said.

Always feel welcome, the man in the passenger seat added.

I feel welcome, Bobbi yawned. Or welcoming at least.

She rolled down the window. The breeze hit her in the face.

That's a start, right? she said. She could feel the wind in her mouth.

It tasted like salt and mud.

When the Tides Attack Your Feet

The cottage was small but Bobbi and Rachel still did not use most of the space. There were two bedrooms, but they decided to share one. The other room remained empty. There was a blanket of dust like dirty snow on the floor. In the living room there was an old television set and a number of houseplants. The walls were too dark for a house by the beach, a deep blue that almost looked black like the sea after the sun had set. There was a screen door that opened out to a small porch that faced the dunes. Past the dunes, the beach was usually empty, private property that belonged to the Hurtt's. Seagulls dive-bombed decaying horseshoe crabs where the sand was wet and dark from the tide. Bobbi and Rachel visited the beach often. Bobbi covered Rachel's head with a pillowcase to protect it from the sun. They lay on towels in the sand. Bobbi walked her down to the waves and tried to pick her up — it was very difficult now — when the foam attacked their feet. More than once they toppled over and seeing they were both all right, laughed.

The Hurtt Family

The Hurtt family were gentle hosts. The children — Thomas, Simon, and Mary — were past the middle of their lives but none of them had a spouse or children of their own. Bobbi did not see them except when they materialized to collect the trash and bring food on trays or to take Rachel up to the big house for maintenance. Bobbi sometimes saw lights flickering on and off inside, heard the sound of light motors inside the Quonset hut.

If the adult children were like ghosts, the old couple was something even more remote. Entities more ancient and insubstantial than ghosts.

During her time there, Bobbi never saw any sign of business taking place. No hearses or long processions, no teary people trying to hold it together in the parking area out front. The only flower arrangements were the roses and lilies left on their counter once a week by Mary. It felt as much like a bed & breakfast as it did a place to honor the dead. We are their only customers, Bobbi told Rachel. We have the whole place to ourselves.

Mary Hurtt had circles under her eyes and hair that was always halfway in a ponytail. She looked moment-to-moment as if she was ready to say something sarcastic but had trained herself not to. Bobbi thought they might form a bond but Mary never stayed at the cottage long enough for deep conversation to take place. There was always something else she needed to get done. Bobbi had the feeling Mary had cared for girls like her before. Women, she thought, checking herself. Not girls. Old, dying women.

Bobbi thought of shelters with stray animals that nobody wanted to pet. She thought of melting ice sculptures and sand castles in the wind. She felt guilty for comparing herself to any of those wonderful things. It was easy to ask for forgiveness. Her prayer was always open.

Thomas and Simon were twins. They were thin with greying orange hair and dressed formally, in dark suits, as if a funeral were about to break out at any minute. They operated efficiently together. They carried trays side-by-side, opened doors for one another, zip-tied garbage bags while unfolding new ones at the same time. They cut sparse patches of lawn with long, sharp scissors.

These were the strangers who watched after Bobbi while the cancer grew and spread and ate her other cells. These were the people Bobbi entrusted Rachel to because they were the only people there were. Sometimes the only thing left to do is trust someone.

Things Kept Falling

Bobbi was often tired and could feel out of breath just walking around their little cottage. She had a low, constant ache behind her face. She sometimes didn't notice the pain, like it had been there her whole life. Her fingers felt swollen but when she looked at them they were the same size they had always been. They pulsed. She barely bothered to bite them anymore.

She kept dropping things. She knocked over glasses, plates, and houseplants. Things kept falling. Someone would always appear shortly afterward to help her clean up. Bobbi said Sorry and Thank you a lot. She had developed a bit of a slur to her speech. Words came out different than she intended them. She repeated them but they still sounded wrong. Memories did not always fit together anymore. Sometimes the pieces of her life needed to be mashed into one another to fit. Her nose bled. She sniffed. The taste of iron made her feel a tiny bit more alive.

Watching Dunes in the Rain

During days when it rained on the coast and the sky was a lamp wrapped in a blanket, Bobbi and Rachel sat by the window in matching sweatsuits and watched the sand grow freckles. The rain dappled then soaked the dunes and the sand around the narrow boardwalk that led to the beach. Sand and rain splashed into the air. The beach eroded into the sea, then washed back up the next day.

Rachel still flinched at lightning, although less than Bobbi now. Bobbi watched the storms with tense muscles, thrilled like she was in a dark theater in front of a scary movie. Sometimes she laughed. Other times tears slipped down her cheeks. Rachel held her hand either way. When night came, there were no stars in the cloudy sky but they sat and looked for them anyway.

A Costume Prepares For Retirement

Bobbi wore a purple sweatsuit with the name of the funeral home on it, HURTT. Beneath that, she was wrapped in an unraveling body.

Consciousness was like wearing a cape all the time and death was finding out the cape was actually made of her own skin.

She looked in her mirrored compact and frowned slightly. Faces are only a mask for the brain, she thought. She had stopped wearing make-up mostly, as had Rachel. She liked seeing how tired she looked in the mirror. You are almost ready to come off, she told her face. You too, she told the brain behind it.

Dust Angels

Bobbi did not research cancer the way she would have when she was younger. The cancer was a part of her body. She didn't want to know its secrets. Besides, there was no computer or Internet connection in the cottage and Bobbi stayed away from the big house and Quonset hut out back. Everything in her life was taken care of and Rachel seemed content at the funeral home. Near peace. Late at night the stars twinkled and in the mid-afternoon when the sun was shining through the windows everything seemed to be glowing.

Bobbi came from the bathroom to find Rachel on her hands and knees, following a spider into the empty bedroom. The spider disappeared in the thick grey dustscape. Bobbi thought it might have suffocated. Or it was hiding. She led Rachel into the room and they lay down on the floor. The air had been disrupted by their bodies and dry grey dust particles were floating down on them like rain. The dust stung Bobbi's eyes and attacked her mouth.

It's snowing, she told Rachel. Spread your arms and legs. We can leave angels where our bodies once were.

They spread their arms and legs and made angels in the dust. They stood in the doorway, both of them filthy and grey. Bobbi could feel her hair dancing with static electricity. She had her arm on Rachel's shoulder and they were looking at their work.

They're beautiful enough for us, she said. I wouldn't change a thing.

Houseguests

The sun was still low and a breeze danced gently with the sand and beach grass atop the dunes. Bobbi sat on the beach and watched it, with her back to the sea. Rachel was behind her. She could hear her digging for little white sand crabs like skeletons buried in the dampness. Bobbi screamed at seagulls whenever they came close.

Her heart flipped in her chest when she saw the two grey hats coming up over the dunes. She tried to stand up but it didn't work. Instead she just waved. Oh Rachel, she said. We have visitors!

The two men looked out of place by the sea, different than they had appeared by the lake the last time Bobbi had seen them. They walked side by side and kicked sand in the air with their shoes. The Snowman was waving back at her. The Other Man did not wave, but he did not look so grim either. He was almost smiling.

Bobbi tried to make room for them on her towel but it was much too small. They stood in front of her and took deep breaths of salty air.

You look good out here, Bobbi.

The Other Man nodded. Bobbi had hoped he would.

My partner is right, he said. The edge of the continent suits you.

Bobbi looked over her shoulder. The sea went on forever. The horizon was blurriness, an exchange of blues. Rachel was still digging. She stayed just out of the tide's reach.

I like it here, Bobbi said. She closed her eyes and turned her face to the sun. I think I am happy.

She began to cough. The Snowman handed her a water bottle that was sitting on the towel. Drink, he said. He waved at Rachel. Hi, Rachel! Long time no see.

Bobbi wondered if that were true. She hoped it wasn't. She had begun to think of these men as guardian angels. She didn't even know their names.

They all went up to the cottage. The men told her they were going to cook brunch. They had already filled the house with food.

The Snowman cooked. He made eggs and pink bacon and scrapple with toast cut into triangles. Fried bologna with mustard, potatoes with peppers and onions. Slices of cucumber and tomato floating in vinegar. Raw oysters waiting on ice. And there was more food in paper grocery bags. Enough for a large family to eat for weeks, Bobbi thought. She had a feeling he would be cooking all day.

She and Rachel sat across from the Other Man at the little table in the kitchen. There was a jug of orange juice between them. The Snowman opened a bottle of champagne and poured it into the jug. Mary Hurtt had dropped off flowers that morning and Bobbi was holding one of them. The Other Man had his hat cocked back on his head and his tie loosened at the neck. He looked calm and patient.

Tell me something nice, Bobbi said.

He reached forward and took the rose from her hand. He smelled it then offered it to the Snowman, who put down his spatula and gave it a sniff. They passed it back to Bobbi, who held it up to her nose, almost expecting the smell to have changed.

I might tell you living only once is like barely living at all, the Other Man said. Say that all of life is only waiting to be dust particles anyway. Eventually we will all play by new rules of physics, the rules that apply to very small objects. He gave her a little smile. But I don't think that would cheer you up.

I don't need to be cheered up, Bobbi said. That sounds nice.

She took a sip of her mimosa. They had brought champagne flutes that shined like diamonds. A toast was proposed.

To stardust, the Other Man said.

Bobbi held a glass for Rachel. Rachel tried to take a sip but it dribbled down her chin. Bobbi wiped her off with a shirtsleeve. When she was finished, Rachel reached forward and touched Bobbi's face with her hand.

Aw, the Snowman said. That was cute.

The Other Man poured himself another glass and food was brought to the table. The Snowman never sat down. He ate off the platters as he served them. Bobbi felt like there was music playing, something tropical, but there wasn't.

She was not hungry, but it was nice to have all that food around. She felt cared for, comforted to be in the presence of so much food, like she imagined an infant might feel being held against its mother's breast.

As the sky grew dark, they lit candles and told Bobbi stories about her life with Rachel. They told her how wonderful it had been. Bobbi listened to the stories with her eyes closed. Whether she remembered them or not didn't matter. She listened and they became real.

The Other Man told her life was funny. That it didn't need to exist but it always managed to anyway. Stuff that is unnecessary is usually funny, he said.

Bobbi laughed. Rachel gurgled in an uncomfortable way that grew into a laugh to mimic her mother. The Other Man and the Snowman laughed too. Bobbi thought she heard faint laughter outside the cottage, coming from the funeral home's windows. She imagined everyone's laughter booming over the dunes and out across the sea. Waves, salt beneath racing laughter. Clouds of fish. Birds and whales calling back to her in squeaks and whistles. She thought about the residue of her laughter traveling through space. She thought about the fact that space even existed.

Life *is* funny, Bobbi said.

Anointing of the Sick

Mary Hurtt came to the cottage that night and touched oil to Bobbi's face and hands. The oil made Bobbi smell like roses. She did not do this every night, but repeated it from time to time. It was a signal to Bobbi that her condition must be worsening. She thought it was supposed to be for her benefit, to give her hope when the situation was growing bleak. Bobbi just liked the smell.

Her guests said goodnight. They were going to follow Mary up to the big house to sleep.

Goodnight, Bobbi said outside the cottage door. She almost said Goodbye, but remembered not to. These days she often felt like she should say Goodbye before sleep.

We always have tomorrow, the Snowman told her.

Not always, Bobbi thought. Then she looked at Rachel, standing beside her with her hands in her pockets. The light over the door was a halo. Her bones felt warm and the air tasted fresh. She had this feeling: Maybe we do.

Last Rites

In addition to being anointed with oil, Bobbi's Last Rites also consisted of Penance and the Eucharist. Every meal she ever ate had been communion and just being alive was a penance, whether she knew these things or not.

Lord, I am not worthy to receive you but only say the word and I shall be healed.

Cremation

Rachel was entertained in the cottage the morning Bobbi's body was carried on a wide stretcher to the Quonset hut where she was to be cremated. Her body was curled in the middle of the stretcher. The stretcher was covered in a white cloth. Thomas and Simon Hurtt carried her between them. Their formal dress made them look like waiters. From a distance they could have been carrying a cake to a wedding party.

The crematorium was an area in the rear of the building that contained a furnace lined with refractory bricks of mineral wool and calcium silicate. The incineration chamber inside the furnace was called the retort. Bobbi's body was placed on a wheeled platform at the entrance. Her skin had already begun to look dead. It was stained with purple blotches where her blood had pooled. Her eyeballs had gone flat and begun to stiffen. Mary Hurtt covered her eyelids with coins before wheeling her inside the chamber.

Temperatures inside the retort rose to 1,800 degrees Fahrenheit. The body took less than two hours to be reduced to bone fragments like sand. The Hurtts did chores while she burned.

Afterward, the cremated remains were further reduced through a chemical process that took place in a stainless steel sieve. The Hurtt family picked through the dust with tweezers and a strong magnet, extracting teeth from her sweatsuit's zipper that were not consumed in the furnace. The remains were then processed in a machine with a rotating barrel that tumbled the bone fragments into more uniform sizes. They were funneled into a thick, clear plastic bag with a zip-locked seal. The bag was placed on a scale. What was left of Bobbi weighed three and a half pounds. The pale grains of bone inside the bag were still warm.

Rachel could not be distracted with board games or shadow puppets on the wall. She stared out the open window at the big house, the Quonset hut behind it, the black grey smoke rising from the chimney pipe. The clouds it put out looked sickly as they disappeared in the windy blue sky. She pushed her head outside. She tried to breathe the air.

I wish every person gave off a unique color smoke when they were cremated, the Snowman said, taking a peek through the window. And your friends and family had to wait your whole life to see what color it was.

The Other Man was at the table holding a magnifying glass, his face buried in Bobbi's copy of *Vitae*. He didn't bother to look up at the smoke. It will always look about the same, he said. No matter what color you make it.

The Wake

The wind kept them off the beach for a day. It had picked up the morning Mary Hurtt discovered the body curled up on the sofa with the TV on. Rachel had been on her knees, washing her mother's feet. Mary could smell extra death in the cottage. Not decay yet, just death. Afterward a very strong wind came in off the coast. By the afternoon, when the cremation was finished, there were clouds and rain. The sky turned black before sunset. None of these were good conditions for a burial at sea.

The bag of Bobbi's bone fragments was brought down to the cottage on a silver tray, along with cups and saucers for tea. The bag was the size of a baby's head. The men sat in the living room and listened to the storm. Rachel leaned her forehead against the window. Mary Hurtt placed a white rose on the windowsill beneath her. Rachel ignored the flower.

The Snowman put his hand on her shoulders and guided her gently into the living room. Steam was rising from their teacups.

I know you are angry at the world, the Other Man told her. The world can't help being unfair anymore than you can help feeling angry.

He's right, the Snowman chimed in. About the unfairness and the anger.

Your mother was a special person, the Other Man said. He picked the plastic bag up off the tray and pulled open the zip-lock. He sat it down on the coffee table in front of Rachel. Rachel stared at the white bag.

It is okay, he said. You can touch her.

She slowly pulled her hands from her pockets. They shook. She reached forward and touched the mouth of the bag. She put her hand inside. The dust came in pellets, little white balls with lumps. It stuck to her skin, clung to the suture on a yellowed wound. She let some of the dust fall through her fingers. She held her hand to her mouth.

The two men slept through the storm on the floor of the empty bedroom. They slept on blankets brought down from the big house. The blankets were laid out in the empty spaces where Bobbi and Rachel had made angels.

The Funeral

The ceremony took place on the beach. The air was mostly calm, except for a slight breeze here and there. The sun looked pale against the scattered clouds. The waves were small. It was as good a day as any for a funeral.

The Hurtt family assembled for the ceremony. Even the father and mother, who were not much more than mummies, were wheeled down attached to oxygen tanks. They sat in the back of the beach, on the small boardwalk that cut through the dunes. Thomas and Simon placed their hands together then left them to join the others down near the waves. Mary had a small boombox with her, like something a child would own. A cassette was playing classical music from the speakers. Violins, cello. A trumpet trying to sound sad. All of it was almost drowned out by the waves crashing against the sand.

Words were said but they disappeared into the sea.

Words didn't matter anyway.

The Other Man kept the plastic bag in his coat pocket until it was time for Rachel to scatter the remains. He put the bag in her hands and pressed them to her chest, then picked her up and lifted her above his shoulders as he waded out, shoes and pants still on. He held Rachel with stiff arms, careful to keep her as dry as he could. Rachel copied him. She lifted the bag of bone fragments over her head.

The weight of the bone fell to the front of the bag and began to spill over the lip. The grains made white clouds in the dark blue water. The clouds were taken south by the current. Gentle waves pushed most of the fragments back toward the beach to mix with the sand, but two small pale patches of bone kept drifting down along the shore until they were pulled out into the deeper water, dispersing, falling apart as the current took them away.

Saint Rachel

Every time a baby is born someone cries in heaven. Tears of joy and sadness drip down onto the earth where the people are already crying, although they don't know why. Everyone gets wet.

Rachel began her time on earth in pieces and like anyone else she struggled the rest of it to feel whole. She copied the behaviors of those around her as best she could. She ate, she drank and she felt death doing the exact same things to her all the time. She loved her mother. Her thoughts were slow and often focused on returning to the womb. She envied rocks and burrowing animals.

Feeding was a sad necessity. If she could not climb back inside her mother or become a part of the earth — and she could not, her mother needed her, would not let her go — then her body and all the parasites that lived off it required she be fed. Rachel ate living things and things that had once been alive. It hurt to take part in the violence of life but eating was an instinct and burden she would carry for love. Life versus death. She held back. She fought her body when it was feeling dangerous. She retreated into death during the peaceful times she spent alone with her mother lying in the trailer like it was a big coffin, just waiting for a mountain of dirt to be piled on top.

They met other people as they travelled across the surface of the planet. The other people were also waiting to die. Rachel hoped they would help her mother in the ways she had been unable to, but mostly they could not. She was not sure people were meant to be happy when they were alive. She was not sure that was the point, even though she wanted it to be. She wanted her mother to experience joy. If she had left the womb whole, then things might have been different. She felt it as an unwanted instinct, like the need to eat. It was obvious they would have been more or less the same.

In the meantime, what happened to Rachel did not matter so much. Not to her.

When her mother left her as bits of pale dust in the sand and sea, she felt more in pieces than ever but she cherished the feeling. She wanted to break down into even smaller bits.

Rachel wanted to join her mother and the rest of the dead, but she did not know how. She refused to eat but the family at the funeral home fed her anyway. She offered her body completely to the parasites that nested in it, but everyday the family cleaned her and scrubbed out her veins. There was no point in pulling out her own heart or severing her head. That wouldn't be enough. She needed to deconstruct completely. Dust was the ultimate goal.

She eyed the furnace whenever she was taken up to the Quonset hut to be preserved. Next to the furnace was the tumbling barrel that ground things into pellets. When she was alone in the cottage, she watched the sea. She saw hungry white birds in the sky.

Rachel stayed in bed with her mother's Bible and all the scraps of paper it contained. She could not read the scribbles but she knew to hold onto the life inside them. She did not let go. She pressed the book against her chest. She took the notes out and held them to her face. Her cheeks left light stains on the fragile papers.

The sky was still dark the morning Rachel walked out onto the beach. She had left the book behind. She wouldn't need it where she was going. She got to the damp part of the shore where she used to dig for sand crabs. The water touched her feet and the salt brought comfort to her skin. She waded a little deeper. Her sweatpants were heavy and the water pulled them down around her knees. She kept walking. The ocean and her body were the same temperature. She waited for the nibbles of small fish and crabs. She went further. She welcomed the pull of shark teeth. Tentacles.

She was all the way underwater now, walking across the sand bottom. The breaking point was behind her. Her skin came off in flakes at her rib cage. The world was black and she closed her eyes. She saw a vision behind her eyelids. She saw bloat taking hold of her organs. She saw it floating her to the surface as animals ripped her to pieces. She saw her body ascending above the waves as the sun appeared, rising high up into the air like a mist, like a cloud preparing to rain. The fish began to chew.

ABOUT TIMMY REED

Timmy Reed is a writer from Baltimore, Maryland. He has published works in a number of places over the years including Akashic Books, Vol. 1 Brooklyn, Curbside Splendor, Everyday Genius, Necessary Fiction, and Atticus Review. His short fiction has been included in the Wigleaf Top 50 in both 2014 and 2015 and he received a 2015 Baker Artist Award B-Grant for his writing. He is the author of the story collection Tell God I Don't Exist (Underrated Animals Press) and the novel The Ghosts That Surrounded Them (Dig That Book, Co.), and Star Backwards (Dostoyevsky Wannabe Books), as well as the chapbooks Zeb and Bunny Build Russian Dolls (Hidden Clearing Press) and Stray/Pest (Bottlecap Press).

Made in the USA
Middletown, DE
19 November 2021